THE BIRD CATCHER

Also by Laura Jacobs

Women About Town

Landscape with Moving Figures: A Decade on Dance

THE BIRD CATCHER

LAURA JACOBS

St. Martin's Press New York

This is a work of fiction. All of the characters, organizations, and events portrayed in this novel are either products of the author's imagination or are used fictitiously.

www.stmartins.com

Book design by Maggie Goodman

Library of Congress Cataloging-in-Publication Data

Jacobs, Laura.
The bird catcher / Laura Jacobs.—1st ed.
p. cm.
ISBN-13: 978-0-312-54022-7
ISBN-10: 0-312-54022-1
1. Women artists—New York (State)—New York—Fiction. 2. Women—New York (State)—New York—Fiction. 3. Bird watching—Fiction. 4. Birds—Collection and preservation—Fiction. 5. Diorama—Fiction. 6. Psychological fiction.
I. Title.
PS3610.A35644B57 2009
813'.6—dc22

2008046207

First Edition: June 2009

10 9 8 7 6 5 4 3 2 1

For my husband, James

CONTENTS

All the birds of the air
Fell to sighing and sobbing,
When they heard the bell toll
For poor Cock Robin.

—ANONYMOUS,
"THE DEATH AND BURIAL
OF COCK ROBIN"

A WEEK IN EARLY MARCH

One

MARGRET STOOD AT THE STONE stairs leading down into the park at 115th Street. The stairs were steep and sinking, pushed in and jutting out. How does such heavy stone get so shifted? Margret always wondered. It couldn't be from people. It must be ice trapped in fissures, freezes impacted like a tooth. Only Nature herself could nudge such slabs, make it look like they had moved in their sleep. Margret lifted her face to the treetops and reclipped her heavy hair back, catching the dark, wavy wisps that were always coming loose and getting in her eyes. You had to concentrate on these stairs, and this hair of hers, the envy of childhood friends and college roommates and now her colleagues in the city—"So Botticelli," they said, "so Burne-Jones"—it was endlessly mossy against her neck, endlessly escaping from behind her ears.

It was seven A.M. and the light was coming in, though you could hardly say the sun was up. It always took longer to find and warm the West Side. Margret went carefully down the steps, then paused to spin the focus wheel on her binoculars, which sometimes stiffened between outings. Like I do, she thought. She began walking with a steady pace, keeping to the wide path along Riverside Park's majestic retaining wall. Up on Riverside Drive, all you saw was a safety wall, three feet high and made of silvery stone rectangles, uniformly spaced. Columbia undergrads sat on the wall, rocking and laughing at each other's jokes, unaware of the other side. Look over, though, and you saw the drop, quite dangerous in some places, enough to send an eely wave up the back of your thighs.

At the bottom of that drop, down in the park and looking up, the wall was something else again, huge stones laid in to heights of thirty feet, rough strokes of coal, bronze, nickel, russet, with scratchy patches of bleach green. Monumental, maternal, it was the fruit of a brute labor the city would never see again. And in the seams and chinks between stones it was alive, a darkness attractive to mice, rats, birds, cats, raccoons. Well, who wouldn't want to live in a wall if they could fit? Even young trees, their slim trunks emerging from crevices four feet above the ground, had roots deep in the dark behind those stones. *Something there is that doesn't love a wall.* But I do, Margret thought; I love this wall.

What if we lived in a wall? she once asked her husband as they walked this path. A wall, he said. He liked to let a question land, to see how it sat. He'd always wanted to live in a cave, he said, with all the luxuries, of course: a stereo system, a library, a sock drawer. Like Captain Nemo in the *Nautilus,* with his Caravaggios. A wall, however, that would be . . . Like living in a corridor, she'd suggested. She was thinking of nuns floating down long passages in stone cathedrals. Their whole lives were a corridor, light entering, piercing, in slivers. So you're imagining a space in there, he said, traveling the length of the wall. Yes, she'd answered. She would have been walking on his left side. He was deaf in his right ear, so you had to be on the left. But why is a corridor so appealing? he wanted to know. Because it's in between, she said. It's nowhere that's always leading somewhere. Like the wind. Whereas a cave is just a hole in the ground. He'd taken issue with that, thought she was being hard on caves. Look at *King Solomon's Mines*. Look at *Journey to the Center of the Earth*. Caves often led somewhere. Not to the same kind of somewhere, she'd retorted. Then he wound her hair around his hand to make a familiar knot at the back of her head. Mar, he said, you cannot use mystic abstractions to win arguments, even silly ones.

Like a rope, Margret thought. He wound my hair like a rope around his hand.

She was entering the north end of the Riverside Park Bird Sanctuary. It was a deserted part of the park, because it was untended, overgrown. The only other people who were out at this time of the morning were runners and people with dogs. They stayed in the south end of the Sanctuary, the rolling Women's Grove, with its attractive path of cedar chips, its pin oaks, lindens, black locusts, and a fifty-year growth of towering, teetering black cherry trees that seemed a kind of coven, ancestral, arthritic, one uprooted with every storm. In the Women's Grove you felt like gentry walking the manor, and that's exactly how the dog owners looked, strolling as if these were their grounds and they should be tamping tobacco into pipes, a shotgun under the arm. They hated having to keep their dogs leashed. It broke the spell, the sense of expansive ownership. Everyone felt possessive of the park. But the north end was Margret's.

People were afraid of it. Here the paths were not fragrant with care, not deep in cedar chips. They were snaky walkways of dirt, young poison ivy crouched along the edges, old poison ivy climbing trees, wild roses throwing tendrils across the path, whippy green arcs with tiny pink spikes that caught like mean teachers and held. The park's retaining wall stopped where the north end began, at 120th Street, because the drop-off stopped there and a steep slant took over. Here the paths traversed a hillside incline, a westward tumble that landed in a slender stretch of meadow overlooking the West Side Highway. From this grassy shelf you could survey the Hudson River and New Jersey to the west, and the vast sky above the George Washington Bridge to the north. The eastern sun had a hard time reaching down the wooded incline in the north end, down through its burly growth dispelled in a slip of meadow, so it was darker in here and stayed colder longer, at least an hour longer than anywhere else in Manhattan. In the morning, Margret always dressed warmer than she wanted to. The north end was a law unto itself.

Which is why it was so lovely. North south east west; none of that mattered here. Not to the birds and squirrels, not to the vagrants who sometimes made cardboard houses in the forked limbs of fallen trees, knowing that no one with authority walked these Indian paths, no one who would roust or bother. When Margret was in the north end she felt she was in the frayed back pocket of Manhattan. A pocket with a hole in it. A place no one cared about and the police shrugged off because they thought it contained nothing. Nothing but birds and weeds.

She could breathe in here. She was free in here. Grabbed at only by the wild rose, the low branch, her hair coming loose across her face, and her thoughts coming loose but not so much in here because she was concentrated on looking. When she walked these paths—the low path that rode just above the meadow so you could spy on the sparrows, or the high path that kept you eye-to-eye with the canopy and everything the sky brings through—she felt left alone by the world and its need for smiles and brightness and the latest movie and the hottest restaurant and all the hungers that made people feel you were fine, just like them. She loved these walks in the north end in the early morning when it was most raw and deserted, because she could feel one with these tumbling woods, in love with them and inside them. It was the opposite of possessing, though in a way she did possess this place because no one else normal came in here. No, it was that these woods possessed her. She wouldn't tell this to anyone. But she felt it. I'm in its body and if I never come out, never come back, no one would know where to look for me because I wouldn't even be here.

The high path was more solitary than the low, maybe because it was like a path through air. This was the path Margret preferred. It was very narrow, very up-and-down, and with the old fallen leaves so wet—damp and matted after three days of cold March rain—it was slippery. But the air had that clarity after rain, that cold, clear sharpness. "Cut glass," her grandfather used to say of such days. And Margret liked that cold-glass feeling against her face. There wasn't much in here now, just the usual blue jays and tufteds, downy woodpeckers and red-bellieds. And a pair of Carolina wrens that popped up like petty tyrants, rasping at you from stumps. I'd love to pocket one of those wrens, Margret thought, touch that creamy breast, smooth one of those bossy little heads. If one of them dies, I hope I find its body.

There was nothing like touching the head of a bird. The feathers were so soft, the sensation of them practically dissolved on your fingers. Margret always had a Baggie in her pocket, just in case she found something fallen. But nothing much fell in here, feathers mostly. She often wondered where the bodies went. Not the ones caught by the peregrines, who lived high in Riverside Church in a west-facing niche and dropped eviscerated pigeons and jays onto the grass triangle down below. No, it was the ones that fell from branch or sky, having lived out their time. They should be everywhere on the ground. But they were nowhere.

Once, heading to the Cherry Walk, Margret and her husband found a dead woodcock in dried asters off the underpass at One Hundredth, no doubt hit by a car. They both stared at it, marveling at its autumn-leaf coloring, the long worm-brown bill, and the strange placement of its huge black eyes, far back on the head and oddly high, like a martian. Margret knelt down to it, to look closer, and said, Let's take it with us to study and then we'll bury it. He said, No, the grass should have it. And when she looked up at her husband and said, But it's so beautiful, he said again, It fell here, we should leave it. They had discussed this subject often: the power of beauty, how it takes you, and the attempt to turn the table and take it, and that's where the trouble begins. But when Margret saw something fallen she felt herself reaching, wanting. Even now, her breath white in puffs, her fingers going prickly with the cold, the Hudson River still and steely through the branchy canopy, and under her feet old leaves slick as salamanders freezing on the path—thinking back on that woodcock in the weeds, she wished she had taken it.

Two

"I'M BRILLIANT. I'm beautiful. I've been on *Charlie Rose* three times in two years. So how can I, of all people, not have a boyfriend?"

Emily Edwards stood directly in front of Margret. She'd planted herself, which is what Emily did. Margret was sitting at a table putting stamps on glossy four-color cards. She liked being busy when the questions started. Emily's hands were on her hips, as they always were when she planted herself.

"You always ask that question the same way," Margret said, "with the answer right inside, staring at you. It's because you *are* all those things that you don't have a boyfriend. You're too intimidating."

Emily threw up her hands.

"That is not the answer I want to hear. That's why I keep asking. Why can't you give me a better answer?"

She paced over to the north window, a casement grid the width of the building, then paced back to Margret. They were in the glassed-in office on the mezzanine level of Emily's art gallery, Flow, on West Twenty-fourth Street. It was Monday, so the gallery was closed to the public, though an afternoon of meetings lay ahead for Emily.

"'Intimidating' is what everyone always says to single women in New York," Emily continued. "I thought men had changed in the nineties. I thought this was the era of the power couple."

"Em, we're not in the nineties anymore."

"Men in this city are warriors. Or trying to be. So why can't they deal with strong women?"

Margret was continually having to come up with new ways to say the same thing.

"Warriors want trophies and handmaidens," she said. "They don't want Xena. I mean, all those spears."

Emily perked, her Little Dot eyes big with interest.

"Does Xena not get dates?"

Margret didn't know. She'd never actually watched the show, just sort of osmosed it from commercials and magazines. Pop culture was easy to osmose—"too easy," she and Emily always said.

"I don't think so. That's why she's always riding around looking for something."

Emily was wearing Yohji today, a beautiful black wool shaped like a space capsule, *Apollo 13* bobbing upright in the sea. The pocket flaps were overscaled, big curves of black satin that hovered like quarter moons. It was one of the dresses Emily wore for meetings, an important dress, and with her shining black hair tight in its signature chignon—"tight as a tennis ball," someone once said—and her china white spoon face over that black triangle of dress, she was like a Russian Constructivist doll, all sickles and angles. In a way, she did look

Xena-esque. Xena in Soviet space! Margret was feeling that lightness before laughter catching at the corners of her mouth. She wished her hair wasn't pulled back because then she could let it fall forward in her face (which anyway, Emily was wise to). So she fought the lightness—it was almost painful. Because you weren't allowed to laugh at Emily more than she was willing to laugh at herself, and this boyfriend thing was really bugging her.

Emily was standing at a distance, her bumpy anklebones almost touching.

"Here I am, living a life of aesthetics, putting my money where my mouth is, so to speak. I mean, the effort it takes. It's Monday, after all. I'd much rather be comfortable, like you."

Margret didn't believe that for a second. Emily wouldn't be caught dead in leggings.

"But I can't. I have to look the part. I don't get to look like a schmo."

"I hardly think I look like a schmo."

Leggings aside, Margret's big white poet's blouse was pristine, and she'd pinned her garnet brooch over the collar button.

"I don't mean you. Anyway, all this and for what? Can't any man see me for what I am? This incredible catch?"

"But you have loads of dates," Margret said, getting Emily back for "schmo."

"I am not," she said flatly, "complaining about dates. Really, Margret. A date's a cakewalk. I'm talking about love. I'm thirty-one and I haven't been head over heels since Jeremy."

Who could forget? Margret and Emily were roommates then, new to New York, both having graduated from Vanderbilt with degrees in art, both having hauled down from the north in the first place. Margret was in a Ph.D. program at Columbia; Emily worked at André Emmerich, upstairs on Fifty-seventh Street. All excited, they crashed a

Columbia party of postdocs one night—it took them two hours to dress "casual"—and from that night on, from the minute her eyes met his and for the next two years, it was Emily and Jeremy, Jeremy and Emily. Seven syllables to say their names! Margret thought of them as the "Ems." And boy did the Ems think they were cool (well, they were), skinny in matching black jeans (Emily's were leather), smoking stinky Russian cigarettes (Jeremy was in Slavic Language and Literature), talking fast over loamy espresso (he dumped in three sugars, Emily took it straight). They were constantly dashing downtown—to Varick Street for gritty films, to the East Village for subversive performance art, to NYU for émigré poets in wainscoted rooms—endlessly jumping in and out of subways like a breathless couple in a Beatles movie. They never held hands on the sidewalk, because it would have slowed them down, and anyway they were too busy gesturing with abandon, deconstructing the things they'd seen. They discussed old issues like Richard Serra's *Tilted Arc*, new ones like the Getty and the Tate, and sticky wickets like Sally Mann's erotic shots of her own children.

"You say she's crossing a line, stealing their innocence," Jeremy argued one Sunday afternoon at their apartment, "but my own niece was diddling away at age five."

"Yuck," said Emily.

"'Yuck' is not critical lexicon, and don't be such a priss. Anyway, no one knew how she figured out to do that, but she did. And the doctors said it was healthy. This whole Victorian fantasy of sexless children. It acquits the adults their sweet tooth," and then he taunted, "*for juicy little packets.*"

"I don't know why you're dragging in the Victorians. It's more than a century later, and we do have boundaries, legal boundaries. Those kids were below the age of consent. Would Sally Mann have let someone else photograph them that way?"

"Probably not, but when it comes to what's legal, they're her possessions. Right? Isn't that what you pro-choice ladies say? And by the way, they're damn haunting pictures too."

"Yes, they're haunting. Because we sense something so wrong is taking place. She's sniffing the linens, and then implicating us as voyeurs. The whole thing is charged with wrongness, but we're supposed to accept it as a complicated aesthetic experience. Bottom line: I want transport. And Sally Mann just keeps dragging us down. She's a high-art version of that awful sex book Madonna did."

"Tres-pass," he said, as if breaking the word into syllables gave it more meaning. "That's Mann's subject. The way family members trespass on each other's privacy. The way knowledge trespasses on innocence. The bite into the apple. The eternal subject. Knowing."

"That's good, Jeremy. Very good. But it's too easy. Exploring a crime by committing it? It's like . . . like Loeb and Leopold."

At which point he lunged for her with a growl and she fell back on the couch squealing. Jeremy admired Emily's wide reaches. Most men did. Margret had been listening to this from the kitchen where she was chopping up sorrel leaves for soup. It was a tedious soup to make, but she loved the transformation, the weedy, dark green leaves so bitter lemony when raw, becoming wistful, pale, a memory of the meadow ladled into bowls with a pristine dollop of sour cream ("a spot of moo," Emily always said). Margret thought they both had points, though Jeremy kept moving the line, shifting the emphasis of the argument to stay ahead of Emily. He didn't argue straight. When he called from the other room, "And what does Miss Margret think?" she called back, "Too many fingerprints on those photos." They knew exactly what she meant.

The Ems were totally pretentious and completely happy in their pretensions, living for art and for each other. That is, until Emily was out of town one weekend and Jeremy went to another Columbia party and met a blond doctorate doing work on Lee Krasner and Jackson Pollock, heady stuff that trumped Emily's job on Fifty-seventh Street. Though professing to be just friends, Jeremy and the blonde got pretty palsy-walsy, meeting for afternoon chats while Emily was selling away at André Emmerich, not the least bit impressed by this so-called friendship.

"The last thing we need is more fancy-pants analysis of those drip-art dysfunctionals. Chaos theory, quantum physics, Lee's penis envy, and Pollack micturating on fires, so to speak"—Emily loved the phrase "so to speak"—"dousing his demons and marking his territory all at once. Haven't we had enough? Which is not to say he wasn't a zeitgeist genius."

Margret didn't mind "so to speak," but she hated "zeitgeist genius." Emily picked it up from Jeremy and waved it around a little too merrily, like a child with scissors. It was always annoying when a female friend was too influenced by a boyfriend, too delighted by his jokes and theories. It was like seeing her slip show. But maybe the phrase bothered Margret because Jeremy was just so zeitgeisty himself, so here, there, and everywhere that you couldn't really trust him. It probably didn't help that Margret was working up her thesis on the Pre-Raphaelites, paintings in which even the epiphanies seemed to happen in slow motion, hushed in heavy silks and self-effacing brushstrokes and almost outside of human time, the opposite of any kind of zeitgeist. Anyway, the Ems' affair, the sweetness of it, was saved by the zeitgeist. Perestroika was in full swing, and Jeremy got a grant that paid the way for two years in Moscow, not quite as nice as Saint Petersburg, but better than Novosibersk. The Ems parted soulfully, their romance ending in grave renunciation and the promise of many letters.

"We had two great years," Emily was saying. "And so much fun. Why aren't men fun anymore?"

It wasn't a rhetorical question. Emily didn't ask rhetorical questions. They looked at each other. Men had always been delighted by Emily—her style, her smarts, her know-it-all Ali MacGraw nose. The problem was they never knew what to do with her once they got her. She just trampled right over them. The fact that she lost interest by date three hadn't really mattered, because she'd never wanted to marry in her twenties. She thought women who did were dumb, and she'd made an elaborate and not wholly convincing exception for Margret, who married at twenty-five. But now, here it was, Emily was thirty-one.

"Are they not fun as individuals?" Margret asked. "Or do you mean the whole pursuit isn't fun? The whole dating game?"

"Both."

"Well, don't forget Jeremy was a student. And the city was cheaper then. Maybe that's part of it . . . how expensive the city has gotten. No one can afford to float anymore, go with the flow. You know, romance slows everything down. Because it makes everything bigger."

"I know. Even just discussing romance slows things down." Emily pushed up her sleeve to look at her watch. "I'm one of the few people who actually likes Mondays, but today I could give it a pass."

This was a big admission from Emily. In all the years Margret had known her, Emily had never once suffered Sunday-night ennui. Margret, since childhood, had puzzled over the tempo of Sunday, the church-silver stillness of morning, the afternoon like something endlessly in the oven or cooling on a ledge, and then by dusk, the day tarnishing before your eyes, the hours numbered. It was a day of depths and shallows, and she'd never figured out how to swim it. But Emily, she just stroked through Sunday. *Masterpiece Theatre* would be on, and as love and death in crinolines ensued, she'd be penciling her to-do list on a sunny yellow legal pad. Her outfit for the next day was already hanging in the closet, a good five inches of space on both sides. "My mom used to call me Little Miss Monday," Emily once said, "but I'm not sure it was a compliment." Emily's mother, recently and gratefully divorced from Emily's dad, tended to be objective.

But lately Emily seemed uneasy. Margret wasn't sure whether it had to do more with the gallery or with men. Emily had enjoyed one success after another since opening Flow. Indeed, she'd cornered a market in Manhattan, a very lucrative market it turned out. In the pin-drop gravitas of the Emmerich gallery, she'd learned the ropes: how to focus an exhibition and how to pace it; when to offer her own assessment and when to slip away, leaving customers to their private and often ridiculous calculations. "But will it go with the couch?" Go with! The bane of Emily's existence. Emily had never been one of those gallerinas who'd rather be reading a book in the back. She knew selling was seduction, and she loved making the match. There were infinite reasons to buy, but there was only one moment, maybe two, to close. Emily wasn't big on support-the-artist. Her view was, they're doing what they're wired to do; they have no choice. She talked instead of "the quest." She knew her customers were hunting for something: themselves. In Emily's hands, customers felt the excitement of the search. With novices she suggested chapters in books, gave them articles she'd xeroxed. A coworker nearly fainted when he overheard her say, "Don't even think of buying this piece until you've seen X at the Met or Y at MoMA. Go now."

"You threw that sale away," the coworker stated when the glass door closed.

"They'll be back," Emily said, "and they won't blink at the price."

And she was right. They didn't blink. They felt they were buying the Met, buying MoMA.

With more sophisticated collectors, Emily was quick in her listening, but quiet, staying out of the way, saying just enough so they felt her thoughts circling, silhouettes they couldn't quite identify. What was she thinking? She was warm but aloof until the moment begged for connection, and having figured out exactly what they needed to hear, she flew in with a simple opinion turned just right, the last click in the combination lock. No one, not unless they're Howard Hughes, wants to buy in a vacuum. Mr. Emmerich himself was known to chuckle when he saw Emily with a customer. "Spinning her web," he would say, in his Swiss-chocolate accent.

He was sorry to see Emily go (her coworkers were not). The local retailers—Bergdorf's and Barney's and Bendel's—they were sorry too, because Emily was so quick with the plastic. But Fifty-seventh Street's loss was Spring Street's gain, and for the next year Emily impressed everyone by managing to sell the most arcane paintings on earth—or at least in SoHo. After that, she jumped to a TriBeCa gallery specializing in contemporary fashion photography, where she lasted three months.

"Oh, Margret," Emily would moan, "when you're around it all day it just seems so faux. It's not that I don't like fashion photography. I had my Penn phase. Remember? When I thought the man was Miltonian. God, I'm pretentious. It's just that there's so little hand in this stuff. It's airbrushed art for airbrushed people, to be put in rooms with no wrinkles. I'm convinced these young couples think the photos will keep *them* young."

"The Picture of Dorian Leigh."

"Ooh, touché. Does anyone say 'touché' anymore? But seriously, you never see older people buying fashion photographs. Right there, that tells you something."

As an antidote to SoHo and TriBeCa, Emily wrangled a sort of internship at the Cloisters, even though they didn't have internships. In other words, she persuaded her wealthy father to subsidize a year of learning because, after all, she'd worked her way up the rungs, sparing him, she was quick to remind, the expense of grad school. Emily was disenchanted with the art world, with the manufacture of art stars whose work became brands and franchises for millionaires only. "It's like John Malkovich designing suits," she declared one night into a third mojito. "Logos and egos running amok, and a Warhol in every hip living room." Almost every week, skimming the Arts & Leisure section in the *Times*, it was the same shake of the head.

"I could be the next Mary Boone if I wanted. But why be the next her? I'd rather be the first me."

Emily was on her own quest, and it had led to the artisan, the guild worker, to the master crafts that were disappearing from earth—*poof*, another one gone—the stonecutter, the wood-carver, Dr. Coppelius, and Jude the Obscure. Daily she rode the subway to the stop at 190th, where you had to rumble up to the earth's surface in an elevator strapped with steel—"like a Morlock," Emily loved to say. Gamely she pushed through the turnstiles against gray winter or pelting rain, her hair as black as a raven's wing in a madrigal, a sack lunch tucked in her tote. Like the penniless beauty in a gothic romance, she trudged up the road to that castle on the hill. You'd never know her father was Dick Edwards, one of the most successful criminal lawyers in America. For a year Emily padded within those stone-heavy halls that echoed with the chink of the chisel, the rack of the loom. Studying in a fortress, bundled up in Aran sweaters and her trusty leather jeans, she was La Belle with no Beast, unless you counted the chief restorer who was always leaning in, breathing a little too close, "mentoring" her. Save us from mentors, Margret and Emily were always laughing together, and then one or the other would add, Except for gay mentors! Who were la crème de la crème—

that is, generous with no sexual agenda. Emily stayed on for another year, now an assistant curator wearing Geoffrey Beene jumpsuits, her tread mute in rubber-soled Robert Clergeries. And all the while during those two years she was making a list, talking to talent, developing relationships with a chosen few. She was laying the foundation for her own gallery, Flow, with collections she'd been guiding for over a year, working hand-in-glove with artisans like the silversmith who'd studied in France at Christofle and now lived and worked in New Hampshire. He'd been doing thimbles when Emily discovered him, thimbles with intricate beading. And also ladles covered with hammerings of carrots, onions. "There's even a wishbone on one," Emily sighed. "God, he needs guidance. But the work is exquisite."

Emily commissioned chalices. She wanted them utterly simple at the lip, but on the stem and climbing the corolla a very fine repoussé of ferns, or curling vines, or thistle and burr, as if the bowl was floating up out of the undergrowth. Emily trusted her instincts. She'd clocked what was happening in the country. First *Ghost*, then *Touched by an Angel*, then *Sixth Sense*. "All this New Age seeing and seeking, this need for heavenly intervention," she said. "When it's right here in the godly human hand."

Chalices. It was perfect, "symbolic," Margret said, when Emily presented the idea over cocktails at Cafe Luxembourg, their meeting point midway between Emily's place in Chelsea and Margret's at 113th and Riverside Drive. In fact, it was Margret who suggested the more naturalistic treatment.

"Have him read King Arthur," she'd said. "White or Tennyson. Or even just watch the movie *Excalibur*. Ask him to imagine how Nature would present the chalice to the air."

A month later, seated again at Lux, cozy in its buttery light, Emily pulled a large lump of Bubble Wrap from her tote, unwound it, undid another wrapping of wool batting, and on the table placed the first one. They both stared at it, a silver chalice veined with winter branches of thorn.

"The Grail," Margret said.

"He has ideas for eleven more." Emily pulled a folder from the tote. "Here are the sketches."

Flow opened with a show called Chalice. Reporters loved the simplicity. Critics loved the coherent package, a gallery that knew exactly what it was about. And everybody loved Emily, an art impresario in the making. The chalices, one thousand dollars each, sold singly (as *objet*), in pairs (as extravagant wedding gifts), and most surprisingly, fax orders chittering in from Los Angeles and Europe, as sets of twelve for table settings. It was a smashing success with a huge back order.

And a success for Margret too, because Emily insisted she dress Flow's window, which was really a box, three feet wide and four feet high, set into the building's facade. It was a lovely thing Emily did for Margret, though also a no-brainer, as Margret was in visuals at Saks, doing freelance jobs on the side. This was a window like the jewel-box windows at Tiffany and Bulgari, only a little bigger. Margret would have done it for free. She even said so. And Emily snapped those Junior Mint eyes on her. "Don't ever work for free," she said. "Not even for me. If you don't know what you're worth, no one else will either."

For days Margret went from sketch to sketch, from the obvious, burgundy velvet, to the impossible, a grotto of grape leaves. She then thought to line the space in gray satin, and frame the window in gray velvet curtains swagged back. The floor would be covered with rocks, and upon a large jaggedy rock in the center would be the chalice with the thorn motif. Stark but theatrical. When Margret showed drawings to Emily, Emily said, "I love the rocks. There *is* something edge-of-the-world about the Grail. But velvet curtains, will they seem too—?"

"Sunday matinee?"

"Yeah."

Margret felt foolish then. She hadn't pushed herself hard enough. Why satin? Why velvet? Why rocks? She finally presented Emily with a small-scale model. Instead of fabric on the walls, she put mirrors, with the sides angled tight like in a dressing room. And then she filled the space with dark thorned vines, swirling and spiraling inward so that in the center she could place the chalice.

Emily took one look and said, "Do it." And when it was done, the chalice floating in a knot of air inside a dense vortex of thorn and light, Margret tucked some emerald green moss into the bowl, a few strands spilling over the lip. It was a secret nod to the great Gene Moore, her hero, who had used moss to such magical effect in the windows of Tiffany.

"It's positively transcendental!" Emily said.

There was something about it. An eeriness that thrilled Margret. The feeling that the chalice was always near, waiting to be found if only you knew where to look for it. The only people who didn't stop to study the window were messengers, flying by on bicycles. From then on it was Margret's window.

Emily's next show was a collection of carpentry: gorgeous wooden niches, arched and vaulted, worked to hang in corners or flush on the walls. Within a week, this too was into a waiting list. It was amazing, the public's hunger for objects touched with a hint of the altar, a spirit of sacrifice. With that second show, Emily truly had found her niche, a pun most reviewers couldn't resist making. Margret could count on six to eight Flow windows a year.

And Flow flowed, though Emily was a little crankier now, four years in and trying to keep the standard high and higher. It wasn't easy drumming up new practitioners of lost arts, or finding artisans who could, or would, take guidance from such a young New York dealer. Emily didn't want to disappoint her following, her fans, but more than that she couldn't stand the thought of disappointing herself. The current show, Ghosts, was the first time Margret saw Emily professionally in doubt. It was only for a moment, but it was a dissonance from the deep.

The collection of torchières and wall sconces, plus three small and strangely beautiful chandeliers, were all made of alabaster, a soft stone much in use during the early twentieth century, but very fragile and now abandoned except for simple shapes like soap dishes and those bland hemisphere light fixtures. The pieces in Ghosts, intricately turned and hauntingly veined in apricot, pale green, and gray, looked like something from the hull of a sunken ship, shapes lathed in white silt and seaweed, bloated with creamy accretion. A few days before the opening, when Margret stopped by, as she always did right before a show, Emily kept moving about the gallery, squinting at the room from different angles.

"Something's missing," she finally said, looking to Margret. "There isn't the coherence."

She strode to the back of the gallery, where her voice took on a faint reverberation. "The quality of light is wonderful, but the collection as a whole . . . it's saying nothing. The silence is driving me nuts."

Margret felt the silence too, the something missing, but the missingness had power.

"You must have called it Ghosts for a reason," Margret said. "Because you were feeling the absence, the presence of the absence. That's what coheres the collection."

Emily was listening.

"Well," she said, "since you put it that way"—she looked at Margret—"does all this make you think of anything in particular?"

"You tell me."

"The chandeliers. They look like things in the apartments after 9/11, that thick coat of ash. Remember that tea set in the *Times*? Like it was petrified? It didn't hit me before, just looking at the pieces in their boxes, or holding them up. When you were doing the window, did you see it?"

Margret shook her head no. She'd been thinking about the skin of the stone, a complexion that was centuries in the making. The window she designed was dark. It contained a skeletal staircase she'd made of copper wire, suspended like a fire escape without a building. One sconce glowed behind it, a night-light for Persephone.

"But now . . ." Emily was turning slowly in the center of the room. "You know, I could really get skewered for this."

"No," Margret said, looking up at the chandeliers. "It's the underworld."

The papers called it "elegiac," "a requiem," "an artistic response to the bombing." Emily, always ahead of the press, was slower to answer, not her usual self. It was that moment of doubt, nagging at her.

"It's coattails," she complained to Margret.

"That's just harsh," Margret had said, "on the show and yourself. If there's anything we know, it's that meanings are unconscious. And atmospheric. You can't control that. You, Emily Edwards, think you can because up til now you have. But a work has a life of its own, and you know that."

"I don't like not having control."

No. Emily didn't like that at all.

It was almost eleven. Margret needed to be at Saks by twelve.

"So what's your week like?" Emily asked. "And stop doing those stamps. Liza's coming in this afternoon, and she'll do it because it's her job to do it."

"Saks today through Thursday. And on Friday a meeting at Lord and Taylor. They called Tom for a recommendation, and he suggested me. And Lord and Taylor really needs help. Their windows are awful."

"Lord and Taylor. That could be good. But was Tom recommending you for a full-time job? Or just part-time when you're not at Saks?"

"I'm not sure. I just assumed part-time. I mean, he said there was a new guy there who wanted to build up his Rolodex. So I assumed that meant having a stable of people to call."

Emily pressed her fingers to her temples and closed her eyes. "I'm trying to picture their windows."

"There's not much to picture."

"They're just big and full of dumb mannequins."

"And yet their windows have a real history," Margret said. "In the forties, when windows were more important than ads, it was Lord and Taylor and Bonwit Teller. Those were the big two."

"Bonwit's," Emily sighed. "Just the sound of it."

"And now it's Nike."

A moment of silence for long-lost Bonwit's.

"Well, I want you to wow them in the meeting, which we can discuss on Friday night. There's a cocktail party at Joel Skelly's, and you're coming."

"But I thought you said Joel was so conceited."

"He is. But it's just a party, and he throws good ones. I mean, just to see the view from those windows."

"I don't have anything to wear to that kind of party. Anyway, I thought I'd go to the Point on Friday."

"Nooo. You keep leaving on weekends for that freezing house. It's so annoying. The place is practically a retirement community, and in winter it's just dead."

Margret wasn't listening. She was looking out the casement window to the building across the street. There was a bird on the second-story ledge that was probably a pigeon, but she always checked twice now, ever since she'd looked out her apartment window and seen a kestrel on a nearby air conditioner, eating a sparrow. It plucked the bird like a cook at the sink, decapitating it; then from the red hole at the neck it ate down and around. When only the bottom half was left, a cup with two spindly legs, from this gruesome goblet the falcon pulled out the guts and swallowed them whole. And most people would have thought it was a pigeon.

"This Friday," Emily ordered, "you'll stay in town, and if Joel's party is a bore, we'll run off to dinner. My treat. Okay? Promise?"

"Maybe," Margret said. "I can't promise."

Three

MARGRET HATED THE TRIP crosstown from Flow. Crosstown blocks were so long, almost four times as long as Manhattan's north-south blocks, which took less than a minute to walk, just about the time it took to quote the first chunk of "Prufrock," up to *In the room the women come and go / Talking of Michelangelo*. That was as far as Margret had memorized the poem, so there was a nice bump of finality upon reaching the curb. In one block you could also get through the opening section of "*Che faro*" from *Orpheus and Eurydice,* right up to that call into caverns—"*rispondi!*"—just as you looked both ways. Margret first heard Gluck's aria her sophomore year at Vanderbilt, was just wrenched by it in Music of the Baroque. "A metaphysical transaction," her elderly professor had said, "melody over matter." Margret still recalled those words, "a metaphysical transaction," still remembered the spring weekend she memorized "*Che faro,*" how beautiful and sad her walk to the library was, the buds on campus magnolias, furred like animal ears, cracking open on tissuey pink petals as if to offer solace.

In one block you could get through the first part of the Carpenters' "Goodbye to Love," a song Margret had sung to herself for years while walking, because of the winding melody, the way it seemed a modern version of a classical aria, that spinning out in air. When she got to the end of the block she was always at the point where the title comes back in that tone of . . . not resignation exactly, more like prophecy.

"What tense is this?" Margret once asked Charles. "The song begins with a declaration, 'I'll say goodbye to love.' And then along the way it transforms into 'I guess I've always known I'd say goodbye to love.' What is that? A future transitive? A past perfect?"

Charles, who was reading by the window, had looked at her with a what-are-you-asking-me narrowing of the eyes. He didn't like pretend ignorance, that kind of feigning not-knowing that so many young women thought cute. He was a professor at Columbia, and around it more than you'd think.

"I really don't know," she insisted. "Grammar is one of my weak links."

"Okay, say it again."

"I guess I've always known I'd say goodbye to love."

"Strange sentence. But tensewise, straightforward. 'I guess,' present. 'I have known,' present perfect. 'I would say,' conditional." He set his book aside. "Play it for me."

Margret slipped in the CD, and that was the beginning of Charles's enthusiasm for a song he'd first heard in college and had dismissed with a sneer. She loved the song because it was so Mozartian, so reasoning. It reminded her of Pamina in *The Magic Flute.* He loved that it was a rock song of renunciation, a total anomaly in a genre of hooch and hedonism, and yet the guitar solo at the end was so out there. "She's Emily Dickinson," he said, "stoned on loneliness."

It was sonorities like "stoned on loneliness" that made him a popular professor on campus, that and the drama of his lectures. He came into the room without a hello-how-are-you and just flicked off the lights, clicked up a slide, and dropped in darkness into the hour, plunging into the spatial poetry of the bas-relief—the power drawn from slim shadows—or hailing the colossi of Nimrud, the monster momentum of those human-headed, eagle-winged bulls, relentlessly striding on five legs. It was a lesson every time the way he began without preamble, as if to say, *Now*—see *now*. It was one way to do it. Not Socratic but kinetic, a match between the eye and . . . everything, his red laser pointer leaping to the screen as he moved out from the lectern like a chess piece, then back, then out again, then back.

He became her adviser in her second year, a sort of stopgap when Margret's real adviser, Maria Silvano, a brainy, bipolar Rossetti scholar, who wore black leather miniskirts and pointy Manolo Blahniks, went off her lithium, wreaked havoc at the faculty Christmas party, and was on indefinite medical leave by the New Year. Margret was told her new adviser would be Dr. Charles Albert Ashur, Ancient Near East, a distinguished Assyriologist who also lectured on orientalism, which took in the Pre-Raphaelites. She'd passed him in the hall and on campus, that dark head, those elegant wools melting over handsome shoulders. She'd watched him listening intently to students who caught up with him after class. And she'd been introduced to him at a grad student tea, where shyness had made her quiet in his presence, boring. He was the most attractive man she'd ever seen.

Anyway, she knew, as everyone in the art department knew, that he was taken. Even the undergrads she overheard in the bathroom—

voices so glossy, they sounded store-bought—even they knew he was involved. She was in a stall when she overheard them, and she drew her feet close to the toilet so they wouldn't know a TA was listening.

"Don't you think he'd be good in bed?"

"Who?"

"Professor Ashur."

"If he promised not to grade you after."

"He's single at least, so it wouldn't be that thing of the married prof cheating with a student."

"Who cares about cheating? I'm pissed about the T he gave my last paper. I mean, very funny. Twaddle? I worked hard on that paper."

"No you didn't. You said you made it all up."

"I know, but it took all night. So how about some credit for creativity?"

"Well, I think he's sexy. Scary is sexy."

"Your saying that is scary."

"He's Assyrian, you know."

"Syrian? I guessed he was Arab or something, because of his coloring."

"Not Syrian. Ah-syrian. As in Assyria. The old name for all those oil countries. Anyway, he's been with a Swarthmore professor like forever."

"How do you know?"

"Jill's dad's a trustee, and he knows everything about everyone, and that's what he said."

"So why aren't they married?"

"Jill's dad says the girlfriend doesn't believe in marriage. You know, politically."

"So she's one of those radical feminists everyone used to be."

"Maybe scary Charles Ashur is pussy-whipped."

Sputters of laughter.

"Oh, god, we're gonna be late."

There was much snapping and scurrying; then the door swung shut with that wood-against-marble thud.

But it was true that Charles Ashur was scary and sexy at the same time. Scary because you did want to please him; you did want to show you could keep up and pull a rabbit out of your hat. And sexy because, well, Margret didn't want to please him, didn't want him to think he was the judge, even though he was. And then there was the way he looked at you, those velvet eyes taking you in under black eyebrows, making you subject and object at once, nervous under his gaze. Bedouin eyes, she thought the first time she'd looked into them. Bed.

"Miss Snow," he said to her in March of her second year. He was unlocking his office door, where she'd been waiting to get his signature on a financial paper. "I'm your adviser, and I have no idea what you're up to. But then I'm not even sure you're in the right century, with a name like Margret Snow." He threw a black briefcase on a metal chair. "So what might you be doing when you're not here? Sitting in a window reading a book about English birds?" He removed take-out coffee from a brown paper bag. "Or maybe you're painting at night in a tower by candlelight? Which would give your work a ghastly glow."

He was on the other side of his desk, looking at her with a pleased expression. He liked that "ghastly glow." She was standing next to the metal chair, flattered that he'd noticed she was avoiding his office, and also struck by the allusion to *Jane Eyre*, page two, where Jane is reading Bewick's *History of British Birds*. Though maybe he made the reference because of the kilt she was wearing, her green and blue, with white anklets in black Timberlands. ("Those shoes could eat children," Emily always said, full of scorn.) The whole getup was a wee bit window seat, but she'd always liked the way anklets set off the curve of her calves.

"I've been communing with a Bewick's wren in Riverside Park," Margret said.

It was a whole other tone that came back at her, like a zoom-in.

"You know birds?"

She nodded.

"Then tell me about Bewick's wren."

It was summers with her grandfather all over again.

"It's like a Carolina wren but grayer, with white on the tail, which is diagnostic. But I was only joking. I've never seen a Bewick's wren."

Margret was about to go into *Jane Eyre*, page two, the whole lead balloon of explanation, but was saved by his grin, the surprise in it. She'd never seen Charles Ashur smile like that; not in class, in the hall, on College Walk, never.

"We're going birding," he said. He pulled open a desk drawer and lifted out binoculars, Nikon, which he waggled in the air and then set gently back in the drawer. "Did you bring your bins to New York?"

She shook her head no. They were back home in Chicago, probably still in the hall closet. She hadn't used them in years.

"You can borrow this pair. So how about Thursday at one? We'll meet downstairs at the door."

That was the beginning. That was how they did it. Climbing hillocks and scanning the sky, they discussed class and her TA duties and her thesis, which she thought she already had a title for. "Still Life: Eternity in Pre-Raphaelite Art." Or "Sensitive Plants: The Dream of Eternity," which would lean on Shelley's poem, "The Sensitive Plant." Or even "Listening to Lilies: Life and Death in Pre-Raphaelite Art." Okay, so maybe she didn't have a title yet, but she knew what she wanted to write about: the Sunday pace of the paintings, humans languishing like hothouse flowers, more plant than animal, practically decorative, and love a gorgeous blossom fading to black. Or something like that.

They would walk the block to Riverside Park or hop a cab to Central Park at 100th, where they wandered the paths from Pool to Loch to Meer for an hour or two every other week, looking and talking. When they started out on their first walks, he'd point wordlessly to his left, a reminder to walk on that side because he was deaf in his right ear, the result of an operation for vertigo. And even when she was over on the left he still sometimes had to drop his head down to hear, and there was something disarming about that, his concentration on hearing, which became one with the close view of his forehead, with its two horizontal lines that were always in the same place, the way branches of a tree are always in the same place. He often grabbed her sleeve when they came to wide crosswalks, sometimes saying, "Whoa, Miss Snow," because he'd noticed that once she got talking she wasn't very watchful. Sometimes he just said, "Snow."

On days when there were no birds, he'd push his hands into his pockets, letting his bins hang against his chest like a forgotten girlfriend. On days when there were a lot of birds, spring song falling from the trees, autumn hunger driving tiny breasts south, he would pause with excitement, like a young hero in a Russian folktale who should have a feather in his cap. It made him look young. He soon realized that Margret knew in her bones what he was studiously good at; he'd begun birding only as an adult. She saw how avid he was, how up on the literature, and that his focus was formidable. He was knowledgeable; she was instinctual. He admired her experience; she admired his reach. They were equals, calling quietly, nodding in ascent; scarlet tanager, blue-headed vireo, chestnut-sided, yes, I've got it. He called more than she did, but kept aware of her, saying what've-ya-got all in one word when he thought she had something good. Sometimes he said it before she even knew what she had.

"How do you know I've got something good," she asked, "when I haven't even locked on to it yet?"

"You go taut like a pointer."

"Like this?" She hooked her right hand like a front paw and pushed out her nose because it was fun to make him laugh. But Margret knew what he meant. When a flit or blur was different, it was almost as if your body knew before your eyes did.

He would pinch up his pants before crouching to look low, and Margret loved the way his thigh muscle bowed against wool or old kakhi. And she loved the pinch, the precision of it, the touch of vanity. He had thin ankles, usually in dark socks that were serious, like the daddy socks businessmen wear, sleek with wingtips but dorky with the running shoes he changed into for their walks. He always had a clean white handkerchief in his left back pocket, folded in a square. He used it to wipe the lenses of his binoculars, or his eyes that teared in the cold. Once he used it to remove a gnat that flew into Margret's eye, which he did with his left hand—he was a lefty—his right hand awkwardly holding her neck. The two of them scrutinized the poor smushed gnat on the handkerchief, Charles saying, "Gnats don't have it so good," which she found hilarious.

His keys were in his left front pocket and sometimes he jingled them, but that was always on the way back, never on the way out. When he wanted to know the time, he swung and cocked his arm, and a silver tank emerged from under his starched cuff. An old Lord Elgin, he told her, when she admired it. "It belonged to my great uncle, who came from Iran." He had a wallet of black ostrich, the same matte black as his hair and eyebrows. Over time she became intimate with the life of that thick black hair, how when it was getting long it began to curl behind his ears, with a wave coming in at the front, and how when it was newly cut he looked shorn, nakedly ethnic, and you could see, on the sides, some silver. He once caught her staring at him after a haircut, and flustered, she heard herself say stupidly, "You're young to have silver."

"I'm not young," he said.

He so well avoided any mention of his private life that Margret avoided any mention of her own, such as it was, sawdust dates in campus dives, or nice downtown dinners that felt a little too grad-students-in-Manhattan. And this mutual unmentioning—it started to feel as if their time together was a kind of private life itself, its own domestic scene, more side-by-side than face-to-face, because their eyes were always in the tops of trees or down among fallen branches. When Margret actually saw Charles with the girlfriend from Swarthmore—girlfriend, that seemed so lightweight; she was his partner, his companion—when she saw them at a Friday evening lecture most of the art department attended, Margret didn't go over, didn't even go near. Instead she stole glances from across the room, taking in the petite woman, probably size six, very buttoned-up in a neat navy suit, and with light brown hair, shiny and almost as short as his. She was a professor of classics, Susan Baughman, and they were a classic university couple, Charles squiring her amid colleagues in ties and tweeds, his handsome hand at the small of her back, his left hand, because she too was on his left. Margret knew that hand well from watching it curl around binoculars.

Susan Baughman wasn't beautiful. "Smart" was the word for her, like a reporter in the forties. The set of her shoulders was brisk. Or was it unbending? Or maybe Margret wished it so. Then again, maybe that's what made Susan attractive to him. Margret had no way to judge. All she knew was that they'd been together for years. I don't feel jealous, she said to herself, as she settled a little deeper and lower into her seat, pocketing herself in maroon mohair. I feel a Mozartian reason, an admiration for him, whom I might have loved in another life, and envy of her, who was lucky enough to be in the right place at the right time. Or, be generous, maybe Susan Baughman is exactly what he wants.

But as the lecture went on, brilliant, endless, Margret felt less generous, less able to concentrate on the voiceless Etruscans. Afterward, with everyone inching out of the auditorium in small steps and quips, and she snaking out faster, slipping by all those male chests under ties and tweeds, and women getting gracelessly into coats, she felt she couldn't breathe. She had to get out as if she hadn't been there. Margret hailed a cab, even though it was an extravagance; she lived only eighteen blocks away, an eighteen-minute walk. She didn't want anyone to see her walking home alone on a Friday night. Emily was out with Jeremy, and it was good Em wouldn't know she was alone. "That's the last thing you needed," she would say.

In the cab Margret tried to brighten. I'll order Chinese, read til twelve, and not think about all the life outside these windows, all the dates and embraces and first kisses and falling in love. But just thinking about what she wasn't going to think about brought tears to her eyes. He was way too old for her anyway, at least forty. Why cry about a fantasy? And yet why did men her own age—men who were calling her—seem too young? Tears balanced on her lower lids as she paid the cabbie five dollars, a "fin" her father liked to say, slang her mother hated. Forty minutes later, tears spilled over, one or two a minute slipping into the Little Bit of Everything soup she'd ordered. Margret read slowly with swollen eyes, a monograph on Millais's *Ophelia* of 1852. Bored senseless, she pulled out her collected Shakespeare to reread that section of *Hamlet*. Reading Shakespeare always made her feel part of something important.

"Too much of water hast thou, poor Ophelia."

Margret cried herself to sleep that night. At first she lay in bed on her back like Millais's Ophelia in the water. In the painting Ophelia's hands were floating open like Christ showing the stigmata, which Margret did for about three absurd seconds before dropping them on the bed. Being on your back was an uncomfortable position to cry in, hot tears sliding down the sides of your face, sticky cold by the time they reached your ears and neck. Margret turned on her side, feeling self-conscious about crying. She stuffed her face into the pillow so it would catch her tears.

She didn't need to muffle sound. Margret never made a sound when she cried, never wanted anyone to know she was crying. Maybe if she'd had siblings she would have learned to cry aloud, to get attention. But as it was, she'd got so much attention that she muted herself when she could. Crying. It was just tears into linens like rain on sand, moonlight watching on the walls. Margret kept telling herself it wasn't really Charles Ashur. It was hormones. And the crushing workload. And her thesis inching along. And Emily dating Jeremy and being so out in the world, so clearly ready to move downtown into her own chic place. Margret would be left in this studenty apartment with its cracking plaster, its thin wood floors that had soft spots like bruises, and those paint drips, decades of paint jobs congealed under windowsills and wall moldings, gloppy cysts constantly catching the eye. She couldn't not see them. Sometimes she just wanted to get a chisel and knock them all off.

Margret missed her next meeting with Charles. She had bad cramps, the kind that feel like an iron hand is squeezing your womb, like Nature herself is mad that you're not pregnant. Margret canceled two hours before. She had nothing to report anyway.

That awful Friday, Margret decided, was good for her, a reality check. She accepted a date with a friend of Jeremy's. And before she met with Charles the next time, she gave herself a shake. Just loosen up. Be blithe. She even unbuttoned her white blouse one more button. Why not? He didn't care about her bosom. He had a classics professor at Swarthmore. She turned sideways to the mirror. From this angle, if you were next to her, there was quite a glimpse. She ran a finger down the swell of softness.

"Her milky breast," Margret said to the mirror. And then she redid the button. That kind of show wasn't her at all. The one time she'd tried to be showy it came right back at her. It was the summer after eighth grade, everyone excited about high school and two boys calling her at home, turning her head. She was up at her grandparents', birding with her grandfather on a particularly sweaty August afternoon, and as they studied some peeps on a mudflat, she flipped back her hair the way her friends at school did, which was not easy with her mop. Her grandfather said, "Stop flouncing your hair like that. You're going to flush something." Then he stared at her for some seconds and squared off. "You're a pretty girl, but is that all you're going to be? Haven't you noticed? Nature has one purpose for good looks, and that's breeding season. Beauty is a trap, Margret. All well and good in its place, but it goes." He motioned farther up the flat. "Look at those scruffy sandpipers heading into winter plumage." She looked. "Don't be a person who courts attention. *Pay* attention."

She knew she was the favorite of his grandchildren—well, she and Jack—and she didn't want to disappoint him. That day when Margret saw her grandfather's look of dismay, eyes blue as a baby bonnet, she knew how ridiculous it was, this flipping her hair as if it were shiny Barbie blond. Pretty was not all she was going to be.

"Let's hop a cab. . . ."

Charles always said it that way, out on Broadway at 116th. This time, though, after they'd scooted into the backseat, Margret said,

"What is that, hop a cab? Do you think it comes from hop a train, like in the Depression? Wouldn't it be fun to hop a train? And hear whip-poor-wills at night?"

She was talking while settling in, trying to get her seat belt fastened, which didn't want to catch. "Though I guess everyone was really hungry," she said, and then it clicked. "Boxcars in the Dust Bowl," she continued, recatching her hair in her tortoise clip. "People who've never lived in the Midwest will never understand." She turned to him for an answer and was jarred by the look on his face. It was the burning look of a boy, the way they look at something they want in a window, something behind glass. She felt it quick in her heart, her back against the seat, and looked casually away as if she'd seen nothing, pretend it's nothing. But it was a split second of everything. And when she heard him say, "I don't know the origin," she glanced back at him and the look was gone.

She tried to be herself in Central Park, but was distracted, excited, tense. He asked her about Friday's lecture, why she wasn't there.

"I was there," she said. "I came late and found a seat way in the back on the left." Well, that was true, the seat on the left. "And then I ran because Emily and I had a party to go to."

"Grad student parties. I remember those."

His condescension was infuriating.

"On the contrary, it was a gathering at André Emmerich. David Hockney was in town." It wasn't a complete lie. Hockney had been in town around Christmas.

"And which was more interesting? The Etruscan tombs or Mr. Swimming Pool?"

"Professor Ashur, those pools are tombs too. Turquoise tombs. 'And in his grave rain'd many a tear.'" She was quoting Ophelia, a line she'd read that Friday night. "No one's ever written about the sadness of swimming pools."

Hop a cab.

Margret thought it almost every time she put her hand up in the street. She was always taking cabs from Emily's, because she couldn't stand waiting for the crosstown bus at Twenty-third, not to mention she usually stayed too long chatting and was running late. She'd think, Let's hop a cab, and she'd remember that day, her turning to him for an answer, and finding the look on his face.

She put up her arm and a hurtling taxi swerved whoosh to the curb, a move unique to cabs, nothing like a chess piece or most things moved by human hands, more like the boxy snap of a cicada, burring sharp and flat to a branch. Margret got in and said, "Sixth Avenue and Fiftieth."

Four

"CICADA."

They listened.

"When you hear that sound, you know it's the far side of summer."

"It's like a rattle."

"Sort of. What else?"

They waited for it to sing again.

"A sewing machine."

"That's good. What else?"

"Like . . . electricity."

"Yes. A pulse. Say the word over and over, and you kind of have it."

"Cicada-cicada-cicada-cicada."

And though the sound wasn't really the same, the rhythm was

right. The repeated word caught the rhythm, trees heavy with heat, electric with longing.

Later that day they heard the sound very near and slowly closed in on it, looking, looking. The cicada was hard to locate, its sound thrown from tree to tree, but finally they found it hugging a young dogwood at shoulder height. Her grandfather plucked it off the branch, gently between thumb and forefinger, and showed Margret its bulldog face, the green-black wing veins and chalk white belly, and then the rattle began, two or three half starts, then the full cycle, that circular rhythm, awesomely loud, the big little body shaking with sound.

She remembered saying, "Cicadas always make it feel hotter outside."

"I agree," he'd said. "The song of the sun."

He told her they were completely defenseless, that they lived in the ground as nymphs, then climbed up from the roots, cracked open on the tree, and emerged as adults.

"Crack open. It's creepy."

Not any creepier, he'd said, than a moth or butterfly squeezing out of a cocoon. Some species lived in the earth for thirteen to seventeen years before they emerged.

"Dirt is eternity," he said.

Margret didn't know what eternity was, but when he said, "It's the same as forever," she liked the sound of it. They were sitting on the huge bald log in a clearing surrounded, shaded, by black locusts, all those rows of little leaves the color of katydids and the branches black as ink. The grass here was tender-looking, long shoots a soft green, soft as hair, so long and soft it looked windblown even on airless days. Sometimes Margret would lie down in the grass for a few minutes and look straight up. When you looked up, the locust leaves were chartreuse with the hot sun glaring behind them, yellow pushing at the green, and in the few spaces the sun got through you saw the force of it, those cathedral shafts, straight as spears and steamy in the morning. She and her grandfather called this clearing the glade. It was a place off the path where they pulled out their thermoses, their apples, their sandwiches wrapped in wax paper.

He insisted on wax paper because he liked the way it folded, and because of how useful it was afterward. You could wrap an interesting fern or flower in it and then press it in your field guide. You could even fold an insect into wax paper, very carefully, and put it in your front pocket so you wouldn't sit on it. They unwrapped their sandwiches, smoothing the wax paper into place mats. She was eight, ten, twelve, and he was in his sixties.

"Do you want to be buried?" she asked.

"Of course," he said. "To say hello to the centipedes. The problem is I don't want to go into a cemetery, where it's boxes in the ground and manicured lawns on top and no good to any other creature than humans wanting things pretty."

Eyelashes are like centipedes' legs, Margret had thought at the time. It was funny how you could remember a thought for decades, just the way you remembered a birthday gift or a grade on a paper. Or maybe she remembered it because, after a minute, she'd said it.

"Eyelashes are like centipedes' legs."

He took a bite of sandwich, peanut butter and jelly, and chewed slowly.

"Yes, they are," he said. "But eyelashes can't eat you up."

And then he'd smiled. A smile to himself. She remembered that she'd wondered why. Now she knew. How do you explain to a child that eyelashes *can* eat you up?

"Does Charlotte want to be buried?"

He took a first bite into his second triangle of sandwich, deliberate and neat.

"Most people only think about going forward. They don't ever want to stop. Have you noticed how people hate stop signs? Roll through them? Your grandmother's like that."

It was true. It wasn't fun driving with Charlotte, because she never really stopped at intersections, just slowed to a nonstop, sort of the way she played Bach, with pauses that didn't quite breathe. She was in the beautiful powder-blue coupe, an old Mercedes that was high court for her high cheekbones and white, white hair. Other drivers let her roll. People were happy to watch that blue coupe do anything. It was a showstopper. Like Charlotte.

"She's like a queen," Margret said. She didn't exactly like her grandmother, which she couldn't say, so she ended up overcomplimenting her.

"But no one escapes," he said. "There's a place in *Hamlet* where he makes this very point. How the fat king and the lean beggar are 'two dishes, but to one table.' And you know who's eating."

"Worms."

"Beetles too."

Milton Beecham adored beetles, though his love was Hemiptera, the true bugs, with family Reduviidae, the assassin bugs, a special passion. Margret couldn't adore beetles, but she didn't mind worms. It was fun to spade into the earth and see them snap and curl, naked and angry, bunched up with fury, then stretching skinny as a tentacle. When you plucked them from the soil to feed baby birds or to use as fish bait, they were surprisingly tough to cut in pieces or to pierce with a hook, as tough as gristle. And even cut in pieces, they still squirmed. They made Margret think of intestines. It was weird to think worms that looked like intestines would eventually eat your intestines.

"But where will you be buried then?"

"I won't. I'll be cremated and have my ashes scattered."

"Where?"

"I haven't decided. I sometimes think Downing Meadow, so I could pass time with my wheel bugs. Or the marsh under the bitterns in the spring. But I have to say right here wouldn't be bad. With the wood thrush."

"That's why I always lie down here. It's so soft."

"Yes," he said, looking up into the chartreuse canopy, "maybe here."

Margret looked up too.

"So, Mar, do we still like our sandwiches cut in triangles, or should we go back to rectangles?"

"Rectangles seem to last longer. But I still like triangles."

"Why?"

"Because they're more elegant to hold"—"elegant" was a new word for her then, and she felt grown-up using it—"and bites look better in them."

"I agree," he said.

Margret looked back on these conversations between an old man and a little girl as if they were part of the leaves and the log, like the song of the wood thrush. Fluty notes and tight trills and reverberating thrums syncopated with silence. "The anthem of the forest," her grandfather once said, as they listened to the slow song that seemed to be everywhere and nowhere, a kind of hide-and-seek. "Like a tuning fork," he said another time, when they were mesmerized by the fractured pitches and sonic vibrations coming from that gingerbread bird with the spotted breast.

"The John Cage of birds," Charles always said. "There should be a Merce Cunningham dance to that song." And you could see it too, the woods a dappled space with strange balances struck and held.

Who'll sing a psalm? It was a verse she knew well from "The Death and Burial of Cock Robin," a poem she and Milton often read together. *I, said the thrush, as she sat in a bush, I'll sing a psalm.*

Margret and her grandfather had once puzzled over what kind of thrush. He had a tape of birdsong, and again and again they listened to the thrushes, Milton hitting rewind with his middle finger, hitting play with the first. Which song was a psalm? The shivery pinwheels of the veery? The tinfoil triplets of the hermit thrush? The Swainson's, like silver through a sieve? No, they finally decided, it was the singing of the wood thrush. Improvised, vaulted, and green.

Five

MARGRET USUALLY TRAVELED south to Saks. She'd catch the subway at 110th, and get off at Fiftieth, where Broadway and Seventh eyed each other, about to converge like two bullies in a race. Walking east on Fiftieth, she'd pass the Time-Life Building, Radio City Music Hall, and Rockefeller Center, midtown in all its sandstone masculinity. It always gave Margret a feeling of the fifties, like in the *The Best of Everything*, a movie she'd seen at college in the fourth-floor lounge, all the girls cracking jokes about white gloves and girdles yet all of them rapt, projecting themselves into big cities. Midtown made your heart leap.

If Margret came up to Saks, usually after seeing Emily at Flow, she took the same subway. One day, well into her third year at Saks, she jumped into a cab and it brought her up Madison—the cabbie's decision, most took Sixth. Margret got out on the southeast corner, and as she stood waiting for the light to change, she saw, well, she would have to tell Charles about it. When she got home she would turn it into theater, make sure he had a glass of red wine and was in the thistle, a chair they had picked out together. They called it that because it was a shade of leather called Thistle, a waxed and crackled greenish brown that Margret had loved at first sight.

"It's so organic," she'd said when they were at the store ordering the chair, a deep, tufted number with an Arts and Crafts feeling. The seat was rather low and the back rose higher than a club but lower than a wing, just the right height for dozing while reading.

"Leather has to be organic," Margret announced. "Either that or go the complete opposite route, lipstick red or glossy black. Not those leather-chair colors. Navy blue, teal, and burgundy, that boardroom look. You have to either be true to nature or just go all the way into unnatural and make it fetish."

"Is that you talking? Or the boys in BR?"

BR was the Boiler Room, another name for Saks Visuals where Margret worked. The office was three levels below street level, down down down past shipping and returns and the lockers and the stockrooms, down amid the pipes and fans and boilers, stairwells getting narrower as you went, walls and floors painted a beef brown or a dirty butter. It got hotter as you descended, a clanking submarine feeling. Not for nothing was the joke in visuals, "If there's a fire, we die. If there's a nuclear attack, we live."

"The BR boys," Margret said, "would agree with me."

When it came to certain aesthetics, the guys in BR could hold their own with any grad student. For them, the semiotics of fetish were child's play. Not that they could do anything with it in the windows. References to Helmut Newton and Guy Bourdin, forget it. Saks had corporate offices right across the street in Rockefeller Center, and the suits were not into semiotics. Barney's up at Sixtieth could be subversive, exhibitionist, even ugly, with a real F-you attitude. At Bergdorf's, the work of Linda Fargo was wildly poetic though obviously expensive. "Jean Cocteau meets Donald Trump," Emily scathed, which Margret secretly enjoyed hearing, even as she knew how difficult it was to achieve such extravagance. But Saks, *its* windows had to find the golden mean between cutting edge and catalog. They could not be extreme.

"It's like we have to wear a girdle when no one else does anymore," Margret had said when corporate nixed their Stanley Kubrick homage—black slabs and sleeping pods—for the first week of 2001. She rarely allowed herself a complaint down there in the Boiler Room, that white room with the low fluorescent ceiling, and though she knew it wasn't the greatest analogy, at least it was unpretentious. Fey Stephen, thin as a straw and not averse to slipping into Galliano gowns before they were shimmied onto mannequins, shivered with delight. "Longline or panty?" He got a laugh, as always, then pushed it like a porpoise with a ball, giggling like Flipper. "And what about those garters attached to the spandex? Those little rubber nipply things that slide into a metal hook. Is there a word for those? I mean, it's the tiniest symbol of S and M ever conceived. Isn't it? Rubber? Nipples? Hooks? Come on, isn't it?"

"Daaaling," Sasha said, exhaling the word as if it were smoke from a Russian cigarette. "You're forgetting the stocking. The nipple and the hook are servants to the silk. They're eunuchs."

Then Joe, the new production manager who was always antsy because he truly was dying for a cigarette, looked straight at Margret and said, "Tell us something we don't know." It was disrespectful, because even though Joe was full-time, Margret had been there four years longer. She realized, as everyone else did too, that he hadn't just been ignoring her; he actively disliked her. Tom, the director of visuals and the man who had to deal weekly with corporate, not just sit and complain like the rest of them, jumped in. "Margret's right. We do have parameters, and let's not forget it."

As Margret got conversant with the boys in BR, Charles, by extension, did too. He was impressed with the way they made verbal play of their work, wove aesthetics, linguistics, vaudeville, into banter nine-to-five. And he thought it wonderful that down in the BR anything could be said, even though that anything might curl your toes. Yes, he winced when Margret repeated the latest on the boys' hookups and breakups, the hot guys on Seven (Men's), and stories of humid doings at bars and baths with the attendant semantics of "cum loads" and "nut sacs." ("It does get a little blue down here," Tom once confessed to Margret, needlessly.) At first Charles cringed, crying, "Too much information!" But then, oh, what the hell. The languages of other cultures, the insider slang; it was always fascinatingly right. And at Columbia, at any university in the country, one word of such jolly genital truth, straight or gay, would get you booted in two seconds, no matter how splendid your CV.

So Margret was always tickled when her husband discoursed on Stephen as if they were old pals, even though two men couldn't have been more opposite. (Was Stephen really a man? Or was his Y chromosome back in Ohio pushing big feet into Mom's size ten stilettos?) And if Sasha called and Charles picked up the phone, Margret knew she could finish whatever she was doing because they would talk for a while, Charles leaning against the living room wall, nodding as she hustled through the room motioning one-more-minute. Margret loved it when those two talked because they could discuss art, movies, books, but most of all they discussed her. She loved going by and hearing Charles say something like, "You should see her hair after she's washed it but hasn't combed it out yet" or "How are we going to get those awful red loafers off her feet?" (Margret, aggrieved, shouted, "I love those loafers") or "This Victorian walked into my office. *In a kilt.*" And then seconds later, his booming laugh. Margret would plant herself in front of Charles, asking, "What did Sasha just say?" He'd hand her the phone so Sasha could tell her himself, except Sasha didn't always tell.

"Daaaling, it doesn't matter what I said to him, though, yes, it was very funny"—Russians had a funny way of saying "funny," as if pronouncing both *n*'s, like "fun-knee"—"but we know what you did, you and I. We know that this man of all men would be susceptible to a kilt, especially a kilt worn by a pale Boston beauty born in a thicket with blackberry hair." Margret glowed as she listened. And she knew there was no point trying to correct Sasha; he'd fixed on Boston and would never trade it for her hometown of Chicago. "Wasn't it Brits who dug up those lions of his? I mean, *really* Margret." There wasn't much you could say. Even when Sasha was wrong, he was right.

"But burgundy doesn't fit your theory at all," Charles had said at the furniture store, flipping through the stack of swatches. "You know very well that burgundy is everywhere in nature, beginning with blood."

"I know, I know. I realized it as soon as I said it. Maybe it's this. When I say organic, I mean the leather is a color it could be in real life, not dyed by someone."

Margret was floundering. They both knew that any theory that got too convoluted was not a good theory.

"But still," she said, "don't you think Thistle is more us?"

His fingers were on the cutting of leather and it looked beautiful against his hand with its black hair, hair that seemed blown low by a strong wind, eastward on his right hand, westward on his left, and stopping just above the knuckles, leaving them naked like stones across a creek. *Us*. It was foolproof. Charles loved his young wife. *Her*.

It was in the thistle, with her sitting on the matching ottoman, that she often told him of the day's triumphs and horrors.

"Imagine this," she said, "but you have to come see it for yourself. So there's Saint Patrick's Cathedral on the northwest corner. Not the cathedral part, but the adjunct buildings, where the priests live."

"And tipple."

"Wearing velvet slippers, don't you think? But this building has spires and flèches, too. And on one of the flèches, the most delicate spikes and stars. So you look up and you see these Christian missiles aimed at heaven, and you'd never think you're across the street from Saks Fifth Avenue."

Charles took a sip of wine.

"Then on the northeast side, Helmsley Palace. The brownstone is so black, it looks burned, which gives it that industrial-age aura of heavy money sitting on its haunches."

"A banker by Daumier."

"It's strung with twinkly Italian lights, and you have to wonder what the priests of Saint Patrick's think of all these richy riches coming and going from Helmsley. It's sort of the irresistible force facing the immovable object."

"But which is which?"

"Oh. Each could be either, couldn't it?"

"It depends on how you see God."

Charles always said that if he was anything, he was a pantheist, in thrall to the sun, the moon, the raptor, and the wind. Raised Catholic, because Assyrians, though Semitic, were among the first Christians, he dumped the saints, their spires, and their sufferings when he fell under the spell of his heritage. No culture ennobled birds, cats, rivers, and trees the way the ancient Assyrians did. Or made hybrid gods of man and beast with such thrusting anatomical precision. Charles shared Philip Larkin's take on the Church: "That vast moth-eaten musical brocade / Created to pretend we never die." Religion was primitive, narcissistic, static. Nature was primitive too, but honest and kinetic. There were no immovable objects in nature. "Movement is the cause of all life," Charles said from time to time, quoting Leonardo.

"I think money is the irresistible force for most people," Margret had said. "And God is the immovable object."

"For a Prod, you're very Old Testament."

"I never could get into the New Testament. Because it always seemed too new. Like everyone was cleaner and hipper in that half of the Bible. I like the dusty old gnarly names in the Old Testament."

"Like the roots of old trees."

"And the vaults and waters."

They both loved Genesis. One of the most eloquent chapters in Charles's first book, *The Incomparable Palace*, was titled "Vaults and Waters." It analyzed the amniotic spaces in Assyrian bas-reliefs—the fixed compartments in obelisks and stelae, the wombs and arteries of the marshes and rivers engraved on Sennacherib's walls.

"So two more corners."

"Okay. The southwest corner is 444 Madison. With Art Deco numbers in gold. Florsheim shoes is there, and *New York* magazine."

"And the southeast corner?"

"Well, I guess it's a fifties building, kind of set back from the street. Like a building you'd see in a stewardess movie."

"Did we really get stews in the fifties? I mean as cultural icons? There were airports in Hitchcock. *North by Northwest*. That was 1959, I think. And there's a lot of flying in James Bond. But stewardesses? Hmmm. Doris Day landed a plane in *Julie*, and I think that was the fifties."

"*Charles.*"

If Margret let him keep going he'd be up and pulling books from the shelves, suddenly set on pinpointing the circa of stewardess movies.

"Anyway," she said, "the building is either the fifties or sixties. The ground floor has a travel agency and a florist, a FedEx and a Rolls-Royce dealership and"—the best for last—"a Turkish Airline."

There was something wonderful about Turkish. The word made Margret think of an old book from her childhood, *The House on East 88th Street*, all about Lyle the crocodile, who lived in a bathtub and ate Turkish caviar. He had a shady owner with a gigolo mustache and a hat like two teepees. It was a book with a happy ending, yet the house was what Margret remembered, a tall thin town house with long hallways and a slant of sadness, Lyle left alone in his tub. When she and her mother first read it together, Margret asked about Turkish caviar and instead Mom told her about Turkish taffy, and it became a ritual, because Margret had never tasted Turkish taffy and was intrigued by it, and because her mother, when spinning a tale, was enchanting. She always began with the same words: "In my day it was made by a company called Bonomo." You bought it in dime stores, she said. It came flat, the size of a dollar bill. You'd put it in the freezer, and then take it out and slap it on the table, where it would break into sharp little pieces. Or you could warm it in the sun, then work at it slowly, pulling long taffy hammocks in the air. Chocolate was the best, but vanilla was a close second, a shade of thick white, like buttermilk. "It really was an afternoon candy," her mother always said at the end.

"But the interesting thing is, there's a building just east of the fifties-sixties building, a sort of taupe-colored brick. You see it because it isn't set in; it goes to the sidewalk. And the wall is covered with stars.

Silver stars. All different sizes. Made of metal. I asked a man who works next door, Why are they there? And he said he hadn't a clue. I asked, Have they always been there? And he said, As long as I've worked here. And it just seems to mean something, but I don't know what."

"Do the stars derive power from their setting?"

"Well, they're definitely absurd. Like the work of an idiot savant, someone with a ladder stealing them up one star at a time so they'll have a night sky all during the day."

Margret was sitting on the ottoman facing Charles in the chair. His legs were open so that her knees, pressed together, were between his. He was looking at her, not the studying way he used to, but the way he did once they'd become lovers, as if from a distance, even though they were only two feet apart. She grabbed the index finger on his left hand and gave it a shake.

"Won't you come see it?"

"No. It's more interesting if I don't, at least for now." He squeezed her knees with his. "Why it moves you is more important than what I think."

They had so many cocktail hours in the thistle. There was even room for them both to nestle into the chair, she between his legs with her back and head against his chest and shoulder, and their four feet on the ottoman.

"This is a great view of our feet," he once said.

"We're the audience and our feet are onstage," she answered.

They didn't do this often, because it was the kind of thing that looked darling in movies but in real life was fine for about five minutes before it got strained. But sometimes Margret would just drop down there anyway. She would pull his arms around her, under her breasts, and then lay her own arms on top of his like a lock.

. . .

Margret hadn't come to Saks from Madison for a long time. She didn't want to see that corner, which she'd never figured out. The employee entrance was on Fiftieth, and she approached it from the west. Its painted metal door, a sickly beige, was nothing like the main entrances with their elaborate bronze canopies. "Urn and fern," Margret called the pattern, a grand craftsmanship that today would cost a king's ransom. Emily said she could think of two such expert ironsmiths in America, maybe three. Still, there was a thrill to the employee entrance, especially when Margret arrived later in the morning and the store was in full swing. She'd pass the security window and the messenger station, and as she walked the bare corridor to the main floor she could hear the store ahead, an immense cape of sound. And then the gleam and glass, the mahogany and mirrors—Cosmetics!—and she was in the sound, the swell, a white noise that was like the sea in the seashell, all eddies and elbows, "Oh, miss, can you help me?" swirling and bumping in the endless search for something, and for Margret a kind of peace.

Six

SHE REMEMBERED THE COLOR. The iron-gray smack, water in her mouth like a fist. It was a recurring dream, being smacked over and over by one wave, her throat locked, the sun snuffed in gray sound. But she was watching too, watching her fish-belly limbs flash white in gray bubbles, brown froth rushing her to shore, the heavy suck of the undertow pulling away, releasing her low on the beach where she lay strangely on her back, alone and unable to move. Am I dead? she wondered in the dream, her back against wet sand, and the whole cloudless blue sky bearing down on her from above. I'm cold. My hair is like seaweed. But she couldn't do anything, because she couldn't move. And soon the next wave would come.

Margret had read about such dreams, that it was a kind of sleep paralysis, the body in strange interim, as if the dream were stealing under your skin. Some people saw these dreams as recovered memory, evidence of childhood trauma or intergalactic abductions. Charles had his own theory: Someone should ask the abductees, Do you have a cat? He thought the typical alien face, with its high cheekbones and unblinking eyes, was really the face of a cat in the night. "It's sitting on their chest in the dark." He was quite sold on the idea. His childhood cat Samson was one of the great influences of his life.

Never turn your back on the ocean.

It was something Margret's grandfather always said, not so much at the shore, but the way other people might say, Pride goeth before a fall. All it took was one smack unawares and you got the truth of it, as Margret learned one summer when she was six, playing in the surf at Gloucester, slowly following her older, stronger cousins. They were supposed to be watching her but they really weren't; they were playing lacrosse in the water at waist height. Margret was working her way toward them. Oh, how she desired to be near the older boys, with their naked chests and slick wet hair and glamorous ropy arms already as strong as piano wire. She was working her way toward Jack, his black hair shining like lacquer, and was up to her chest when someone yelled, *Common eider!* Margret turned to look for it, because everyone loved ugly eiders, and a gray wall slammed her from the side, hitting her like a roar. She was under the water, rolling, scraping the bottom. Just as the ocean scuttled her near shore, a frieze of her mother rising on white legs, the undertow dragged her out again. She saw bubbles popping on the sand, vaguely heard her mother's scream, and felt a sharp claw of salt water up her nose.

It was the lifeguard who grabbed her back, who carried her coughing and gasping to shore, relinquishing her with rough slaps between the shoulder blades. He would be the object of her adoration for the next year. His peeled nose, his baggy red shorts, the white blond hair on his legs, thick as a pony's. Mom wrapped her in two towels and stuck her under one of the family umbrellas, the yellow-and-white one, which ever after seemed sickly, and said, No more swimming for the rest of the day. Charlotte sent one cousin to the concessions, a mile away it always seemed, for a cup of tea for Margret, who sat wan under the umbrella, motionless under the convalescent heat of the round white sun until Milton got there. She watched him talk quietly to Charlotte under the blue-and-white umbrella, and when he came over to Margret and her mother, he said, "So you got clobbered."

She nodded.

"The old one-two, the tide then the undertow. And a snootful of salt water, I bet."

Yes. That was what happened.

"Well, you have to go in again, right now."

She didn't want to. She pulled the towels tighter around herself, and pushed her toes into the sand. Her mother next to her watched but said nothing.

"Did you come up on your own or were you pulled up?"

"On my own."

"So you got rolled, that's all." He reached his open hand down to her. "I told you, never turn your back on the ocean."

"I know," Margret said, "but I did, and . . ." She wanted to say, I got hurt, but clearly she wasn't hurt; she was perfectly fine sitting there in two towels.

"Come on."

Her grandfather pulled her up and they walked to the water. "The fact is, we all get hit. No one can watch for every wave."

In the dream she could only watch the sky because she couldn't move, could only wait for the next wave to come and take her out. On the sand, waiting for the wave, she was like a bride on a bed: scared, still, her eyes on the ceiling, feeling the enormity of her body, alone with that feeling, alone with the growing thrum of the unknown, soon to be possessed, wanting to be, not scared. It was always the last dream before waking. And when she woke to the room, light shy in the curtain, she felt abandoned, thick with tears. The wave hadn't come.

Margret never dreamed this before Charles disappeared. It started after. She never told it to anyone, because your own dreams, when they aren't just boring to others ("No one is interested in other people's dreams except shrinks," Emily once said, "and they're paid to listen"), are too revealing, and this one was so obvious and sexual. On her back on the sand, her body irradiated with heat, an ache like the heaviest petting, the orgasm only fingertips away, this waiting for him, waiting for the wave that could only be him, reaching from northern waters where the plane went down. The plane that left on a Thursday at dawn for a three-day trip to see razorbills and dovekies and murres, seabirds for his life list. She remembered his wee-hour leave-taking as if that too were a dream, his body on the edge of the bed in the dark, his arms worked under her shoulders, lifting her and the warm blanket together. His whisper, "I'll call you at noon and see you on Sunday," and her saying, "I hope you see a dovekie." Then the four kisses they always did before going to sleep, not pecks, but not sex, something in-between, like flannel nighties with nothing underneath, each kiss slightly different. And then a squeeze of a hug, his just-shaven cheek still cool, smooth, pressed against her own, the scent of spice, Blenheim Bouquet. Then the click of the front door; she remembered hearing it as her head sank back into the pillow, the distant click, or maybe she just thought she remembered it. And then he was gone.

Seven

HER DAYS AT SAKS were Tuesday, Wednesday, Thursday—window days—but in the last year she'd been asked to come in on Monday, a planning day. Margret was permanent freelance, like staff but with no benefits. That was how you began in windows. Part-time. Dressing and toting unwieldy mannequins that weighed sixty pounds; setting up the windows, then painting out the floors. And part-time was pretty much where you stayed. In Margret's six years in Saks Visuals, years in which retail wasn't doing so hot, positions that came open were left open. Only Tom and the three managers beneath him were full-time: Tina in fashion, Joe in production, and shy Holt in lighting. Everyone else was Tuesday, Wednesday, Thursday. It didn't matter. It wasn't about climbing or cutthroat. It was the greater glory of being a tiny team doing an impossible job, twenty-six windows every week. And every week they did it.

They were all there for different reasons. Tom, their fearless leader, had been in theater, first as an actor. "I was Hamlet in high school, Horatio in college, and Gertrude in an all-male production at the Minetta Lane. That's called goin' south." He then went over to set design, specializing in touring shows, which meant a lot of time out of town when all he really wanted was to stay put in his Chelsea one-bedroom instead of constantly subleasing it to others. For Tom, the windows were showtime *sans* actors, directors, critics. "Lovely," he'd sigh.

Tina was a tomboy in a tank top, a lanky lesbian of Greek descent. She had a curving collarbone you could shoot arrows from, except Tina didn't need arrows; her big matte mouth shot darts just fine. She'd been reading *Vogue* since the fifth grade, and with a design degree from FIT, Tina knew fashion not only as well as the average fashion queen, but better. "It kills me how male designers all claim to love women so much, but heaven forbid they cut a seam for tits bigger than a radish. There should be a class for every fag in fashion school called Boobs: Deal with 'Em." Tina didn't say this only to Margret. She'd examine the bodices on dresses, the good stuff from Designers on Three, and show the guys just what was wrong with the seaming, as if it were their fault. "You want to use our bodies as a blank slate for your dreams of success. Well, hell-o, our bodies have dreams of their own. I mean, I'm a B cup, and I can squeeze into most of this stuff, but look at Margret. She's at least a C. She could never fit those boobs into this Galliano. And if she can't wear it, why bother?" It was nice of Tina to feel this way, and Margret would have been flattered if she hadn't been completely mortified, her bra size suddenly the topic of the day. "Escapism is easy," Tina summed up. "Reality is hard."

"That's why we don't like reality," Stephen sassed back. Then with a sympathetic glance Margret's way, he said, "But we do like your breasts."

For Stephen, Saks windows were home. He'd loved the store since his boyhood in Cleveland, where he was the mini-me of his continually remarried model mother. "Mom wasn't a smart Suzy Parker who married menschy Bradford Dillman," he once explained. "She was dumb Dovima who married thugs." Stephen's mother used him til he was ten as a showstopping accessory in Saks fashion shows. When he was fifteen, she got him a part-time job as a sales clerk in accessories. "I started in Hosiery. Nude, sand, beige, taupe, *and jet*." "And jet" was one of Stephen's catchphrases or, rather, his mocking comment on the world. He said it fast and to the side as if it were one word. At first Margret thought he was invoking the French photographer Atget. Even when she knew better, the usage was difficult to explain. "It's a fashion eternal he admires," she told Charles, "but he's also laughing at it. I think what gets him is that women think they're so racy buying jet. So it's kind of a judgment. Someone or something is 'and jet' when they think they're racy but they're not."

Of course, then Charles wanted to look up "jet," saying, "It's a material of mourning. I think it's made of fossilized wood." He always wanted to know what things were made of.

"I knew it was a bum gig," Stephen continued, "the job no one wanted, so I was a dervish in my station. I organized hosiery so only I knew where everything was. Which was really stupid because then I was totally stuck there. But you know, I loved those flat boxes, and the flat stockings inside, with the foot shape that dangled when you held them up. Oh, god, how I miss those reinforced toes." Stephen himself was a sheer silk stocking, and Saks was his box.

Joe in production. Husky, sexy, sleepy and fidgety at once, slim in the hips, burly in the chest, the kind of chest that seems too big to fit into his belt, yet you can't call it a pot; the kind of scowling guy girls sigh over. He was a Yalie, a hated-being-gay struggling novelist who'd worked summers for his father's construction company and was actually pretty visual. He joined the group around 2000, when the previous production manager moved to Florida. Joe referred to their work in windows as Chic Simple, after that series of little fashion books, even though he knew it wasn't simple. Sasha, in fact, had a theory they were all going to end up as silly eccentrics in a book Joe was writing, which was yet another reason to be wary.

As for Sasha, it was almost as if someone had strapped him into *Sputnik,* shot him off, and after orbiting the moon a few times he'd landed in the Boiler Room, where he'd been singing hymns to lunar beauty ever since. A fashion illustrator in the hours when he wasn't at Saks or on the phone, Sasha drew in a luminous style. His figures glowed and floated like opalescent aliens, faceless descendants of Paul Iribe in the teens and Georges Lepape in the twenties. Sasha's problem was compromise. He couldn't do it. If he didn't like the voice of the editor on the phone—and they called Sasha in droves—he just hung up. And if he didn't like the clothes they wanted him to draw, he just sent them back. But when he did finish a job, maybe two or three a year, and always after a string of all-nighters and probably one thousand and one cigarettes, the illustrations were an alternate universe, faceless women ravishingly dressed, ghosts clothed in pointillist watercolor.

Margret thought Sasha a genius, but it was clear he couldn't sell himself, and in New York City salesmanship was as important as, often more important than, talent. Emily too thought Sasha could be big. She'd seen a sketch he did—of Charles no less—one evening when the whole gang except Joe trooped up to 113th for a night of vodka and complaint. "Fuck Tea and Sympathy," Tina had said, speaking for all. The drawing was a pencil sketch on a stiff piece of laid white paper with gilt edges (the back of a wedding invitation, one of Margret's Boston cousins). Emily had pored over it for a long silent while, then said, "He's caught that thing in Charles, the softness inside the drive." "I know," Margret said, "and the eyelashes."

Emily was puzzled that an artist so quick with character preferred his people faceless. Margret thought maybe Sasha saw the truth of others too clearly and was overwhelmed by those naked faces. Maybe that's why, when he wasn't holed up on East Eleventh Street, in a teeny one-bedroom with a wood floor that slanted perilously to one corner ("It catches the pencils and pennies that think they can escape"), he was in windows. Meanwhile, Emily, in her slow-then-fast mongoose way, was figuring out how to spark Sasha to the next level.

Except for Joe, Margret liked everyone in visuals. In fact, she couldn't even say she didn't like Joe. She was just so aware that he didn't care for her. It made her afraid of him, and then resentful that she was afraid. She never knew what to do with her arms when he was near. She wanted him to see that she was oblivious of his dislike, but this made her self-conscious, as if she were in a phone booth with no money. She rarely met his eyes. And when they worked in the windows she gave him a wide berth, which wasn't always easy considering the windows were so narrow, more like hallways than rooms.

Once, walking up Fifth Avenue, Margret and Charles stopped in front of Bergdorf's wonderful windows, and she sighed, "Squares, rooms, depth." And he said, "So living in a corridor isn't all it's cracked up to be?" She had to admit there were drawbacks. Use them, he counseled, don't wish for a different space; let the space you have tell you what it wants. He described a famous ballet by George Balanchine, *The Four Temperaments*, how it unspooled like a cylinder seal, classicism flattened until it appeared primal. "And it was all because he had to finish the dance on a wide, shallow strip of stage. Stravinsky said, 'The limits generate the form.' It's all an artist needs to begin." It was then Margret realized, with a stirring that surprised her, that Charles viewed her as an artist even though she'd never created anything.

The limits generate the form. When the whole gang was in one of the narrow windows in stocking feet, nailing, painting, wiring, whining, futzing—freezing in winter, for the windows were unheated, or broiling in summer, for there was no AC—it seemed to be all limits, all elbows and exhalations. And the air in there, especially in the summer with the sun outside and the hot fluorescent floor lights within—sweat mingling with spray deodorant and spritzes of tester perfume, someone's garlic dinner from the night before, someone else's doggy socks or was it funky jeans? Margret lived in fear that on a first or second day she'd bleed past her Tampax, and that period smell would join the fray. What would Joe make of that? One particularly hot day when the sun was sinister and they were all exhausted because they couldn't salvage a concept, it just didn't work, and it was going to be a week of awful windows they'd have to walk by without seeing, as it was too painful to look—though corporate would probably love it because they always loved the failures—someone silently passed gas, the rotten-egg kind, too thick to ignore. As everyone fanned the rancid air, saying, "It wasn't me," Sasha, who really couldn't cope with bad smells, held his throat and gasped, "*It will melt the Dolces*," which did have 20 percent polyester in the blend. That's when Stephen said what was in everyone's heart: "Well, isn't this glamorous?"

It was in such moments that you wondered why you were in windows.

"It's fashion, theater, poetry, art, all in one," Margret had told her bewildered parents over the phone after she'd accepted the job at

Saks, exactly one month before the spring semester ended, having no plans to go back to school in the fall. She didn't know then that it was sometimes the most tedious aspects of fashion, theater, poetry, and art. Pulling dresses off hangers on Two, Three, and Four, the saleswomen eyeing you skeptically as if you were carrying off their gifted children. Figuring proportion, the spacing of things on walls. And prop painting, gummy latex gunked in your cuticles and pestlike in your hair. Why was she, with a master's from Columbia and a doctorate waiting only to be written, in windows? That was the plaintive question her parents howled from Chicago and were still silently sighing even as they tried to show support with questions about mannequins (Dad: "Designwise, they haven't really changed much over the years, have they?"), window aesthetics (Mom: "But the Saks windows on Michigan Avenue aren't the least bit conceptual"), pay scales and advancement (Margret: "Seventeen dollars an hour is really good by industry standards").

They were furious with Aunt Bett for calling her bosom friend Frannie, aka Frances Patrick, formerly head of promotions for Saks Fifth Avenue, and asking the semiretired PR diva to talk to Margret. The two had met for lunch at a place called Michael's, a restaurant on West Fifty-fifth Street. It was in that beige brick building with round bays all the way up, sort of a 1950s version of turrets. It was the kind of place where everyone noticed everyone else, like the Maxim's scene in *Gigi*. Frances was at the table—*her table*, it turned out—and Margret rehearsed Emily Post as the maître d' brought her over: the older woman doesn't stand; you make eye contact, offer your hand, then sit down; and don't touch your hair unless you have to.

Frances looked so groomed and natural, so crisp and languid, with her ash blond hair and hazel eyes and mouth lightly glossed but not quite colored. Margret already felt hot under her hair, thought her lipstick too red and her white blouse boring. And the jacket Frances was wearing. A pale green wool, probably cashmere, it was mottled like the shagreen compact Charlotte carried in her purse, polished ray skin so smooth and beautiful, it was like holding the sea in a circle in your hand. In places where the body emerged—the cuffs, the neck—the edges flared to reveal a soft inner facing of oyster. Margret had never seen such workmanship, as if someone had whispered what the wool should do and it had listened. "Ralph is a genius," Frances said when Margret complimented the jacket.

"And his advertising," Margret agreed, "it's historical in such a modern way. You can practically deconstruct a Ralph Lauren spread." She saw a skip in the older woman's expression.

"It's Ralph Rucci," Frances said gently. "He's a brilliant and still underrated American designer. A Ph.D. in philosophy, by the way. I think of this jacket as a meditation on nature. It came from a collection inspired by a trip to Crete."

"It seems alive," Margret said. "Like it's both predator and prey."

"So you see. A degree from Columbia could fit you beautifully for fashion."

Margret felt the glow of the wine they were sipping, a chardonnay to go with their wild mushroom risotto. She wasn't used to having wine at lunch and felt loose and swimmy. Every now and then someone would come over to say hello, men with a fresh-pressed swing to their good wool suits, men with no swing at all, their double-breasteds seeming to hug them from behind, and icy women acting warm in breakneck stilettos. Frances introduced Margret as "my best friend's niece; she's considering a career in fashion," to which they would nod or say things to Margret like, "Well, you're talking to the best." Frances had obviously been a mover. And then it was time for dessert, which Margret thought they would skip. But no.

"I have to have my sweet," Frances said. "I'd rather swim ten extra laps than go without dessert. One of the reasons, Margret, that fashion has such a bitchy reputation is that its women are mad with hunger. Diet pills and cappuccino, that's what they live on. I was tough in my day but never short-tempered. Because I kept my blood sugar up. So have you ever had panna cotta? No? We'll get two. With chocolate sauce. It's a dream."

It was a dream. Each little mound was as white as the plate it came on, creamy white the way Margret imagined vanilla Turkish taffy, yet quivering like a little breast, milkmaids in Thomas Hardy. Margret thought she'd never tasted anything so simple and delicious. And, oh, the warm chocolate.

"I see I have a convert," Frances said, and Margret blushed.

"It's such a contradiction," she replied, "baked cream. But so much art begins in contradiction. My thesis adviser is, or was, always urging me to see ballet, an art of the body that's about transcending the body."

"But it's the same in fashion," Frances said. "Look at Geoffrey Beene. He'll use the most humble material—horsehair trim, for instance—on a gown that makes you think of goddesses on Mount Olympus."

"Is it a reference to Apollo's chariot?"

"The horsehair. You got it."

It was exciting for Margret. To see her expertise in art applied to the real world, which was full of art too. She took a sip of her cappuccino, the tablecloth empty around it, a vast white space, and she felt, *yes*, life was more than Columbia University and the professor with beautiful hands who belonged to someone else.

"Visuals."

Margret snapped back to attention.

"That's it. I'll put you in touch with Tom!"

"Visuals?"

"The windows! It used to be called window dressing. It's the siren song of the store, the call to the customer. Windows have an illustrious history. We've been getting stiff competition from Bergdorf's these last few years. You'd be perfect for it. Why not windows?"

Why windows? her parents wailed over the phone. Why not give grad school one more year?

Because she was sick of the books, the papers, the stress, the solitude, the lonely nights with her nose in moldy tomes. It was always the same. The mornings in coffee shops, frothy cappuccinos fresh and full of hope. This is where you're meant to be, she'd feel, as she emptied a packet of brown sugar onto white froth, which accepted it almost lasciviously, the sugar sparkling, then melting and sliding, the crystals capsizing into aerated milk. It always made her think of the first boy in *Lawrence of Arabia*, the one who disappears in quicksand. By the afternoon she felt she too was disappearing, sliding slowly to a future she couldn't quite see. It was like driving a country road at night, a short view through the windshield, a bowl of brightness with blackness on all sides.

"No one sees into the far future," Emily said, when Margret first admitted she might want to leave school.

"You do."

"That's different. I'm not like other women. I don't get waylaid."

"I don't see how I've been waylaid."

"No. But you're comfortable with negative capability. You're like Christabel in the root of a tree. Only for you the root is grad school. In fact, you're a lot like your dad. And I'm like mine. I have to see results right away. I know where I'll be in five years because I need to know."

"Oh?"

"My own gallery, probably downtown. But you. Doesn't this not knowing where you'll end up go with the territory—you know, being an academic? I mean, we've always assumed you'd get a great gig. But I also assumed you were aware of the market. Or is this like when you lost your virginity? Regretting the whole thing when you find out it's not so hot at first?"

"It wasn't so hot. Anyway, I'm tired of being on a track. I don't even know what that means anymore. I feel like my whole career, which so far consists only of being in school, is one recital after another. I'm like a lightning bug in a jar."

They were drinking martinis that night, and when Margret heard herself say this, she knew she was getting drunk. Emily could hold vodka better than Margret could, and she was still pretty alert, her head not dropped low, like a wounded general, the way it did with one too many.

"I went down this path because I thought it would be sure," Margret said. When you've drunk too much, sentences like that hung boringly in the air.

"What are you saying?"

"I think I took a path that made everyone happy, and so it made me happy because they were happy. I know I'm overusing the word 'happy.'"

"You keep using the word 'path.'"

"In my family, people take paths."

Margret didn't have to explain. Emily knew that Margret's cousins, all male, had taken paths. Medicine, law, business, they all had letters or "Esquire" after their names. All except Jack, whom everybody loved, even Emily who'd met him only once, Jack with the moonshine smile and the shoeblack hair who left girls melted in puddles behind him and who silenced bullies with a glance. Jack wouldn't know a path if it hit him. His favorite book as a kid was *Kon-Tiki*. His favorite writer in college, Randolph Bourne. He was caught in his own charisma, fighting to be free of it, but weak with the freebies, the females who wanted to taste him and tame him. A taste was all they got.

Margret revered Jack. He'd apologized to her that day at Gloucester, when they were all walking to the cars, laden with sandy beach stuff. He'd pulled her aside, knelt down, and looked her in the eye—this older boy with his blade-naked chest breathing in and out, still hairless but banded with new muscle—and said, "Margret, I was supposed to watch you, and I didn't. Will you forgive me?" He did that for a six-year-old. And taking his lead, the other cousins came over and apologized too, but not in the same way. She loved Jack much more than she loved the blond lifeguard with the pony-hair legs. But she knew, even at six, that Jack was beyond reach, and not because he was a cousin. In fact, the family wasn't quite sure where he was, though last Margret heard, he was thought to be in the rain forest working with indigenous tribes, though Aunt Bett said he was hunting undiscovered plant species for pharmaceutical research. Jack was the exception that proved the rule.

"I don't know." Margret was trying to sound sober, but felt like a clock with old cogs. "I've just been so busy . . . you know, winning the next round, showing off."

"But you've never been a show-off. That's part of your power. You come on real quiet, hiding behind your hair, and then you write these papers that blow everyone away."

Which made Margret feel worse, getting complimented when she'd never told Emily the truth. Yet even then, in that sodden conversation at Café Luxembourg, Margret couldn't tell her. Things you didn't tell even your best friend somehow didn't exist. Not until you discussed it. She couldn't tell Emily, because Emily wasn't romantic that way; she didn't pine, she was a warrior, and she would think Margret was acting like some weak woman in a nineteenth-century novel. Margret couldn't say to Emily, and certainly not to her parents, that she loved this man who was older and coupled, a man she couldn't see even at a distance without feeling a jump in her heart, a pressure in her chest like white gauze pressed to a wound, ecstatic circulating blood, and couldn't be near without heat in her face, which she turned away from him, turned in his office upon the spines of books on shelves, or out birding lifted to the sky for hawks and falcons. Books and birds, near and far, these knocks and bumps and hollowing plunges—she felt she was being rattled out of grad school. She loved him and she believed, she really did, that down in the basement, down in the dark below the weekly walks and books on shelves and ambitions on the ceiling of a Sistine sky, down the stairs where the corners were in shadow, a cardboard box was pushed to the wall, top flaps folded inward, and in that box, marked "Margret Snow," were his feelings for her.

You don't have to stay, she said to herself. *You can leave.* There it was. Margret could always come back to grad school, but the important point was that she could leave too. And with the word "leave," a little fissure in the world, a leaf falling from a tree, falling to the ground, and then it rains, and then it dries and the wind blows and a stencil of the leaf is left on the sidewalk. Or the leaf falls at his feet and he's moved to pick it up. She sometimes lay in bed at night thinking the force of her fantasies, like the weird glide of that little window on a Ouija board, that somehow her heart in the night would move him, glide him, to her.

Leave. Her parents would freak, of course, but they were in

Chicago, and it was her life, and anyway they had each other. She was testing him. But in a way she was testing everyone, the first time in her life that she was doing the testing. Margret left Columbia and went straight to Saks. No, she went straight to him, then Saks.

When Margret got to the Boiler Room, Emily's words were still in her ears. *You leave on weekends for that freezing house.* Tina was nowhere to be seen, probably upstairs somewhere. Tom stuck his head out of his office, "Hey, doll, sketch up some gypsies." Joe was on the phone. The musical *Gypsy* was coming back to Broadway, a show about the stripper Gypsy Rose Lee, and Tom loved it as a hook for Resort, mannequins in the new swimsuits with long white gloves and feather boas. But how to make it sing? That's what they had to figure out.

Margret had her own space in the back, with a little desk where she could sketch out ideas in peace. It was in a corner, just beyond the wall where they stacked the mannequins, a white-plastic battalion of blank faces and a real twilight zone at night. Not that she had seniority over Stephen, but his specialty was hair and makeup, and Sasha, needless to say, wouldn't have known what to do with a desk. Tom had devised this little space for her after the accident, his way of saying, or so Margret took it, that the Boiler Room was home.

She had thought she would do a collage of inspirations on the strip of wall above her desk. In magazines she'd seen how designers and decorators had bulletin boards crammed with pictures and postcards, magpie nests of eye-catching culture, all the things that inspired them. Hers would be neater, she thought, more composed. But every time she'd put something up, she soon took it down. A black-and-white photo of Martha Graham as ancient Jocasta, chin and heel slashing. An old French print of a peregrine falcon, *le faucon pèlerin.*

A dripping velvet Ophelia gown from a *Vogue* photo spread on Brit Chic. A color print of a hummingbird nest, tiny as an egg cup, decorated with a spider's web and lichen like something from *Cinderella*. She put them up and she took them down. She spackled in the tack holes and painted the vertical strip above her desk a color called Blue Cloud, which was a whisper of sky. The BR guys didn't like it one bit. The whole ethos down there was gorge-the-eye. We're gorgons, Sasha said. But Margret liked her blue wall.

I'm not going to Joel Skelly's party, she thought, sitting down at her desk, and Emily can't make me.

Eight

MARGRET WAS STANDING at the main-floor information booth. She was holding her coat and waiting for Mr. Jay Marti. The woman in the booth hadn't said whether he was coming up or coming down—"He'll be here shortly," is all she said—so it was hard to guess from which side of the store he'd approach. Margret had on her best suit, actually her only suit, a black wool pinstripe with a nipped-in waist and a loosening hug at the hips. "Very French," the saleslady had said, "very Dior in the forties." "Very very," Margret always thought when buttoning it up. She'd always been a little stiff in this suit, bought during her first year at Columbia for her first TA lecture. It was a purchase forced on her by Emily. "Enough of this Brodie-girl look. Twirl up!" Even on thin days, Margret felt the jacket stern through the torso, like it was going to lecture her. She'd wanted to go up to a size twelve, but Emily insisted on the ten. "It fits you to a T."

"But I feel all structured up in it."

"That's how you're supposed to feel, as long as it's not binding"—Emily had given the waistband a tug—"which it isn't. Good clothes are demanding. That's the point. And besides, with that mane of yours, you can't afford to wear billowy clothes. *Something's* got to be reined in."

Charles loved it, always had, he told her when she wore it for their third date, a concert at Carnegie Hall. When she opened the door for him, he said, "That suit!" and placed his hands right on her waist. They heard Beethoven's Third that night, and the height of the hall and the scale of the symphony seemed to capture how big it all felt, the thrill of finally being a couple together. And that it was the Chicago Symphony Orchestra playing, the city where she had grown up and where he'd gone to grad school—at the University of Chicago—and where maybe they'd walked right by each other in Hyde Park, he in his twenties and she seventeen years younger, not even in her teens. She'd worn pearls that night, a choker that Emily lent her, and Charles had loved that too, pinstripes and pearls. Three months later, for her birthday, he gave her a pearl choker so that she wouldn't have to borrow Emily's. He'd looked at many strands, he said, white pearls with a blue cast, a pink cast, a gold cast; but the strand with the silvery cast was it. And when he went home with Margret for a weekend in the fall, to meet her parents and discuss the wedding, she showed the pearls to her mother, who thought them beautiful but couldn't help musing, "You would have been the professor in pearls." To which Margret wanted to say, If you need a Ph.D. so badly, *you* go get one.

For her whole life Margret had watched her father apologize for what he wasn't—a rainmaker, a moneyman. Yet what he was—an expert on infrastructure in buildings of the Chicago School—was really cool. So what if he wasn't going to be a millionaire like Milton?

Or make as much as Bett's husband, a doctor, or Bethany's, a tax lawyer who had them living in a loophole? Why not make a career for herself? None of the Beecham girls, strangely, had finished college—each in her turn dropping out to marry—but Aunt Bett had gone back for a degree in garden design and had a thriving consultancy, and Bethany ran a cute boutique on Newbury Street. Why hadn't Mom gone back to school?

"Everything came so easily to Bonnie because she was so pretty," Bethany said to Margret one summer, an explanation that Bett, the oldest, promptly squashed.

"No," she said, "everything came easily via Mother, who spoiled her rotten, and then Daddy couldn't stand to be around her because she was such a snot. Whenever he tried to include her in his interests, do something with just the two of them, she threw tantrums. We *all* had to go insect hunting with him."

"And bird-watching at dawn."

"And we did it. But Bonnie would scream and cry and run to Charlotte. He gave up on her. I'm not saying he was right. As we all know, Milton Beecham could really shut the door. But Bonnie manipulated."

Margret's mother was going to be an artist, and her early paintings—small turbulent oils of the Charles River, Gloucester inlets, and a vast Atlantic—were quite good and a little scary, sort of van Gogh-ish. Bonnie was a windblown romantic in those days, "always spinning out the door on dates," Bethany said. And impulsive to a fault. That's how she met Margret's father. She threw a snowball at Gregor Snow's head, whom she didn't know from Adam, because he'd blushed when they passed on the steps of Widener Library. When she was later introduced to him and learned his last name was Snow, she burst out, "Snowball!" After their first date she decided

Gregor—the shy heartthrob of Harvard's Graduate School of Design; the lean son of Karl and Anna Snow, working-class Croatians—well, he was just what she and her Waspy family needed. Pictures of them newly married were pinwheelingly lovely, he with his sensitive gray eyes and she still unaware of her own riptides, still simply a wide smile, a tumble of dark hair, her deep-set navy blue eyes like slashes—the prettiest of the sisters. The way she gripped to Gregor in those photos, as if he were a buoy in a wave, as a girl Margret had thought it showed *la grande passion.* Now, if you wanted to, you could see it as a sign. Poor Dad, she thought, he never knew what hit him.

Lord & Taylor was a far cry from Saks. It just didn't have the bustle, the gleam. And designwise the main floor was a mess. The parquet was stained an awful purplish, the likes of which Margret had never seen before. The columns were mirrored in skinny vertical rectangles, like a motel banquet room. And the wall colors, cream and pig pink, cringed in the overly bright lighting. The only remnant of grandeur was the high, arched ceiling latticed with strips of relief work, garlands and ovals with Greco-Roman motifs. Unfortunately, someone had slapped it with gloss white paint, more fitting for a gym. This once magnificent space bore many fingerprints, all of them guilty.

"Margret Snow?"

She turned.

"Jay Marti," he said.

They shook hands.

"I thought we'd talk in the store restaurant"—he motioned for her to follow him—"it's on the fifth floor, and way more pleasant than the offices on eleven. It'll be empty now, except for the staff setting up."

They got in the elevator and stood silently to five. She followed him past dress racks into the restaurant, An American Place. He was small and wiry in skinny black jeans, Doc Martens, and a red gingham cowboy shirt with a string tie. He had silky black hair pulled back into a short ponytail, and a round face with huge dark eyes and a pencil mustache, just like the man in *The House on East 88th Street.* They sat down at a little table in the corner, and his eyes—Incan eyes—seemed to see into her soul.

"So Tom's got a lot of talented people on staff, but he recommended you. Why do you think that is?"

Right to the point. Margret slid into doctoral mode.

"I was wondering that too. I think it's because I have imagination, which most people in visuals have, but I'm also dependable. I understand deadlines. And I try not to get bogged down with ideas that are too complicated—you know, the ones that will never work within the limits of time, space, budget, and manpower."

"How long have you been in windows?"

"It's six years now."

"So it's time for you to move up or move on."

"Well, I think I'm ready for more responsibility."

He had a focus about him, a stillness of the senses. And those large eyes, almost black . . . she wouldn't want to anger those eyes.

"That's all?"

Margret couldn't say she wanted to have Tom's job someday, or Jay Marti's. She couldn't say she wanted to run a visuals department, with all the logistics. If he was asking what her ambition was, she didn't know. She took a deep breath.

"Before I went to Saks, I was studying for a doctorate in art history at Columbia, but I left without getting one. I realized I didn't know why I was getting one, except to satisfy other people. So I left with a master's. Visuals was a place where I could use my education, without having to declare an ambition. I guess I still haven't. I just love being creative in that space in between."

"What else do you love?"

"That's like when you're asked your favorite poet. You can never think of a single name. I love crystalline things like Satie's Gymnopédies, and "The Aquarium" in *Carnival of the Animals*, where you feel life, emotion, swimming in its own little world. So much of art projects outward. I like to be pulled in. Is that an answer?"

"What one thing would you save from your apartment if there was a fire?"

She'd never thought this before, that more could be lost.

The sea-green Harris tweed.

"A jacket," she said.

Jay Marti didn't say anything for a moment. Then he asked, "What do you think of our windows? As spaces?"

"The eight little boxes on Thirty-eighth are seductive. The larger ones on Thirty-ninth, the usual. The challenge is the big windows on Fifth. They're hardly partitioned. More panoramic, like a time-space continuum."

"So what would you do with them?"

"Well, I'd be thinking long and hard about how to use that space to your advantage, with concepts that are more dynamic—you know, ideas that move through the window. Even though there's a frame when you're on the street, from the sidewalk you can see into the other windows as well. That could be used to give the viewer some surprises."

"My background is in architecture," he said, "and when I first saw those windows, I thought, they're definitely wonky. But they could also be lots of fun. So here's the deal. I'm talking to a lot of people. I'm asking everyone to send me photos of their three best windows, with an explanation of why you did what you did. If it's something you worked on as a team, then tell me what your contribution was. Can you do that?"

"Yes."

"Good. Warning, though. I may be a while getting back to you. I don't rush. I grew up in Peru, and I've been in LA for some years, so I don't jump to New York time. Josef Sudek used to say, 'Hurry slowly.' That's my motto too."

"And Lord and Taylor doesn't mind that?"

Saks was rush-rush-rush.

Jay Marti laughed as he stood up, a light skimming laugh as light as his eyes were deep, and said, "Not from the looks of things."

"It was a pleasure to meet you," Margret said at the elevator, extending her hand into his.

"And you, Margret."

It was the shortest interview she'd ever had, almost as quick and wiry as Marti was. She hadn't been nervous before it, not the least bit, but now, alone in the elevator going down, she felt uneasy, as if the four walls were close around her, witness to something that had already happened. It was one of those undertones, the dark form that glides under your raft—or is it just a shadow? a tidal swirl?—but still you pull up your legs and aim the raft in. She was feeling anxious, like suddenly things were going too fast and her life was changing. Like Marti would call and she'd have to take a job though she didn't want to. I don't have to send the photos, she thought. I could just forget about them. Really, why did I go to this interview when I'm happy at Saks? It was Emily, of course, pressuring her. And because Tom thought she should do it. She wanted to impress them. But why do I have to impress them? Why do I keep doing things for other people? And why do they keep pushing? Yet she knew Tom had done this for her, so she could make more money.

The elevator door opened and the main floor looked as motley as ever, and empty, a bad sign on a Friday morning. Saks by eleven was a madhouse. She walked past the counters and pushed through the old brass-and-glass doors. She didn't even look at the windows as she headed north on Fifth Avenue. It was going to take a lot of work to bring back this store. A lot of late nights and long weekends and love. By the time Margret got to the Times Square subway, she'd decided she wasn't sending the photos. The gliding anxiety was gone.

Nine

THEIR PARKING GARAGE was up at 130th and Riverside Drive. It was extremely reasonable for New York City, $150 a month, but it was seventeen blocks from 113th and not pleasant to go to at night. One or the other of them would get the car during the day and search for a spot on the street, and eventually one would be found, though sometimes it was closer to 130th than 113th.

They liked to leave by four in the morning. It got them to the Point fast, no later than seven. They once tried leaving on Friday night at eleven, but they still hit traffic, and the day stretched so long on the rack, they practically crumpled out of the car in Cape May. Four A.M. worked better. There was something lyric about stepping into the dark street, tomb-quiet, as if they were lovers alighting from a ladder. It was fun flying down wide-open West End Avenue, the stoplights pointless and genial. Then the swoop left and around into the Lincoln Tunnel, no inching, and then emerging under the slumbering cliff homes of Hoboken. Winging onto the Jersey Turnpike, Charles would sing, predictably, Simon and Garfunkel.

I said, Be careful, his bow tie is really a caaa-mera.

He had a beautiful voice, not big, but warm. Like melted caramel. Margret had always wished she could sing. That, and run fast. She had a nice speaking voice, a nice low voice, people said. "It goes with your gray eyes," Emily decided early in their friendship. Margret was a good lecturer, laying the stress just so, the way she played piano, and finishing with a sweep. But her singing? She was somewhere between soprano and alto, no register really, and to her own ears, ardent as they were to hear beauty, she sounded breathy and tinny. Which is why she sang only to herself, quietly on sidewalks or in the tub, where the sound, as Charles liked to say, was small but true. His singing, though, she loved. He'd sing in the car on the way down with Margret driving—she drove down, he drove back—maybe one or two songs before he sank into sleep, the rock and folk of his teens or, strange taste of his Assyrian parents, the classics of deep-voiced men, from Ezio Pinza to Johnny Cash. A favorite was "Old Man River." He'd grown up listening to the Paul Robeson recording.

"Seventy-eights," Charles once said on the drive. "Profound things happened on seventy-eights." Margret hardly remembered forty-fives. "Heavy black plates, brittle as biscuits, they were thickets of sound, a density in adagio you can't imagine, and vibrato that bounced around the room. Beethoven's *Grosse Fugue*. My father played it for me, and I was lying on the living-room floor looking up at the light fixture and I thought I was in Einstein's brain. And the packaging. Not those skinny LP jackets that came later. These were like special editions, boxed sets. They were serious—and dangerous. The seventy-eight that obsessed me was the crash of the Hindenburg, the actual broadcast. For me and my friends, that record had the power of *Playboy*. We were mesmerized. Not because of the loss it held but because of the naked truth. For boys, destruction is sexual. Boys are terrible, Margret. We can only have girls."

All this from the passenger seat.

"'Old Man River' . . . I loved that voice. The strength of it and the sonority. I was working my way through Eliot's 'Four Quartets.' I was around sixteen, and there was this line, 'I think that the river / Is a strong brown god,' and that was Robeson. One man singing a hymn to the river. A voice moving like a hand. It was a moment for me. It let me go back . . . into the sands."

Back to the greatest riverbed of all, the Tigris-Euphrates, cradle of civilization. And back to the Assyrian empire, to Khorsabad and Mosul, Nimrud and Nineveh, where the first music was notated and the first library built and the first thunder cut in stone—the clash and clatter of armies, the tooth and claw of big cats. All he'd wanted, he told her, was to be an American boy, to escape mawshe, hareesa, bushala, the old meals cooked in stewpots and stored in mason jars, all the old-country dishes he'd come to relish making for her, even to the point of stirring hareesa with a branch stripped of leaves, as his great-uncle had. All he'd wanted was to be Anderson not Ashur, to speak English, not the guttural Aramaic of family gatherings, the men arguing in throaty slashes, with their lustrous eyes and the Mesopotamian plains baked into their skin, and the women, even the loveliest among them, having shadowy mustaches and the deeply carved nostrils of their ancestors—this in a country that worshiped everything upturned and blond, where even Cleopatra, that ridiculous Liz Taylor, had alabaster skin. He played baseball, rode bikes, and pretended that the near priceless rugs on his family's wood floors, the old Kermans and Kashans, Tabriz and Talish, all brought over from Urmia, Iran—the city on a salt lake where his parents were born—were just the same as the wall-to-wall carpeting in his friends' houses. Until he heard that song.

He sang it one or two times a year, because she asked him to. It was hard to sing. But she loved his silky way with its intricacies, the slow roll downward on "jail," his control of it, how she could hear his throat around the word. And that it was bound up in that adolescent moment, the incandescence! It summed him up, the success he was, and the invisible things he'd seen from inside his tribal skin, a pigment that spoke of kings and concubines, sandals and almonds, stamping horses with tasseled reins, a Byronic stain that excited Margret—*The Assyrian came down like the wolf on the fold*—and made her want to lay her fingers on his forearm, on the history in his skin and the black hair that graced it. When he hit the lowest note, he'd always give her a glance. And he could run fast too.

It was cold out. She could see her breath in the air. Being out on the street at this hour, with the stillness and the March cold, was like being in a living room in the dark, a familiar landscape turned cool and aloof with shadow. She wondered if the Skelly party was over, was yet another dark living room, only this one in TriBeCa. Emily was probably home by now, asleep and dreaming. But of what?

Margret got to the car on Riverside Drive, put her stuff in the backseat, and then slid into the cold compartment, to let the engine warm up. She and Emily had been friends for how many years, and she still didn't know Emily's deepest desires. She knew Emily tended to sleep in a fetal position, a big pillow cupped in the curve of her body, her cheek against the top edge of it. It was surprising, considering how curveless Emily was awake. She could be very charming, but she was just too slim and too driven to be sweet or soft. When she tried to be sweet it felt more like largesse, alms for the poor, sort of irritating. Yet Emily did want love—Margret was sure of it. So why couldn't she find it?

It had been fun when they used to go to parties together, both of them dolling up, Emily chic in her extreme silhouettes, tent skirts of stiff duchesse satin that made her look like a little bishop, paired with a simple white or black or striped T-shirt, and her hair slicked back in boy-glam beauty. And Margret doing the best she could with her standard party outfit: straight skirt to the knee, either the black gabardine or the pinstripe skirt of her suit, and high black pumps, which Emily forced her to buy at Bergdorf's and in which she had to take clipped geisha steps that made her feel like Jell-O in a mold. Whatever top Margret wore, whether it was a tucked-in blouse or one of Charlotte's old cashmere cardigans, Emily would unbutton it to the bra. "Think sexy librarian," she always said, shaking her head at the wasted potential. "You look better on less than anyone I know." Charles, who had seen them dressed like this at an art department cocktail party in the year before he and Margret were lovers, had said of Emily, "She's a Modigliani inside a Braque," which was perfect, Margret had to agree. And yet her cheeks heated at his appraisal of Emily. She wanted him to notice her, just her. He did say, "Miss Snow"—he always called her Miss Snow at school functions—"you're taller all of a sudden." This was, of course, due to the pumps, the most elegant shoes she'd ever owned (and at $240, the most expensive; in fact, Emily had split them with her as a birthday gift). Then he was gone into his weekend, which Margret imagined was rippingly articulate and monastically quiet and ripe with red wine and rare books and late-day walks under ancient oaks on the snowy Main Line.

Margret and Emily had bundled into a cab a while later. It was a cold night, the kind of cold that makes your perfume glassy. They'd clattered downtown to an *Artforum* party in Gramercy Park. It was one of those parties that doesn't quite have a center, but instead carries on in clumps, one in the kitchen, another near the living-room windows, another in the hall outside the bedroom, with too many laughing women drinking fast and the men either gay or taken and the others hardly standout. Margret had plopped down on the couch while Emily worked the clumps, and eventually the guy who was the best of the bunch, a tall, skinny Elvis Costello, geeky sexy, plopped down next to her, and they had a long talk about the hair in *The Wizard of Oz*. Dorothy's, the Cowardly Lion's, Glinda the Good Witch's, and that weird munchkin hair. "Spirit gum," he explained. He loved when she told him how back in the third grade, a nasty classmate had called her Glinda the Mud Witch because her hair was like Billie Burke's, only brown not blond. Margret didn't add that when everyone laughed she went into the girls' room and cried silently in a stall. It might have been different if Burke hadn't had that ridiculous glockenspiel voice. Anyway, Costello went on and on and Margret realized he was working out a theory, and thus she sank lower knowing she was trapped, because nothing comes between a young man and his theory. Such was the pitfall of plopping into couches. Emily—this was the greatness of Emily—rounded down on her when he went for drink refills. "I know he's the cutest guy here but he doesn't let anyone get a word in edgewise, so get off that couch and let's leave *now*." Emily's "*now*" was like cold water in a hot pan. Margret popped right up.

When Margret no longer had to go to those parties, she felt sorry for Emily, who had to go solo. The odd recurring dream that started once Margret and Charles married, an upsetting dream that made no sense at all—the only way to explain it was Emily, who was still out there looking. In the dream, which always made Margret cry in her sleep, she was single. Charles had never married her, and he didn't want to see her anymore; so she had to start dating all over again, knowing he was out there looking for someone else. It was awful, she and Charles not together, Charles having left, and she in a strange room that was much like one from childhood, the narrow front bedroom at Karl and Anna Snow's, the room her grandparents had used for storage. When Margret woke from this dream to find Charles next to her, his body a familiar mountainscape under their pale yellow blanket, she felt a fairy-tale happiness. They were married. He wasn't going anywhere.

Margret put the car in drive and inched out of the parking space. Charles had always gotten the car from the street. He didn't want her alone out there after midnight. The first time she went for the car in the night, the rustling elms bronze in the darkness, the street sepia, Margret saw that "always" was over. They were like moments of private celebrity, these flashes veiled in black. The arrival of the Carnegie Hall subscription series, tickets in pairs. Membership renewals from the Met, the Frick, gregarious and unknowing, addressed to him. Glossy auction catalogs from Sotheby's for the rugs he loved and studied, but couldn't afford, and every other month his beloved *Hali*, airmailed from London in thick cardboard. The reach for things in stores—the book on Moorish design, the moss green socks in Men's, the package of salted pumpkin seeds—her hand reaching before she remembered, then mutely dropped.

The empty seat beside her in the car.

She continued the four A.M. drive to Cape May. She loved the shroud of it, the silence and the dark. Not the Lincoln Tunnel, Hoboken, and Jersey Turnpike part—left, then right, then left, except she was never sure, still had to watch the signs, more now that he wasn't there to help. But the liberation as she left the turnpike for the Garden State Parkway. It was the end of left and right, and the start of just going south. South in the quiet of the car, south surrounded by trees, south in the small of the night. You saw a lot of ghosts, driving alone at night. Shadows, coronas, and blurs; probably floaters too. Margret liked that, liked that sleeping-breathing feeling around her, the peace she felt being awake when others were lost in dream. Awake with the owls gliding on silent wings, deep and unseen in the fields, barn owls white as specters, great horned owls hoo-hooing the hour of the hunt. Awake with the night herons, their croaks under stars, their wing beats like oars. Awake with the mockingbirds, singing in the dark as if no one had told them the day was done. Blind troubadours, Margret once called them.

Poets never stop singing, Charles had said, no matter what you take from them.

She felt he was beside her on the drive, getting some rest so he could have an early morning of birding when they got there. Shadows, coronas, and blurs; they were his owls and herons and mocks beyond the headlights.

The bowl of brightness before her, the tunneling feeling of driving in the dark, road signs rearing up suddenly, their lettering phosphorescent—it was the same short view she'd grown to hate in grad school, though then it was only a metaphor; she never had a car at Columbia. But now the short view, the no view, was comforting. It made her feel safe. She passed by Asbury Park and thought as she always did, Bruce Springsteen. She noted the exit for Tom's River, a long way to go still, and an image of Nathaniel Hawthorne, of puritans in bonnets and axes behind sheds. She drove through the prehistoric pine barrens with its witchy trees. Then New Gretna, Absecon, Atlantic City, all going by with a speed you never got in daylight, a cruising speed of seventy, which didn't feel fast at all. Then "the big dick," a smokestack that was laughably phallic. And then the bridge at Great Egg, like going over the hump of a giant camel. The top of this bridge felt very close to flight and made Margret anxious. No matter how many times she drove it, she gripped the wheel hard all the way up and over, Charles sleeping beside her, sometimes snoring. On the way back, as Charles drove, he'd be exuberant; his parents had never let him go on roller coasters as a kid, on anything really, because his mother was so protective of her little Assyrian prince. He'd tease as he drove faster—"We're going to fledge"—and Margret would grip the seat on both sides. As the landscape fell away near the top, the sky in their ears and that top-of-the-ferris-wheel feeling, he'd give Margret a look, and she'd bark, *"Watch the road!"* He only laughed. But heading south to the Point, Margret drove and Charles slept.

On the other side, seconds later, ring-billed gulls lounged on every highway light, blasé in the grayness, a welcoming committee of little yellow eyes. She wanted to wake him here, but by agreement she'd sit tight past the last miles of salt marshes and fishing inlets. She'd wait til the Garden State Parkway ended, a tangle of merges and swerves, docks, bait shops, and oyster bars all funneling into Lafayette Avenue, a dog of a strip in traffic but a flying carpet at dawn. On Lafayette she'd reach over and jostle him so he'd be awake by the time they reached Collier's, a big green barn of a liquor store and the official end of Lafayette. Curving right at Collier's, they'd take another right into the Wawa, run in for papers and coffee, black for him and hazelnut extra light for her.

Then came the best part of the trip: the two-mile drive westward on Sunset Boulevard, which led to Sunset Beach on the Delaware Bay. On the right side of Sunset was West Cape May, a borough of homes old and new, farmland beginning about a mile in. On the left was the world-famous South Cape May Meadows, a hundred acres of fields, ponds, and mudflats, the ocean just over the dune. The place was a birders' paradise, a tumble of surprises during migration, and graced any old day with simple treats like snipe in the weeds, bobolink calling *pink* on goldenrod, and nighthawks dusting the sky at twilight. Cape May Point was beyond the Meadows, near the end of Sunset Boulevard, so those two miles were another kind of bridge you crossed over.

How they loved that stretch of road, loved the phragmites teeming to the left, great sheaves weaving, rowing with the wind. Loved the way summer hung heavily on Sunset, heat waves slurring the air, haze paling the greens, graying the blues, chalking the sky and sand so you felt the entire place was sick with sun, leeched and reeling with ghost crabs, the translucent housewives of the beach, and pallid grasshoppers ashen in the dunes. In fall, they loved how everything stiffened, golden stalks breaking, and the last dry leaves on trees laughing madly in the wind. And winter, the cold fist of it, the sun a white fuse, the Cape May shops putting Victorian capelets on dress forms at the door, and bosomy estates serving plum-pudding teas. In spring, frogs caught their headlights at night, a pinging brightness in the road that made them brake. It wasn't fun to squash a frog. And dawn. So often at dawn, clouds lowed in the Meadows, heavy on the grasses, sometimes rolling over onto Sunset, whiting out the road like a Turner and slowing them with contentment. They tried to describe it at first—clouds grazing, or camped out in sleeping bags, or hiding from the sky—but eventually it was enough if one or the other just said, "clouds."

Margret didn't stop at Wawa. She needed to sleep for a few hours so she could work later in the day. She worked better down here than in her New York kitchen, if only because there was more space. As she rolled west onto Sunset, she cracked open the window. The cold air was fresh mixing with the heat in the car. She loved that sensation, sharp and cozy, a cold cheek against a warm one.

She had begun with the warblers. She had two palm warblers in the back, thawing in a cigar box, and she hoped to get them both done this weekend. I have a black-and-white, she thought, a male yellow, two ovenbirds, my beautiful pair of black-throated blues, and also the pair of common yellowthroats. That makes eight waiting. They'd been in the freezer, some for almost ten months, while she practiced on other species, white-throated sparrows and most recently two very plain yellow-rumps. The smaller they got, the harder. She was working her way to the warblers with white, especially the male black-throated blue, his belly like fresh snow. You had to be careful with white, that's what the books said; white feathers could stain at the seam, and once stained you never got them clean again. You might try and think you succeeded, but in time the seam would reappear, a shadow through the feathers, though whether it would be grayish or brownish or yellowish, Margret didn't know; she hadn't worked with white feathers.

The white breast of the male black-throated blue was so white. Maybe because the black and the blue were so dark, like midnight in a children's picture book. What struck her when she held the tiny body in her hand, its little head lolling, was the deep green in the blue, the kind of color only nature can do, a mossy blue. And the female. Who could say what color she was? There was no name for that beigy green, that dingy celadon. No names, Charles used to say, for so much of nature's palette. The black-throated blues both had that little white square on the hip—a "hip-pocket handkerchief" birders called it—so charming on the male, and diagnostic on the female, who moving in the trees looked like other mousy warblers.

The sun was coming up behind Margret, roaring in her rearview mirror. Spring migration would begin in six weeks and go strong through May. I have to be ready, she thought, for more warblers. I have to swoop in like a swallow. She smiled, thinking of the barn swallow at Harvard's Peabody Museum, where at least once a year she and Milton had gone for an hour's stroll, heading up the metal stairs to the third-floor display of stuffed birds. The collection, from the late 1800s, was amazingly complete, a corridor of American birds behind glass, made in the days when people bird-watched with a shotgun, not binoculars. At the entrance to the corridor, the barn swallow was mounted in flight, just leaving a nest of baby barn swallows. Talk about tiny taxidermy. Her feet, minuscule tangles beneath her, were all but vestigial, as if the air were all that mattered.

In the summer, Margret and Charles saw barn swallows near the garage at 130th. They flew in great swaying circles, streaks of blue curving up to a fifth-floor balcony, streaks of rust sliding down, scooping into the shade under the elevated West Side Highway. Back and forth they flew, up and down, the same circuit of curves, an amusement park of air. They have their routine, he said. They love their routine, she answered.

Margret turned left between the pair of white brick walls that marked the entrance to Cape May Point. She'd be home in two minutes, in bed in ten, in the arctic air under the white down comforter in the blue-green bedroom, the one room where the sun couldn't pry until its afternoon descent, and then crept in like ivy.

NIGHT FLIGHT

Ten

THIS WAS NOT THE SAME as going to the Point. For this she rose at five. She dressed quickly in old cords, a sweater, and a jacket. Early morning was still cold in April. She pulled her hair tight into a ponytail and jammed a baseball cap low on her head, grabbed the tote with the Scott towels and a mini cooler, and was out the door by five fifteen.

The walk to the subway was always unnerving. The quiet was different at this hour, not rich and round as it was at three or four, but tense, the skin of it stretched thin. Even the whoosh of cars that passed on Broadway, never on the side streets, felt furtive, as if hurrying to get away. And the yellowish light from the streetlamps, it was so . . . scrofulous. Pockmarking the darkness. What was that poem by Frost?

I have been one acquainted with the night.

Anyone who walked the streets predawn was suspect. They might have been partying too late. Or escaping a bad one-nighter. Or in need of something from a pharmacy. But they tended not to be these. The few people she passed were themselves predawn, sprung, it seemed, from the queasy dream of the yellow light. They were like the vagrants she sometimes saw in the bird sanctuary, men living on the rim of the normal, sleeping in the northern opening of the Amtrak train tunnel, their strides too long and loping, their clothes not quite their own, and the look in their eyes quick, calculating, even when eager to be trusted. Living in the cracks.

Milton used to talk about his beloved assassin bugs, how the dangerous ones in South America, the species that spread Chagas disease, lived in the crevices of adobe houses. At night the heat of sleeping victims, the breathing and the blood, drew the assassins out and down. They fell from the ceiling like horrible rain. Kissing bugs, they were called in the States, because they liked to bite around the mouth. She remembered her grandfather telling her that the locals had another name for them, something with a *V*. It translated, he said, as "those who let themselves fall."

When Margret emerged from the subway at Chambers Street, it was still dark. She'd timed it that way. She wasn't a member of the dawn patrol, and she didn't want to cross paths with whoever was on duty. Because they started at first light, she began a little before. Still, there were only three people who might recognize her, and it had been eleven months since they'd seen her, on an orientation patrol the previous May. Margret and two others, a thin young man who was an architect and a jittery older woman who kept mentioning her doctor husband, had tagged along with a woman named Robin. Whether or not Thin and Jittery had assumed patrols, Margret didn't know. But Robin's patrol day was Sunday, and this was Monday.

Margret knew what she was doing wasn't right. By coming earlier than the patrol, she was undermining its numbers, stealing data. In fact, taking the corpses was illegal. She knew this because Charles had frequently chided her for picking up feathers, citing the Migratory Bird Protection Treaty of 1916. And yet Robin had admitted that they didn't get all the bodies, that the birds taken to New York Audubon, the numbers filed, were not really representative. It was commonly known that street sweepers and corporate doormen whisked the dead into Dumpsters as if they were trash, like the empty bottles and paper cups that landed in gutters overnight.

The birds did land overnight, in many cases safely. It was this Cubist trap of mirrored windows and lobby gardens that beckoned the hungry and broke their necks at sunrise. The biggest trap in Manhattan was here at the southernmost tip, the financial district with its bad feng shui, its greenery in dribs and drabs—shrubs in cement tubs and small trees planted on promenades. Margret didn't like this part of town. She too felt trapped down here, never able in all her predawn days to figure out the lay of the streets, the logic of north, south, east, west, which bottlenecked into a maze of too many head offices on too little land. It was a place with no vistas, all shoulders, and bullying ones at that. To think of creatures weighing ounces making the same night flights as airplanes, beating slim wings through cloud, mist, and under moons of all phases, then landing exhausted in this maw of moneyed ugliness . . .

Every morning, for a month the previous spring and already a week this spring, Margret had come. Not last fall, not after September 11. Then she went to midtown, to the sidewalks around the Empire State Building. But down here she had a pattern. She started on the West Side, at the World Trade Center, now a vast cold hole. She worked eastward in a clockwise sort of circle, a necklace of buildings, moving around this one, then that, the asphalt hard and hateful in the heavy gray air, and still no hint of what the day would be as the sky waited for sun, so it always felt overcast. It was the opposite of birding, this not looking up but looking down, scanning the sidewalks, the alcoves under overhangs, and the curving corners on either side of revolving doors.

"Injured birds try to hide," Robin had told them, "so check corners." It was heartbreaking, how they sought a point where the vertical and horizontal meet, a geometry that had nothing to do with them. But it was rare to find them alive, Robin had sighed.

An unpracticed eye would never see them. The bad crashes were greasy smudges, bills broken, sometimes just a head, the body already eaten by gulls. A birder's eye needed to adapt, to look for something without movement, blur, flutter, twitch, the opposite of everything you're taught. In fact, Robin said, most birders had no interest in the wreckage caused by cities, and they certainly weren't big on the patrol. Birding was supposed to be about nature, life, "a happy hobby," she said, "and this is a downer."

But not for Margret. She heard Robin talk and felt desire in her ribs, felt it circle like a cat in a basket, purring and waiting. She'd listened as the architect nodded his head and talked about green design and how backward even the big firms were. He was going to change the world, and Margret respected him even as she thought he looked too thin for his ambitions. And Miss Jitters, a woman seeking a calling—anyone could see how sincere she was. When the three looked to Margret, she felt her secret flatten, as if something too large was passing too close. She heard herself saying, "I grew up birding. My grandfather taught me. I think he'd be concerned about all this, so that's why I'm here." Appreciatively they nodded. Which made Margret feel all the more apart. It wasn't that she was a real birder and they weren't. It was the other knowledge. They were here to give, and she was here to take. She couldn't explain it, how she almost stopped breathing as she closed in on what might be feathers, a body. How her heart was pumping. How the world fell away.

To find them and lift them off the ground.

To hold them weightless in her hand.

To smooth with the side of a finger the nape of a broken neck.

It filled Margret, this ownership of something that cannot be owned. Every scrap in the distance raced her heart *pink* like the bobolink. Then when she was upon it—a banana peel, a hair scrunchie, a crushed and blackened rag—a gulf of loss, even anger. Once she ran to a blue jay on a curb only to find a twisted white gym sock with two blue stripes. She felt a fool, yes, but more than that, robbed. It was unseemly, she knew. But just as unseemly, the lifting elation as she knelt down to stillness.

"What are you doing there?"

Margret hadn't seen anyone around, only a little bump of something on the asphalt, a catch of orange; she'd run to it and knelt. Quickly she nipped the thing into a paper towel, then rose and turned in one motion.

It was a policeman, fresh-faced and on foot. Margret smiled.

"A policeman walking the beat," she said.

"A young woman crouching at the curb."

"I'm part of the dawn patrol. Project Safe Flight? We pick up birds for New York Audubon. To get numbers. You know, how many are killed by skyscrapers during migration. Do you want to see this one?"

He hesitated. He held a cup of coffee in his hand. He looked a little like Patrick Swayze. He was bowlegged in his blues, with a broad Irish chest, like a shield. He took a step toward her.

She brought the loose white clump forward, and let the paper towel spring open to show a tiny warbler inside, its feathers glowing orange and black against snowbank white. A gorgeous male, strangely early. You never saw Blackburnians until May.

"It's a Blackburnian warbler," Margret said.

"It's tiny."

"Look at the orange. Doesn't it remind you of a Creamsicle?"

His left hand drew back the paper towel for a better look. He wore a simple gold band much like hers.

"It *is* like a Creamsicle," he said, then stepped back.

"It's come up from South America to breed, and it crashed into a window, so I'm retrieving it for data. I assume that's okay with you guys, because we're a group that's known. Project Safe Flight."

"Right. The gal with the bird name."

"Robin."

"Yeah, that's it." He took a sip of his coffee. Men looked funny sipping, yet she'd always loved watching Charles sip, so delicate. "You know, you should be more careful at this hour."

"I am. I'm a birder so I'm aware of everything that's around me."

He gave her a long look.

"You weren't aware of me, and I was only twenty feet away."

The dark blue of that uniform and the body breathing inside it . . . Margret was starting to feel imposed upon, as if he were standing closer than he was, and all the energy in his body was in his chest.

"That's because I was concentrating on not damaging his feathers."

"Right. But if you were my wife, I wouldn't let you do this alone. You should be patrolling in twos."

"I'll suggest that at the next meeting."

"Tell them Officer Mayle said so. It looks safe down here until all of a sudden it's not."

She nodded. He seconded the nod and walked on. She watched him go, and when he gave a short look back, she waved and turned.

It was seven and the sky was coming in azure. It was time to get home, get these guys into the freezer and grab an hour or two of sleep before Saks. Margret wondered if Officer Mayle would tell Robin about her. Well, so what? They didn't own these birds, which they'd just throw into a giant freezer at New York Audubon to be tagged and measured God only knew when. Anyway, the patrol didn't know Margret's real name; she'd used her mother's maiden name, Beecham. So they'd never find her. Or this blazing Blackburnian. Or the hermit thrush she'd found first, so much smaller in the hand than when you see them on the path, looking faintly over their shoulder the way hermits do. Both, but for broken necks, were pristine.

Eleven

WHEN MARGRET ARRIVED, Emily wasn't there yet. Margret had said yes because Emily was going to kill her if she said no again. So here she was with three strangers in an apartment on Sutton Place, an East Side enclave so quiet and exclusive, you felt you were in the deep pocket of a creamy cashmere coat. And the sofas in here *were* creamy, a sort of café au lait velvet pulled over plump upholstery, *so* plump that when the young man next to her dropped down like a bomb, Margret popped up on a surge of goose feathers, then slid toward him and his deeper indentation. It should have been funny. But because he didn't even notice, it was just annoying, as was his reddish blond hair and his reddish brown eyes and his tangerine tie shouting "special me!" over a pink paisley shirt.

He'd come into the room and hardly looked at Margret, who was attempting conversation with a man and woman, clearly a couple, a conversation in which words felt like wooden blocks of red and blue. There was a round of hellos among the three, and then the hostess, Nan Schifman, who'd streamed out to take a phone call from her sister—"My kids are with their cousins for the night"—streamed back in and said, "Margret, this is Oliver. Ollie, Margret." The married couple, Fred and Leslie, immediately started teasing Ollie about his orange tie, and you could tell he was pleased as punch—Hawaiian Punch, Margret thought—all the while dropping knowing bits like "David's piece on Putin" and "that poem by Updike" and "Anthony's latest," as if this were *What's My Line?* and Margret was supposed to guess. Margret had never seen *What's My Line?* but her father had referred to it throughout her childhood. "Oh, for the wit of *What's My Line?*" He once explained the glimpse it gave him, the slice of city sparkle that existed in the world. Not the soot of South Chicago alleys still narrow from cart-horse days, but urbanity smooth as silk and smiling like Arlene Francis and Bennett Cerf.

Obviously, Ollie worked at *The New Yorker*. What Fred and Leslie did, Margret didn't know. When Margaret had been led into the living room, Nan said, "Leslie, Fred, this is Margret Snow, a friend of Emily Edwards." Which made Margret feel like some horrible hanger-on. And yet, according to Emily, Nan really admired Margret's windows for Flow, and specifically asked for her number.

Vague introductions had always bothered Charles. He hated to see people left hanging, especially in New York, where you didn't quite exist until people knew the nature of your work. If you were too shy to blare it out you could be invisible for hours. Whenever she and Charles had gone to looming dinners, gatherings of professors in their primes and department heads like lords, he made sure she was well introduced. That hand she'd seen at the lecture, guiding Swarthmore through the crowd, when that same hand first settled on the small of Margret's back it was like something in the Bible, possessive and poetic at once, as if palms and psalms were the same thing. His pride in her was a moat around her.

Margret reached for the third Bellini that had been placed in front of her, knowing she shouldn't; they were stronger than you'd think. In this stylish living room, its spaetzle sofas a calculated contrast with the taut Wiener Werkstätte furniture angled in expensive islands of space, she was stranded. She couldn't break into the conversation, because it was a world she knew nothing about, and she couldn't get up and browse the art, because that would be weird.

"No, no, no. It wasn't Tina who hired them; it was Bob," brusque Leslie was informing orangeade Ollie. "She was stuck with a lot of bad hires because of his queenie taste."

Margret scanned the room. They were all here. The Ross Bleckner and the Rothenberg horse. And this latest development, a John Currin, female faces something between marzipan and Mattel, a yucky combination. There was a Basquiat in the study, or so Emily had said, and in the bedroom a Joseph Cornell shadow box. A unique form of withholding it was, putting the thing most worth seeing in the one room you couldn't wander into. The Bleckner was nice, but that was the problem; Bleckner was always nice. But Cornell.

Margret was pretty sure they didn't put coats on the bed here, not even light spring coats. The maid who took Margret's shawl had disappeared through a door cut into the foyer's hand-painted scenes of white swans on silver leaf. Mute or tundra or trumpeter, you couldn't tell. The artist who painted them didn't have a clue about bill formation or silhouette; he or she was caught up in the swoop of arched necks like *S*'s. Charles once told Margret about a trip to Ireland, to

Galway, where he'd seen hundreds of swans feeding in a river, their white necks reaching to the rushing bottom, "Very straight," he said, "like the arms of girls." The Cornell—that world behind glass, her world—was in a room you couldn't go into. Oh, to lie down in one of those boxes. To take a nap in it right now.

It had been a rough week. With Tina out of town and Tom out sick with the flu, it had fallen to Margret to manage Stephen's window concept, and instead of collaborating he'd just screeched at everyone, while Joe constantly disappeared for a smoke. Margret tried to keep the peace, but the concept was crummy and turned out awful, as anyone could have predicted. Giant cardboard robins pulling Lilly Pulitzer shifts out of Astroturf. Early birds catching worms. It looked like Walgreens. On top of that, her eyes were now tired from the Bellinis even as her stomach was sharp with hunger. Why, she thought, did it have to be in the bedroom?

"Fanchon!" they heard their hostess exclaim, the foyer suddenly spilling with people. Fanchon must be the French-looking woman in the spiraling dress, a gauzy blue-black with ruffles at the hip and hem that seemed to stir her tall slim figure like a drink. She had a low, soft bust, sort of jouncy, and her hair was up in a French roll of such gleam, it filled Margret, who smoothed her own bramble behind her ears even though it would never ever be smooth, with envy. Following Fanchon was a gay couple. The short thick fortyish blond was very Waspy in red velvet slippers, black flannels, and an ivory turtleneck—he had to be a decorator—and the young, tall, lean, dark one had to be the catch. With his amazing posture and wearing a starched blue button-down that ballooned in back like a sail, his jeans gripping tight at thigh and calf, he looked like an archangel just dropped to earth. After them, thank heaven, came Emily, also in blue-black, one of her tenty, tea-length skirts with a matching cashmere T-shirt. Margret couldn't wait to see what Emily would make of Fanchon. Both women were slim, chic, inky, but where Emily was still and focused in her wind-shear duchesse satins, the Little Dot eye of the storm, Fanchon was soft and swingy, like sexy wind chimes. Indeed, Fanchon was braless, Margret now saw, as the creature took a seat across the mirror-top coffee table, which accounted for the jiggle. Ollie was hanging on every swing and sway. Leslie leaned back, watching.

More Bellinis arrived, and so finally did Lee Grovenor, the host. But only to say, and not without a mist of censure at the lateness of these four, "You may bring your Bellinis; dinner is served."

He reminded Margret of a saw-whet owl, with his small stature and square forehead. Despite his socially prominent wife—one of a brash new breed of philanthropists, and very successful—you could tell he was solitary. Emily said Lee was the most respected dealer of rare books in Manhattan, "but at parties he's happier in the kitchen, sending out culinary wonders on big white plates." He turned on his heel, and in his wake a chastened flurry of intimacy, names exchanged, and quick sips from tubes of fine crystal. Emily plucked the sleeve of the archangel and brought him over to Margret. He had a smile that makes a mother weak.

"Margret, this is Azam. He's a dancer with the Martha Graham Company."

Azam had a strong brow, a long beautiful nose, and black hair that swept back as if he were rising on a current. His skin, a more golden tone than Charles's, was of the same Near Eastern sands, and the green of his eyes was striking against black lashes and the blue of his shirt. Olive, sand, and sky.

"Do green eyes read from the stage?" Margret asked.

He threw back his head, lofting that smile.

"I had a teacher who said I must wear contact lenses for auditions. But I was too afraid they would slide behind my eyes and get stuck there. She said, You're a stupid boy because that's impossible. But"—he gave a charming shrug—"lucky for me, my eyes look darker when I dance."

And probably not only when he danced, Margret would have said to Emily if she could. They were both studying those eyes when Nan herded everyone into the dining room.

"Why were you so late?" Margret whispered on the way.

"My next exhibition finally arrived," Em whispered back, "at four. I was in crates for hours."

"Well, I was stuck next to that awful Oliver. It seemed like hours."

"Poor you. He's really conceited. And he's just another editor in a city jam-packed with editors."

"It's not only that. Nan introduced me simply as a friend of yours, as if I've done nothing else in my life."

"You can't take that personally. She just assumes that if you're here, you're known. So dive in. The bigger issue is no eligible men. Azam is beautiful, but he's with *him*."

They both looked at Velvet Slippers ahead of them, doing the Truman Capote shuffle.

The dining room was oval, something Margret had never seen before, so there was nothing on the walls, which were lacquered a peaceful blue gray. "Fifteen coats," said Velvet Slippers, whose name was Steve. The table of dark wood was shaped the same oval as the room, and the napkins were white linen with rolled edges, pressed yet airy. The wineglasses came from Emily's gallery, from the exhibition called White

Horses—one of Margret's best windows, though it went mostly unremarked. The artist, a glassblower, had somehow infused a whitish glow into Josef Hoffmann shapes. The glasses were "in dialogue"—Steve again—with the chandelier of white opaline that hung above. The silverware looked Werkstätte, so stylized and flat, and the table was finished with white carnations in mercury-glass globes. It was simply but exquisitely done.

"I hate highfalutin," Nan was saying. "Carnations are beautiful in bunches. And they go with the whole Secessionist ethic. Hardworking. Modest. And no scent to upset Lee's creations. Orchids don't have a scent either, but they're so narcissistic, don't you think?"

I love orchids, Margret thought, they're like the nuns in *Black Narcissus*, breathing thin air. But everyone nodded as they took their seats, assigned in laid-paper rectangles, each wedged into a sterling silver honeybee. Each bee was different—flying, crawling into a flower, posed on a petal—all of them adorable.

"These bees," Margret said to Nan, "they're so correct . . . I mean anatomically."

"We saw them in a shop in Paris, and Lee loves the idea of the hive; you know, the utopian thing. So we bought them, and I can tell you you'll never get a deal with the French. I would have walked away. There are only ten and I really feel it's twelve or nothing. But Lee had to have them."

Which was odd, in a way, because Lee seemed so not part of the hive. But instead Margret said, "Whoever made them had really studied bees."

"Maybe that's why Lee wanted them. He so rarely wants things—it's either books or art—so how could I say no?"

Emily had said often enough that it was Nan who had the money, a family fortune made mid-century in greeting cards.

Lee and Nan were seated at opposite ends of the table, Lee on the end closest to the kitchen door. Margret was on the left of Lee, with Azam on the right, across from her. Their host's empty chair looked not much sat in. On Margret's left was Fred, then Emily, but it might as well have been miles away, since they were on the same side and couldn't exchange glances. Then came Ollie, then Nan, and then coming back, Fanchon, Steve—who had indeed decorated this apartment—then Leslie, then Azam. Thank God it was Emily stuck next to Ollie. Emily could make conversation with anyone.

They all sat and a young waiter who was dressed in black went around the table pouring white wine into glasses. "A Sancerre," Lee told them when he announced the first course, brought out in twos by a young woman waiter, a terrine of terrapin with a drizzle of honeyed blackberry sauce. Terrapin! From the other end of the table came a deep Fanchonian wave of appreciation.

"*Tortue de mer*. I love turtle. Even more than *lapin*."

As plates were placed in front of them and Lee took his seat, the talk was of turtles, though Margret couldn't stop seeing Fanchon strangling rabbits.

"My mother flushed my turtles down the you-know-what when she heard they carried salmonella," Steve said. "Tom, Dick, and Harry. I was inconsolable for days."

"My turtle escaped," said Ollie. "Shelley was his name. Get it? Shell-ey. We never knew where Shelley got to. We think he was living in the garden, because flowers were always disappearing. But frankly, I didn't mind that Shelley was gone. Turtles are rather dull, you know."

"Maybe Shelley found you dull," Leslie suggested.

"Our dog ate mine," Azam announced. "I waited for the shell to come out the other end but it never did. Unless I missed it."

Everyone laughed because Azam was so attractive.

"Emily Post was famous for her terrapin stew," Emily said, hoisting the conversation up to higher ground. "I know all about my many namesakes, and there's a whole chapter on terrapin in her biography. They were breeding in her basement, down in the mud, and they would snap at the ankles of anyone who went down there. Emily had to carry a shovel and wear boots. I'm surprised it didn't hatch deep primal fears in her son, who wrote the book. But the chapter was very sunny, and the soup, according to him, was sublime. The key is, turtle has to be fresh. Which is why they let them breed in the basement."

"That could be a title for a book," Leslie said. "*Bred in the Basement.*"

"But would it be a mystery or a melodrama?" her husband wondered.

"It's a memoir," Steve snapped. "A memoir of the American South. And I would know, 'cause I was a gay boy down there in my teens."

And then he shuddered.

"That's such a stereotype," Nan cried. "I don't disagree with it, but it is a stereotype."

"Where did you live?"

"Louisiana."

"I nearly went to Tulane."

"New Orleans has the best *antiquaires,*" Fanchon declared. "I could shop there for weeks."

The far end of the table focused on Fanchon's charm bracelet, rattling in the air, because she had recently added a charm bought in New Orleans—a gold bat. Lee was back in the kitchen.

"In Chicago," Margret said to Azam, "there's a restaurant called the Cape Cod Room"—she knew this was boring but now she couldn't stop—"and it's famous for its Bookbinder soup, which is made from turtles."

"Last year I was in Chicago on tour," he cried, "and I was wowed. I was thinking about Al Capone and Scarface, and when I went into the ring—"

"Do you mean the Loop?"

"Yes, yes, the Loop . . . it was like time did not move."

"That's one of the things about Chicago. It holds its history. The alleys, the shadows, the El . . . it's like a steel monster shrieking by. But if you haven't seen it, you can't understand."

"And New York isn't like that. As great as it is."

"No."

Then Lee took his seat to a little round of "wonderfuls" and "lovelies." Margret turned to him.

"Lee, I'm Margret Snow. I do the window for Flow, and I'm also in windows at Saks. And this is Azam, who dances with the Martha Graham Company."

"Did you do the window for White Horses?"

"I did."

"It was interesting."

"Could you tell me what caught you?"

He took a bite of his terrine, in no hurry.

"It was surreal," he said, "but in a quiet way. I kept thinking about it. And I never notice windows. Or they never notice me."

"What was it about?" Azam asked.

It was difficult to articulate.

"Death," Lee stated.

"It was layers of white and ivory tulle," Margret explained, "stretched across the space. And I found a real horse's leg in a prop shop and placed it a few layers back, as if it had stomped on one of these goblets. And I powdered the leg with baby powder, because it was actually gray, to make it white like a Lipizzaner."

"The Lipizzaners!" Azam exclaimed. "Horses that are dancers. I've always wanted to see them."

"The metaphor of the Lipizzaners," Lee said to the last bit of terrine on his plate, the squarish silver fish fork so perfectly elegant in his squarish hand. "I have trouble with it. The reins, the nostrils, the white engine of them. The French turn pleasure into art; the Germans, power."

"But they're just dancing horses," Azam protested.

"I don't see them that way."

"And yet you bought the glasses," Margret said.

"We did, didn't we? Do you like the terrine?"

She wasn't sure. The taste was dark, hard to find. Or maybe the drizzle overpowered it a bit.

"It's different," Margret said. "A new taste for me, because it's much more pure in a terrine, I think, than in a soup."

Lee nodded, then left for the kitchen.

"What's going on down there?" came Nan's voice from the other end.

"We were talking about the Lipizzaners of Vienna," Azam answered, with his crushing smile, "and these wineglasses."

"I fell in love with them at Flow," Nan said. "Tell the story, Emily."

"That *is* the story. You fell in love with them at Flow."

"It's not the whole story. Don't you remember? You and I were talking about milk glass, and how it's fallen by the wayside, and you said, I have a designer who's making milky crystal, and I said, Do it, do it, I'd buy it."

It was a measure of how much Emily liked Nan, Emily who was never led to a decision, that she merely smiled and said, "Having smart clients makes all the difference. I just follow their lead."

"But of course," chimed Fanchon. "I learn so much from my clients."

Leslie asked her what she did.

"I set up the appointments in Paris for big American collectors. Paintings, jewelry, antiques, even the couture. I go with them. I get them in. I am in the cracks, which is not a bad place to be."

Margret looked to Azam. "Have you ever been to Paris?"

Just then Lee announced the next course, a mousse of black mushroom, dolloped inside a large cap of white mushroom nestled in baby greens. Everyone oohed and aahed, then followed Lee's lead and dipped into their mousse.

"I just got back from Paris," Fred said, for the first time turning his attention to their end of the table. He held his already empty mushroom cap in a rather plump hand, pink at the knuckles, and was nibbling at it like a chipmunk.

"You're so lucky," Margret said.

"It's not luck. It's business. I'm in illustrated books—art books. Northanger Abbey? So of course we do a lot of European buys."

"And how do you know Nan and Lee?"

"Leslie and Nan go way back. And Northanger Abbey is looking into a book on their collections. Which are obviously not all here. There's also the house in the Hamptons and the London flat."

"They're so young to have more than one collection," Azam said.

Not to mention a place in London.

"Well, they have the passion. Look at little boys with baseball cards. It's all about the passion."

"Maybe," Margret said. "But it's about means too. Sometimes

what you love, what you're passionate about, is completely beyond what you can ever afford. You study it every way you can, but you can never collect it. You watch others with more cash but less understanding walk off with your baby. I think that's why people become scholars . . . so they can possess with their minds what they can never hold in their hands."

The whole table was listening.

"I agree with you completely," Nan pronounced from the far end. "We study everything we collect. We comparison shop; we submerge ourselves in books. And no one submerges like Lee."

"Steve," Leslie said, relaxing into the wine, "you're a decorator. What do you think when confronted with a client's collection?"

"Obviously it depends on the collection. A wonderful group of paintings, bring it on. But so often the collection is arbitrary. Why this and not that? If it's based on color, like blue-and-white platters or old creamware, that's easy. But a collection of hat boxes . . . you want to slit your wrists."

"Give us an example," Ollie demanded, "of something really egregious."

"Oliver wants more," Leslie said.

"I think it's more interesting when people tire of their collections," Emily interjected. "They're the people who come to me. They're looking for something . . . immaterial. There's a critical mass point with collectors, when they have so much stuff they're almost sick with it."

"Sick *of* it?" Azam asked.

"No," Emily said, "with it. The collection starts to make them smaller."

"It confines them," Steve agreed.

"And yet the act of collecting," Margret said, "it's where you're most alive."

"A true collection is very intimate," Steve said. "Which is why it can be a little freaky, a kind of case study. I'm not talking about Tartan boxes on a glass-top table."

"But what makes a collection true?" Fred asked. "There's fetish collections and really fine collections and just damn silly collections."

"Like?"

"Hotel hand towels versus, oh, I don't know . . . antique globes versus—"

"Shake-'em-up snow scenes."

"I love those."

"Here's another thing," Steve continued. "Collections create dimensional problems, they take up space. Suddenly a home is a museum or a curiosity shop."

"I still want examples!" roared Ollie.

"*Voilà*," Fanchon said, "I have many examples. My skinny little Seattle millionaire who collects flow blue. Why flow blue? Because it reminds him of the blue of the computer program that made him rich. My couple from Greenwich who collect European buttonhooks. Not American, only European. Why? I don't know why. But those buttonhooks scare me. They have them hanging in the hallway to their bedroom. I never ask."

"Puppets," Steve exclaimed. "That was real freaky. This Hollywood actress in Gramercy Park—no, I'm not telling you who. She has about forty puppets from around the world. On strings. I was like, can we hang them from the ceiling and open a restaurant? I mean, what the ef do you do with forty puppets?"

"What *did* you do?" Lee asked, seated again.

"I found a lone white wall, perfect for an overhead spot, and said, This is the puppet gallery. You will have a rotating exhibit here, one puppet at a time, just like MoMA."

"Bravo," Fanchon said, and everyone else clapped as Steve lowered his head for a bow.

Lee half rose to say, "Quail. Plum sauce. Mashed parsnips." The plates came in. Also a Bordeaux. Waiting for everyone to be served, they all sat L-shaped in their chairs. No, h-shaped. Dinner parties took a lot of attention, and then in the end you wondered, what for? The surprise affinities, the spontaneous friendships, they were only that, surface glitter that slipped away with the tide. How many people really did dial up in the days after? No matter how wine-warmed and suddenly chummy she'd been, Margret had never called another professor's wife for the lunch they vowed to do. Because she didn't need anyone new in her life. And Charles never pushed her, because he was basically solitary, wary of friendships between couples. "So Pinter," he once said.

Margret looked down at her quail. It was golden brown and butterflied, and so much tinier than in life. Margret knew only too well how little the musculature was under its mantle of feathers. For everyone here she could have illuminated the process, what it was like to flay the skin, rolled back like the inside of an eyelid, larded here and there with saffron-colored fat, and the hard burgundy carapace underneath. How you had to make key cuts all the way along, the leg bones up within the bed of leg feathers, and the tail, severed from the body without snipping the feather roots. It was like slipping the hand from a glove, a hand that didn't want to go. The hardest part was the head, the way the skin cuticled inward at the ear holes. The way you had to cut around the eye socket, careful not to nick the lid, then scoop out the eyeball, and the brain too, like in a Frankenstein film. There *was* something Frankenstein about it, a semblance of life created from something dead. As Dr. Pretorius said in *The Bride of Frankenstein*, it was always better to grow life from a seed. It was one of Charles's favorite moments in movies, down in the tombs when Pretorius brings out his little lab experiments, the tiny homegrown creations he kept in bell jars. A king, a queen, a ballerina, and a mermaid. She and Charles both loved the mermaid in her jar of water, her hair floating like seaweed, and also the way Pretorius picked up the king with a pair of tongs. It was the movie they watched on the New Year's Eve preceeding 2000. It seemed so right, so millennial. Afterward, fifteen minutes before midnight, they walked out to the wall on Riverside Drive, and looking into the park through the cold black branches against the cold black sky, they wondered at the burning lights across the Hudson. In the icy dark they listened for countdowns from the windows on the Drive, *ten nine eight seven*, and then for cheers and "Auld Lang Syne" to tell them it was twelve.

"What are you thinking?"

Margret looked up. Azam was staring at her. He'd asked what she was thinking.

"You looked far away," he said. "Or else feeling sorry for your bird."

He had a piece of quail on the prongs of his fork, his index finger long upon the silver, European-style, his hand big and bony, swallowing the silver. Charles's hands were long-fingered but fine, not bony; the black hair across the top was smooth. The hair on Azam's hand had curl in it, but it was so like Charles, so black.

She picked up her knife. "I guess I was thinking how tiny the wishbone must be." Yet she knew there was no wishbone in this splayed quail, a Rorschach of legs and breast.

"So you must make a tiny wish," he said.

"The wishbones are gone," Lee said, "because the quail are butterflied. So there can be no wishes, not even tiny ones."

Lee began eating with such quiet concentration that everyone else followed suit, and the conversation dwindled to murmurs of appreciation and happy sips of wine. It was very good wine, anyone could tell that, and Margret didn't demur when the waiter filled her glass again. She was feeling floaty, across from Azam, so attractive even if he was with Tweedledee Steve, who was quite smart and funny. She liked Lee, so compelling in his serious and disappearing way, and Nan too, so energetically there. Fred was pretentious, but he was stuck with Leslie, who seemed angry in general, yet possessive of Ollie. And Fanchon, unflaggingly French, rolling her *r*'s like an engine—she was a good guest, doing her duty and diving in, just like Emily. Their perches in the marketplace gave them exclusive views that were very seductive. Margret had an inside view too, what sold at Saks and what didn't, not to zillionaires but to real New Yorkers. But it wasn't Paris, London, Sutton Place. Saks was small in this setting, though when Charles pushed her windows into Columbia conversations, the professors, it turned out, were fascinated. Margret took another sip of this beautiful wine.

"Your friend says you are a fan of Martha Graham."

Azam was talking to her again. Margret nodded but didn't say anything, because Emily had exaggerated her interest in dance. She'd been to Graham only twice, both times with Charles, because there were masterpieces he thought she should see.

"What do you love about Graham?"

"Well, I've only been twice," Margret answered, realizing her mouth wasn't working so well. "I mean, the one about Oedip . . . Oedipus."

The wine was warping her consonants.

"*Night Journey*," he prompted.

"Is that the one? It was like an Assyrian," she said slowly, "bas-relief. Those little palms and things in profile."

Her face was hot. Why did he keep looking at her?

"What I want to know," Emily said, pointing a pretty finger at Azam, "is why Graham men are always in such skimpy costumes? I mean, really, Azam, it's jockstraps and loincloths. Do you guys ever, among yourselves, admit she was sexist?"

"Noooo." He smiled lazily. "She just liked to see men's bodies. You know the famous line?" He squared his shoulders. "Walk like you carry the seed."

"What seed?" Nan called from the far end.

"Sperm," Fred said.

"What are you talking about?" Ollie demanded.

"*Martha Graham*," Emily, Fred, and Azam said in unison.

"And you should see Azam onstage," Steve announced. "Who would have thought little ol' me could have a cousin who looks like that?"

"My Persian mother married his Scottish uncle," Azam said.

"Second marriages for both," Steve explained. "They met at a medical convention."

"I was fifteen then," Azam said. "When I came to New York last year, Steve found me an apartment and decorated it. So even though we are step, he's really like my older brother."

"I laid down the law," Steve said. "No waterbed. And no mirror on the ceiling."

"But we love mirrors in the bedroom," Fanchon purred, looking first at Nan, then Emily. "No?"

"So you see," Azam whispered to Margret, the two of them Lee-less again, "I am more than a Graham man."

Margret said nothing. She focused on her parsnips, which were the best course of the night. The taste was so simple and strong, carroty yet white. Charles had loved her sorrel soup, and her chicken and barley, and the oxtail she'd made maybe twice. Only twice in six years. She took another sip of wine. Felt it warm and woody down her throat. Then another sip because it was so good. And why shouldn't she finish her glass like everyone else? Who cared if she got a little drunk? It was Friday after all, and the evening was going on so long. Margret tried to see what time it was on someone's wrist, but there were no watches in sight. She took another sip and decided to go to the bathroom before the next course came out, to find the Cornell and not talk for a while.

"Will you excuse me?" she whispered, and Azam nodded amiably. She took a deep breath, hoping she could walk okay, and headed back through the living room ever so slightly atilt, that lag time between thinking what you want to do and doing it. She looked for a maid or someone who could point the way. When none appeared, she wandered down the hall. She found the bathroom but crept farther, pushing softly at every door—child's room, another bathroom, child's room—until one door opened onto a corner room with an ebonized bed, lavender walls, and heavy green velvet curtains, simple and rich. Only a bedside lamp was on, like a lantern in the dark, but it was enough to see the Cornell hanging between two curtained windows. Margret went to it, stood in front of it, then backed up a few steps and seated herself on the foot of the bed.

It was one of the Aviary series from the 1940s. Mystical. Magnificent. The back was papered in birds, an old illustration of warblers on branches. Flat bars spaced vertically under the paper gave the backing a jailed effect, like a cage of air. Yet in the foreground were real twigs, and on the twigs, paper cutouts of warblers, glued as if perching. It was warblers deep and near. The inside rim of the box was papered with yellowing numerical tables, rows and rows, hundreds of numbers. A spring fallout, Margret thought, countless birds in spring migration, desire filling the trees. Desire, she thought, leaning back on the bed for just a second, letting her tired eyes close for a blissful moment, is like a cage. . . .

She woke with a start, Lee's owl eyes looking down on her, his hand hovering at her shoulder. She jerked upright.

"I'm so sorry," she cried. "I wanted to peek at the Cornell and I was staring at it and I guess I just slipped off. I'm really sorry."

He gave a little wave of the hand.

"Usually it's my chair that's empty at the table. Anyway, everyone's leaving."

"*Leaving?* How long have I been here?"

"About forty minutes. Don't worry, the table decided to let you sleep."

The table!

"But I'm on your bed," she said.

It was so embarrassing. But he was looking at the box.

"So what do you think? It was a wedding gift from Nan's parents. Her grandfather, a very smart man, bought it in the fifties."

"It's one of the most beautiful things I've ever seen."

They looked at it without speaking.

"Quick question," he said. "When you broke the wineglass for that window, how did you break it?"

"You know, I wrestled with that. Because those glasses are expensive, and you can only destroy something once. I put it in a ziplock bag, and then holding the stem I closed my eyes and knocked the bowl against the stone wall in Riverside Park. It broke beautifully."

They looked at the Cornell one last time.

"I'm not sure that's true, though," he said.

"What?"

"That you can only destroy something once."

"Here comes Goldilocks," Leslie hailed, as if Margret were now her best friend. Emily simply raised an eyebrow, her once-again-you've-gotten-away-with-murder look. Fanchon said, "It's so charming to be young," even though she couldn't be more than five years older. Then she grabbed Emily's arm. "We must have dinner . . . just us, to discuss everything." Emily had no choice but to agree.

"Tomorrow we talk," Emily said, as she hailed two cabs. Before Margret stepped in, Azam rushed up and pulled both of them into a bear hug. "*You two must come and see me dance.*" Then finally Margret lay her heavy head against the backseat's fake leather, the taxi shooting west, then breezing up Park Avenue, the lights stopping them every few blocks like a fickle woman saying no. And then the drive through Central Park at Ninety-seventh. Stone walls, curves, stars, the sky blue-black like the dresses, and brazen spring so fresh and fast, racing in the open window, invading her aquarium of air, her hair blowing across her mouth, her cheek, and the driver in front not bothering to talk. The night doorman saw her to the elevator and pressed the floor for her. The evening seemed to have spanned years. The apartment when she entered did not want light, or she didn't want it, so she went through darkly, straight to the bathroom where the moon splashed luminous in the old white tub into which she threw her clothes. She washed her face and brushed her teeth and drank cold water sideways from the tap. In the bedroom she pulled down the blanket and crawled into bed with only her underpants on, her chin still wet, her breasts heavy against the cool sheet.

She fell asleep thinking of his hands.

Twelve

"FALLING ASLEEP *in the master bedroom!*"

Emily always called around nine the next morning, eager for the postmortem chat.

"It's your fault," Margret said. "For telling me the Cornell was in there."

"That's what I told the table. I said, It's my fault. And Nan, who found you and very nicely left you there, said, Why didn't she just ask? And Steve said, Because it's hard to ask. Then I said, For Margret, shadowboxes are like store windows. She really studies these things."

"It's true. I do. And Nan was so offhand in the beginning."

"New Yorkers are much more understanding if you make it about work. Anyway, I think even Nan was ready for a nap. People are pretty tired by Friday."

"She and Lee are such an odd couple."

"Because he's so sensitive and serious?"

"Yeah."

"Well, she is a steamroller, but she has to be. And everyone wants her on their board. I think she actually forgets how intellectual she is . . . French lit from Brown. She was working on a book when she and Lee met. Women of the salon, eighteenth-century. She needed to find some obscure French text. Anyway, Nan's really loyal and she sends me lots of customers."

"So what was dessert?"

"A perfect chocoloate mousse made the old-fashioned way, with raw eggs."

"He likes mousses, doesn't he? He likes to take things and turn them into something else, turtle into terrine, mushrooms into mousse, birds into butterflies. I wonder what it means."

"He is a bit of a mad scientist. By the way, have you heard from that guy at Lord and Taylor?"

"Jay Marti? No. But he said it would take a while to get back to people."

"It's been two months."

"Which is a while."

"Why don't you give him a call? Just a reminder. I mean, I'm not pushing you, but Saks isn't getting any easier. And those giant robins . . . that couldn't have been your idea. Could it?"

"It was Stephen's. It was his turn and he thought it would be witty, but the execution wasn't."

"Isn't it your job to oversee when Tom's out?"

"Yes, but Stephen's a screaming meemie."

"Mar, you have to learn to shut that down. The responsibility for those windows was yours."

Margret didn't say anything. She knew Emily was right and she knew Tom wouldn't be happy, but Tom also knew how Stephen was, and Tom had okayed Stephen's idea.

"I'm just not paid enough to work the kind of hours it would have taken to fix it, if it could be fixed. And I have other things I'm working on."

"This is Margret Snow talking? Margret who pulled all-nighters for papers not even in her major? And what other things are you working on?"

Margret was silent again.

"My own projects."

"I bet you just blew him off, didn't you?"

Why was everyone so keen on her career? This was just what Margret was sick of.

"We still haven't finished talking about the party," she said. "You know, it turns out Azam is straight. He made a point of saying so, not in so many words. Of course it never would have been a question if Steve hadn't let everyone think Azam was his boyfriend. Anyway, maybe you can date him."

This time Emily was silent.

"First off, I don't see why I deserved that, especially after watching out for you last night. Second, Azam may carry the seed, but I don't think I'm at the point where I have to start dating men ten years younger than me, and a dancer at that. Third, I have enough on my hands with Fanchon, who was hitting on me."

"Really?"

"She was seducing everyone at our end of the table. Every time Oliver flagged, she just jiggled her boobs. And she kept looking at me like we understand each other or something."

"Maybe because you were both in the same blue-black."

"Oh, yes. She said we were both wearing the ink of the octopus."

"She does seem successful."

"She's got her game, that's for sure. And she doesn't have to generate a scene like I do. Doesn't have overhead. Just get people entrée and then advise them. I wonder how she charges? If it's a flat fee or hourly or both? Anyway, you've changed the subject, as usual. You've become a master at changing the subject. At least you don't say things like, This conversation is over, or I'm done here, which seems to be the new thing. I love how women have become empowered to not deal with things."

"But I don't do that."

"I know; I'm ranting. I'm just so disappointed with our gender. All these women who just want to be supported by their husbands and have babies. America got attacked and we'll never be safe again, so let's move to the suburbs and buy an SUV and devote ourselves to our kids, each and every one of whom is gifted and don't you forget it. So what was the point of feminism if women are just crawling back into their hole?"

"What brings this on?"

"The usual weekly phone call from Joy."

Joy was Emily's older sister—Donna Reed on speed, to put it mildly.

"You know, Emily, it was you who changed the subject. We were talking about the party and then you switched to Lord and Taylor, so it wasn't me. And anyway, why is everyone so concerned with my career?"

"Is it a career? That's the question. It's not that I'm not glad the insurance was there and you have this financial cushion, but it sure doesn't seem to be helping you . . . get ahead."

"'Cause that's what it's all about?"

"You know what I mean. Those plywood robins, pulling schmattas out of Astroturf!"

Yes, it was embarrassing. But it was also committee, and that's what happened sometimes when other egos were involved. Emily couldn't understand, because she had complete control at Flow.

"I'm not complaining about the windows you do for me, and you know I'd be the first to complain. But all those hours at Saks. I keep wondering, do you get pleasure out of your job anymore? Why are you there? What do you want?"

To be alone with my birds.

"I wanted to talk about the party," Margret said, "but I guess we're finished with that. Are you doing anything fun tonight?"

A sigh from downtown.

"A date . . . yes, a blind date. With the brother of a customer. We're going to City Opera's *Madama Butterfly*, then dinner afterward at Mr. Chow's. Pretty creative, eh?"

"It sounds fun."

"Mr. Chow's is always fun. What are you going to do?"

Margret heard the forced cheer in that question and ignored it. She knew exactly what she was going to do. She was going to reread chapter two in Hasluck's *Taxidermy*, "Stuffing and Mounting Birds." She was going to rent *The Bride of Frankenstein* and watch it after dinner. And she was going to be up and out by five Sunday morning. She'd heard that the gallery housing the Temple of Dendur, its north window, was a death shear for migrating birds. It might be spooky to lurk around the Metropolitan Museum at first light, but it was way closer than Wall Street. She'd see.

"Sasha said we might go to a movie. I have to give him a call."

Thirteen

WELL, THAT WAS WEIRD. Fifteen minutes standing on Fifth Avenue looking up into the smile of the first man she'd ever slept with. How many years ago? Thirty-one minus twenty-one. Ten. "Margret," he'd boomed, pulling her by the wrist so that she spun to face him in front of Rockefeller Center, tourists plowing by. It took a second to place him, to focus. William Ferris. "*Will.*" He looked the same, such blond handsomeness, everybody's image of the good-guy frat president, which he'd been, with his beer-sleepy smile, and his clean blond hands respectful even on Saturday nights. He was in town for a neurosurgeons' conference, and was staying at the St. Regis. His wife was inside Saks, buying some shoes, and he was outside waiting for her, watching New Yorkers on a Wednesday afternoon, the last week in April.

Will wanted to know everything, *everything* she'd been up to since graduation. Margret was speechless before his sweeping enthusiasm. Her everything was what he wouldn't want to know. Too sad. He was a doctor now, the doctor he'd always wanted to be, a man who fixed things with his hands, fixed brains, and he would hear her story and see it couldn't be fixed. Her everything would ruin his weekend. So she ran with the ball, just like the Commodore quarterback in that great game their senior year. I'm second in command in Saks windows (the robins were down, and not a moment too soon), and I freelance around town. Oh, yes, my ring; I'm married, very happy. And Emily's here, a great success with her gallery Flow, down in Chelsea; you should go there if you get a chance.

Will was generous, as generous as always. "I just knew you'd make it wherever you went. And Emily too. Both of you such stars." Stars. It made her heart lurch. They were standing facing each other, and he kept putting both hands on her arms, as if to convince himself she was really there. "You must come see us if you're in Ohio. I'm in the book, in Oberlin. Do you promise? And your husband too. You'll love my wife, Sarah, and she'll love you." And then they hugged each other, and Margret backed away, waving goodbye until the crowd closed him off. Then she turned west to Sixth, to take the M5 up to the garage at 130th.

She loved the M5. It was one of the joys of New York, all the better because it was sort of secret. Well, not a secret exactly, but it claimed a stretch of Riverside Drive that was arguably the most beautiful boulevard in Manhattan. In a way, the Drive was part of Riverside Park, because both were designed by Frederick Law Olmsted in the days when the West Side was the ritzy part of town. Unlike every other boulevard in the city—Fifth or Park, both very handsome, but stiff and straight—Riverside Drive rolled and curled, lifted and swayed, cutting a voluptuous swath. Like an Ingres, Charles said. And with the same kind of quiet. Margret loved how the bus, when it turned on Seventy-second and headed toward the Hudson, seemed to be leaving the city behind. It was never very crowded, could even feel private. And once the bus turned north, whatever side you sat on, there were great things to see. To the east, prewar buildings with curving facades and limestone mansions like little kings, and to the west, gardens, lawns, sycamores, elms. Sometimes she saw ducks from the Hudson flying behind the trees.

Margret boarded the bus at Fifty-second, where it was still crowded. When a woman laden with shopping bags from Toys "R" Us bunched out of her window seat at Sixty-sixth, Margret slithered in, just in time for the park view, the green grass dotted with daffodils, and squirrels chasing squirrels up trees. It had been a spring day like this when she and Will finally did it, having not done it almost all of senior year. When the time came, silently after his fraternity's spring formal, in a room he'd rented in the nicest hotel in Nashville, the whole thing felt stage-managed, like they were doing a nude scene in a movie. None of that luxurious petting through clothes that makes you feel swelling and empty at the same time. ("Do you think men get that sensation?" Margret had asked Emily. "No," she said, "they're trying to empty.") Will made a great ceremony of removing their clothes deliberately at the start, which made Margret self-conscious. Still, she didn't want to ruin it, his plan to deflower her beautifully. Once he climbed aboard, though, it was push-push-*push*. Margret could have sworn she'd heard something crunching inside. She knew she probably hadn't, but it felt like something crunching, like when you bite down on rubbery white chicken cartilage; that's how she remembered it, like there was cartilage in there giving way.

All those evenings they'd gone deeper into the night, his hand under her sweater, her bra, her fingers pressed under his jeans and catching in the muggy opening of his boxers, where his penis, all akimbo, was aching to get out. All that necking and petting until they were like sunken ships, waterlogged bodies settling into sand . . . she felt like all he had to do was pull off her clothes and slip into her like an eel. But no. Will was saying her name in great gusts, marching orders from his cock, which soon had him marching double-time he was moving so fast, and she a stretch of cold white road beneath him. It wasn't like anything in Colette's *Cheri*, that undulating abandon. It was blunt and sharp at the same time. Raw and unpleasant. And then his tense freeze above her, the stampede of shudders before he crumpled down on her in a sweaty heap.

"Most women are deflowered by incompetents," Emily said the next day.

"When I told you I might do it, why didn't you stop me?"

Emily looked surprised.

"Because there's no way to know for sure. No cues, no matter what anyone says. You can't tell who'll be good and who won't. It's like ordering from a catalog."

"It was so cold and naked."

"But I thought you were in love with him," Emily said slowly. Margret could tell Emily felt terrible then, for not stopping her, though everyone knows you can never stop a friend from doing what she's been thinking about doing for weeks and weeks. And Margret had felt in love with Will, because everyone treated them like a golden couple, and because of the unopened treasure chest that lay hidden within those sunken-ship sessions on his bed, the riches all the books and songs go on about. She felt tricked by ego, tricked by sex, and tricked by her own inexperience, which led her to believe that her body's hunger was also her heart's. She knew it was unfair to hold this against him; he wasn't wildly experienced himself. When he'd fallen on her in a heap, she had to remind herself she'd cared enough to go this far—they were lovers now, at least for the month left until graduation. But she felt sick. She thought she knew what love was, and all she knew was this wasn't it.

How different with Charles. Just thinking of Charles that first time, just touching the surface of the memory, created a glide inside her, a shimmer of contentment. How bold she'd been. How unlike herself. But then dropping out of school, that was unlike herself too. She remembered all those phone calls with her parents, with Emily. But not a peep to Professor Ashur. She was afraid he'd think all the time they'd spent talking and birding was wasted.

She hadn't been on campus for days, and hadn't seen him for probably three weeks, but she had a book he'd lent her and that was something. Margret knew she needed to speak to him before she closed the door on Columbia, but every time she thought she'd stop by his office something held her back, the fear she'd be standing on the other side of his desk and he'd see her as a lightweight, finking out on her thesis. She kept looking at the book on her bedside table, a serious book with the forbidding title *Arrest and Movement: Space and Time in the Art of the Ancient Near East.* It was published in London in 1951 and had those glazed pages, as shiny as white porcelain, on which the print sits slippery and spidery. He'd lent it to her because the book contained a majestic passage on the dying lions of Nineveh, that pinnacle of Assyrian art and a masterpiece almost ill with empathy, mortality. It made her think of Masaccio's *Expulsion.*

She knew she was going to use the book to see him. To see, finally, if anything was there. But should she call first and tell him she was going to drop by with the book, or should she just go over? She fretted the question during those days of neither-here-nor-there, the interim weeks when she was checking off academic obligations while going twice a week to Saks to get her feet wet. She still felt the north call of Columbia, the hold of 116th, with its sixties stoicism, its quad of stone squares and circles, its chess-champ intensity, and cappuccinos at Café Taci. She felt all this intellectual solidity set against the pull of midtown, where the big windows reflected laughing lives, not lonely paths through glazed pages. Margret found she didn't mind the interim, the floatiness of it. And her question about the book kept drifting in and never went out, like a buoyant beach toy the tide can't seem to carry away; it just bobs there twenty feet from shore and makes you think of physics you never learned and has you saying to yourself, there are some things even the tide can't do. So by the last Friday in April, Margret had lived with the question for so long that it was like a colorful bobbing thing she had only to go out and grab. She decided to go.

Margret bathed around six. It was still bright outside, and the long thin bathroom window which had so thrilled Emily and her when they rented the apartment three years earlier—"A window in the bathroom is a prize," the Realtor had said—let just enough light get to the weary white tiles so that a hint of shine caught here and there, and you could lie in the tub and pretend you were at an old Swiss spa with a forest on the fringe. Margret liked to fill the tub up high and then just languish. She liked watching the stillness of her body under water, the way her legs looked stunned, pink, the skin newborn like the lower half of a mermaid who has suddenly lost her tail. She liked wiggling her toes up the foot of the tub so they peeked above the waterline and kept from drowning, and she always wondered at how her breasts floated, twin islands so light in the water lapping around them. There's no stillness quite like a bath, Margret had thought, drifting in that space between the end of the week and the beginning of the weekend, a dimensionless passage so often pitched with longing, isolation, even desperation. The "Fri" in Friday had always made Margret think of fright and frighten. But now this hour seemed like a path of lavender, though maybe that was because of the soap. She glanced over her body again and decided she was looking as slim as a size ten could look. Her period had just finished so the bloating was gone. Heat was leaving the water so she soaped up, then rose to rinse with a steaming blast from the tap.

Margret dressed as she usually did—nothing fancy, her blue-and-green kilt with above-the-knee black stockings—but put a little color on her lips, so Charles Ashur could think she was going out later. She left the apartment a bit before eight, because that wouldn't look so premeditated. Who drops by unannounced on Friday night? By eight he might have already left town to visit Susan Baughman at Swarthmore. Or he might be out, or be eating dinner, or have a guest. It just didn't matter, because it was all a lark, a chance, and if you tried to plan these things it got too calculated and it wasn't chance anymore. The one thing Margret had decided, had written in stone to herself, was that if he wasn't there, she'd leave the book. His not being there would be a sign for her to let this go. The note in her pocket, which she would put in the book if she had to leave it, was simple. After composing many variations on "goodbye"—in one she even made a lyrical reference to "migration season," instantly awful—she wrote: *Thank you for everything. Margret Snow.*

The walk over, the chill air, she remembered it still, April having waved its wand over the black enamel lampposts, the mica glittering in the sidewalk, the chartreuse shoots on trees, pointillist dots of spring green. Everything gleamed with the same spring need: *reach for me.* Why was it that spring twilights made your body feel so big against the air? So all-or-nothing?

The building was at 113th and Riverside Drive, no. 404. Before she came in view of its entrance, she stopped, pulled her ponytail tighter in its clip, and took a long look at the river, because if he wasn't there a phase of her life was over. It had to be over. She'd loved him for too long. She was nervous and could feel her pulse under her earlobes. Entering the impressively marbled lobby, she wondered if other students ever came to see Charles Ashur, something she'd never wondered before. When she got to the doorman she told him her name, and then, because she didn't want to be like those others—if there were any others—she overexplained. "I brought a book for Professor Ashur, and I can leave it with you, but if he's here I can take it up. It's really up to him. If he's here."

"He's here, I think," the doorman answered, and she felt a sway inside. The doorman picked up the intercom phone and said, "A Margret Snow is here to see you . . . *with a book.*" He listened and said, "Uh-huh." Then he turned and said, "Ten-E." She took the elevator up, and when it opened she saw B to her right, so she went left, following the hall around a corner. Charles Ashur was standing in his doorway, leaning in the wedge between door and jamb.

"A Margret Snow," he said, as if naming a species.

The look on his face was a mix of interested and aloof. It was a look she'd seen from time to time, in class when he got an inane comment from a student, and once in Central Park when a know-it-all birder planted himself right next to them and started explaining things as if they were beginners. It was a look Margret wasn't happy to be receiving herself.

His black hair with its silver at the sides was a little long. He was wearing a French blue button-down, which made his eyes very dark. She found those eyes hard to look at because she wasn't his student anymore. His sleeves were rolled up, and the dark hair on his arms . . . that was hard to look at too. In the two years she'd known him, she'd never seen his cuffs unbuttoned. She'd never seen his arms. Only the hair on his hands.

"I thought I'd bring you your book," Margret said, holding it up like show-and-tell, rather dippy, she realized too late.

He looked at the book, then back at her.

"I didn't call first because I just thought I'd leave it to chance, either catch you here or leave it with the doorman."

She held out the book. But he made no move to take it, and she felt his silence was a test.

"I know it's Friday," she said.

A non sequitur. But in that cul-de-sac of hallway with a yellow ceiling light behind her, and a nighttime silence behind him, and the cool spring evening of blooming forsythia outside these prewar walls and halls and doors, it seemed Friday was everything.

"Well, come in, Margret Snow. I'll give you a glass of wine, and you can tell me why you're jumping ship."

He saw her into the apartment and then led her to the library, which was actually a small square dining room, lined on every inch of wall with books to the ceiling. He slipped *Arrest and Movement* into a slight cleft on the shelf, which Margret thought was so charming.

"What a wonderful room," Margret said. "Is it a perfect square?"

"Almost perfect. It's the only almost symmetrical room in this extremely asymmetrical apartment. Do you like square rooms?"

"I never thought about it before."

"I bought the apartment because of this room. Because when you walk through the front door you face right through to the east window, with that little bit of Saint John the Divine. I couldn't resist. And then you can go that way"—he nodded to the right—"to the kitchen. Or this way to the living room."

She followed him in, and then he left to get the wine. Margret scanned for signs of Swarthmore, but saw nothing in the way of photos, and no sign of a woman at all. Just windows with no curtains, a large stooped tree in a green glazed pot, and walls a shade of white that made her think of milk. Really, there was very little in the room. A beautiful mirror on one wall, the black frame alive with pearl inlay. A nineteenth-century photograph of a stork's nest on a mosque. A stereo, records, and CDs in an old rosewood étagère designed like a mihrab. A brown leather chesterfield. A low Chinese tea table. And on dark wood floors, Oriental carpets slapped down side by side and in perpendiculars, not the formal kind with arabesques, but more folkish and geometric, with octagons and angles. Blues and browns, reds, creams, and corals, it was the rugs that had color, voice. Everything else seemed to be thinking.

He was a gracious host. He sat her down on the big old couch against the wall, surprisingly deep, the leather worn and thin. He said he had nothing in the fridge, but he brought out a plate of green grapes, a French cheese, and some soft butter—"I love butter," he apologized when he set it down. There was also a baguette he said was almost stale, but it tasted wonderful to Margret, especially with the butter that was so soft, it was almost crepey. Margret's grandmother Anna Snow used to leave butter on the counter for hours, maybe days, and it never went bad. It was as if with her graying wooden spoons and fistfuls of flour, she knew the eternal secrets of such things. Butter. Milk. Arms. Certain words were striking Margret with the meaning of life.

They sat on the couch side by side as he grilled her on what she was going to do next. She told him about the position at Saks in visuals, another word for window dressing, an assistant position, and she was excited about it. "I just need to be in three dimensions, not living in monographs and photographs and flat things on walls."

With a quick nod, he seconded her decision. "You know what you need to do now?" he said.

"What?"

"Start seeing opera and dance."

"Because?"

"Store windows are stages. You'd be learning from the masters. David Hockney's *Magic Flute* at the Met. And Martha Graham, the Noguchi sets. You want dimension? *Appalachian Spring*. Nothing like it. Also *Night Journey*. I think Graham and Noguchi were channeling the Assyrians."

Always the teacher.

"And you have to see *Davidsbündlertänze* at the New York City Ballet."

"I've played pieces from *Davidsbünd*."

"You have? What's it like?"

"It's hard. Like Chopin in a void. Like Schumann hears the notes through a scrim of silence. So you have to find your way there too."

They talked, and it was comfy and lovely and the phone never rang. He poured more wine, a pinot noir that was making Margret feel exceedingly happy.

"Except for your very white walls, which are *très* sixties, though I'm sure you're aware of that, you seem to like colors with earth in them. Everything in here—the wood, the rugs, this leather couch—everything seems steeped in native soil." Though why she was making a reference to the caskets of vampires, Margret couldn't say. Maybe it was because Anna Snow had occasionally spoken of vampires. Werewolves too.

"Even the wine," Margret said, "has a fertile taste. It's earthy."

Margret didn't know why she was making pronouncements like

this, except that in this different setting, indoors with Charles on his territory, she was feeling free and uncareful in a way she'd never let herself be outside.

"If I spilled wine on this rug," she continued, "it would blend right in. Don't you think?"

"Miss Snow, that's a very old Baluch under your toes. So please don't spill. But I agree with you. People forget that art is organic. Wood in the wine, minerals in the oils, ivory in the music."

"You mean elephant in the music."

"And madder in the rug."

"Madder?"

"An herb that makes this particular shade of pinkish red."

"Madder," Margret said again. "But I always thought red came from an insect. Something with a *C*."

"Cochineal."

"That's it. Cochineal. My grandfather used to mention it."

"And what did he say about it?"

Margret put her fingers to her temples, a pose she'd picked up from Emily. "I'm trying to remember. He was teasing my grandmother about her chinoiserie corner cabinet. The red one."

"Cochineal is the insect from which a blue red, a bloodred, is derived. It was also ground up for the first true lacquer. Can you imagine? The wings of an insect were the basis for lac, which was painted on ships that carried spices and dyes like indigo and cochineal. Barrels of color!" That was Charles. In thrall to something long ago and far away, history in a barrel.

Then he launched into news from the art department, doing vicious, spot-on imitations of colleagues, which she never guessed he was capable of doing, because he was always so proper. They were right next to each other on the couch, close as they often were when birding, but in those moments they were walking and climbing, caught in a cat's cradle with the birds in their binoculars, connected and separated by what they were seeing, as well as by the fact that he was a teacher and she was a student. Not to mention the age difference.

But now they were sitting. And there were no birds here in his living room, no Columbia, no rules. They were sitting and unmoored, a foot of space between them, twelve electric inches, and Margret was paying strict attention to her kilt, which kept opening because the dry cleaner had lost the safety pin and she didn't have another. So she was smoothing it closed, and it stayed closed until she moved, and then she had to smooth it again. He asked if she'd seen the great crested flycatcher in Riverside Park.

"Is there one?" She tried to sound bright even though it was the last thing she wanted to talk about. "I haven't been going in lately. I don't think I've been in since our last time. I've had so much else to do."

He was looking at her strangely. Margret felt she had just slighted their outings together, and their friendship, by feigning interest in the flycatcher as any other woman would. But everything had been so giddy and exciting, and now he was on to bird-watching, which felt like backtracking. So it was all just birds. What if he cut to the chase and asked, Why are you really here? What would she say? Margret was suddenly sad. She'd misread everything. She was looking at the place where the safety pin should have been. The lull reminded her of those silences on a long drive.

"I guess I've been going in for both of us," he said.

She looked from her kilt to his thigh, the muscle under the fabric, a thin gray flannel, and she touched him. She put her hand on his thigh like it didn't even belong to him. But it did. The muscle went taut. And then his hand was in her hair, his lips on her brow, then on her mouth, and it was perfect, like she was in exactly the right place at the right time and the locks were unlatching. This was what they were ready for, their kisses longer and deeper, creating widening ripples in the room, their bodies dropping down into the couch, floating in the center of four legs and four arms, their flesh elated under wool. He was a good kisser, surely one of the delights of life, finding that the man you've wanted knows how to kiss. She remembered how his hand brushed the front of her kilt aside and sought the top of her stocking, where the nylon met the skin, and how he played at the rim, running his thumb along the plump little ridge there, then spanning his hand around her leg, gripping it. "More," he said into her mouth, and his hand moved up the cool clime of her thigh, Margret not stopping him, not stopping him at all, feeling a spike of wildness as his fingers grew insolent at the edge of her underpants, and not the least bit bothered by the comic geometry when he pulled them off and they caught, caught, and caught, a slow motion snag at knee, calf, and heel, as if they were some kind of cotton conscience and didn't want to go. It was funny but Margret didn't laugh. Just go, she thought, pulling closer.

"Condom," he said, a word that sounded like black robes, and she said in less than a whisper, "Withdraw." She trusted him and didn't care, and her arms were around his neck.

He loosed her arms to lift himself up from her, his eyes black as he reached to turn off the glaring lamp. Then she heard the ragged sexy opening of his pants, the tug at his shorts; the movement was like quickness in a crowd. She reached down and closed her fingers around that hard hairless curve.

They pressed together on his couch the size of a coffin, the smallest room in the world, and her hair undone was everywhere around their faces and necks, growing and shrouding, while he inched into her. It was something quite different than she had known. So close, so slow, so dark, so wet. He was slow and thick in her, his arms around her back fixing her to him as he worked silently inside. Not the unthinking strokes of her first lover and the one after, sailing away or stubbing her out. No, this was dreamily close in and slow, a drenched, pinned sensation, a kissing above and below. There was a sucking sound like mud, the madder moaning. It was strange the way she began to feel pleasure far off, felt it in the dark, a wall of pleasure coming from way out like a wave you watch, first a seam on the water, then a riffle, then a rise coming in, a rise growing til there's no horizon, pleasure is rolling up and up, climbing the wave. She was climbing under his face so close over hers, his cock glued into her, then drinking him in ecstatic waves like wingbeats, the heavy beats when a gull lifts off, flooding and falling into lightness and looseness. So this is what it was, sex and love. Oh, how she loved him and at that moment was gone from him.

"Finally," he breathed, "finally fucking Mar."

When he said that, she swam up and grabbed the hair behind his ears. He thrust harder, then pulled out so fast, she was sorry for the slippery loss between her legs and also that this distinguished man had to come on her thigh, breath breaking, like a teenager.

He rustled, reached for something in his pants pocket that was down near his knees. A handkerchief. He wiped her thigh with it, then closed the kilt over her. He settled tighter to the couch, drawing her into a spooning position. It should have been uncomfortable, but it was wonderful.

"I love you in your little kilt," he whispered. She liked that he was whispering. It had all been so quiet, as if that made them more alone together, or maybe it was just that they were used to being quiet, like birding when they thought they had something. But was he saying he loved her? Or he loved her outfit? Men had a way of saying odd things, no matter how smart they were.

She wasn't sure what to do next. She hadn't thought this far ahead, had never really imagined this would happen. She'd never had a one-night stand in her life. But then, this wasn't that. This wasn't even friends falling into bed. Because they had never been friends, really. But he could have called me, she thought, called when he learned I was leaving school. What if he just took something easy, something he wanted yet was unwilling to risk anything for? But he'd called her Mar. No one called her Mar who didn't love her. And the way the word carried into her climax and his still coming . . . she'd never heard Mar like that before. It seemed a land of warm tides and soft sands for only them.

She had to trust her judgment. It was like making the call in the field, like those late summer days when her grandfather grilled her on the beach at sunset, as the gulls and terns were flying by in streams: "Call it, don't think, call it." She called common tern, ring-billed gull, black-backed, least tern, common, herring gull. "Wrong . . . keep going." So she did, and every summer there were fewer wrongs, a growth you couldn't measure against a wall but she could see in her grandfather's face, the set of his chin, a calm that was the closest he came to giving a compliment.

"I can't tell you that first impressions are one hundred percent right," he once said. "But if you're paying attention, they're ninety-nine percent right."

She glanced across the room to a digital clock in the mihrab. It was 1:20. The moon beyond the two windows had laid two silver veils across the floor. Maybe she should leave, sneak out like a wraith in the mist. She hadn't moved, because she felt like an open bottle, but she shifted her hips to test the situation and his arm tightened. He wasn't dozing at all. But what was he thinking? Probably, what have I done? What are we doing?

"Don't you dare think of leaving," he said.

She turned to face him, her arms folded between them like a mantid, and touched his chin. It was scratchy with beard.

"I don't want to leave," she answered.

Margret didn't leave. Not til Sunday evening when he walked her home and kissed her at the door of her building as if it were the end of a thrilling first date. It was then that she asked him, "Why did the doorman say uh-huh on the phone?" He drew back to look her in the face. "Because I couldn't believe it. I said, 'Margret's here?' "

It was the end of the ride. The M5 was crossing the long viaduct that served as a bridge from Columbia's campus into Harlem. One hundred thirtieth was on the other side. Tomorrow it would be one year since his Thursday flight to Newfoundland. She'd told Tom she would be away after Wednesday, down at the Point, and he'd given her a quick nod and a silent hug. There was nothing to say. Nothing but not hearing from him at noon, when he said he'd call. And the phone calls to his hotel, where he hadn't checked in. And the call from that voice, a voice in a suit. And then life folding at the knees.

GOLDENRODS

Fourteen

MARGRET WAS A LONG WAY away from that pretty female cardinal, her first attempt. A long way from the scalpel incision she had feared to make, the steel tip pushed through a bed of tiny breast feathers—a half-inch deep, that delicate bed—gray feathers going red at the edges. The silver tip went soundlessly past the feathers and through the skin. And though there was moisture within, it wasn't blood, and though the skin was thin, like wet paper, the scalpel freed it easily, and over the legs the skin could even be rolled back with one's fingers.

The skinning had seemed to be going well, so well she wondered what all the fuss in the books was about, until she had to snip the bird's windpipe and spine, and blood leaked through its nostrils and stained one wing. She should have put cotton in the bill. When she got to the cloaca, having released the body at wings, legs, and neck, she couldn't tell where to cut. The flesh down there was wobbly soft, like an oyster, and full of bowels she didn't want to disturb. Yet the tail feathers were there, anchored among the buttery glands and bobbly tissue. With her scalpel she worked the skin down to the orifice, but she scraped away too much and the tail fell off. She moved to the head.

Margret had read that peeling the skin over the skull was difficult, but this seemed like it would never go. She made an extra incision behind the head and slowly turned back the skin, which moved easily until it reached the ears and eyes. She thought she would feel sick popping out the eyes, but she didn't, even though they had to be scooped out. They were like blueberries flattened on one side. When she held the first eye between her fingers and ever-so-gently squeezed the round part, the flat side popped forward into a hemisphere, like in life. The morning sun coming through the window caught the eye, and she saw an amber ring inside, and within the ring a pinpoint black pupil. She saw liquid moving in the eye, a mysterious liqueur creating this rich color, this life. She felt the glory of it, the sun rising in the eye.

Next she made a hole at the back of the skull and scooped out the brain, a pink phlegm, spilling at first, then finishing in a membranous lump. The empty skull was thinner than a fingernail—you could see through it—and almost golden. She released the throat organs as far up as possible. Then, with a meaty tug, like getting the last bit of raw shrimp tail out of its shell, she pulled out the rest of the windpipe, including the tongue, which looked like a miniature trowel, stiff and silvery gray.

Margret had done everything by the book, but when she took stock of the bird, which still needed flesh trimmed out of the wings and off the legs, still needed clay pushed into the skull and eye sockets, it looked mangled, the edges greasy, probably because she hadn't boraxed as she went along; she'd been afraid she wouldn't be able to see what she was doing. And the head was twisted in the wrong direction, having somehow looped through the second incision she knew she shouldn't have made. I need Q-tips, she thought. A sharper scalpel. A tougher tweezer.

Before the cardinal she'd studied books she bought online. She had Montagu Browne's dark blue tome from 1896, *Artistic and Scientific Taxidermy and Modelling*, and Paul Hasluck's slim green volume from 1907, *Taxidermy*. Browne was flowery and high-minded, curator of the Leicester Museum in England, and clearly full of himself. Hasluck, more of a headmaster, was cut and dry, with now and then a sigh that seemed scolding. "Do not copy stuffed specimens," he intoned, "for such a course is simply to perpetuate mistakes already committed." They both beat the drum for taxidermy as an art, a practice to be mastered, and not, as Browne disdainfully put it, "a clown's pastime." Margret got the feeling that bad taxidermy had been a Victorian blight. Birds with bulging or asymmetric eyes. Birds with bellies way too big. Birds in wonky postures you'd never see in the field. One came away from Browne and Hasluck feeling that every oaf with a knife and some tow was setting up shop and stuffing birds.

Margret didn't know what tow was before she'd opened these books, that it was wood softened and spun into a kind of hair, good for filling out necks. And she'd never heard of excelsior, which sounded like something from Arthurian legend but was really just fine curled wood shavings. The books were full of words from a dust-mote world of stuffing tables and ceiling hooks: bradawls, gimlets, spokeshave, pinion wire, flake white. The preservatives alone filled Margret with foreboding: mercury, arsenic, carbolic acid. Even plaster of paris, used in those days to absorb grease from the skin, was now known to be carcinogenic. When Margret was a girl, Milton had told her about President Franklin Delano Roosevelt, how he'd been an avid taxidermist as a boy until the arsenic dust made him so sick, he had to stop. "He turned green," her grandfather said. It was a cautionary tale. By ten she was helping Milton with his insect collections, handling killing jars saturated with cyanide. "No green fingers" was all he needed to say.

Certain names recurred—Waterton, Granger, Houseman, Webster—a strange coterie she pictured in profile, sitting in front of fireplaces, or in long white aprons as camphor bubbled in the back. Each man had his own techniques, beginning with his preferred cut for the flaying, the single cut from which the insides would emerge, a subject of heated debate. Hasluck went longitudinally down the breast, unless the feathers were white; then he went down the back. Browne insisted—was bitterly adamant—that the only way to skin out was from under one wing. Cutting down the center, he wrote, had "not one single advantage to recommend it." Yet that was what most taxidermists did. Then there was the preservative of choice and how to apply it. After that, the best way to make a body, which was excelsior, or wood wool, pressed into an egg shape and twined with string. And finally, the most successful strategy for wiring the wings and feet.

They each had their pets and peeves. Regarding glass eyes, Browne thought German eyes far better than English, and French eyes, which were rounder and fuller, the best of all. When it came to wire, Hasluck preached galvanized iron, stating there was nothing more annoying than a finished bird "all shaking and trembling." Margret had to agree. She remembered a stuffed oriole on Milton's bookshelf that bobbled helplessly whenever you took a book, even from the bottom shelf. No one respected that bird, which was there because Milton's older brother, killed in World War II, had stuffed it as a boy. Both Browne and Hasluck suggested that beginners start with a starling because it wasn't too small and because the skin on the back was so tough. On most birds, the skin is thinnest on the back.

Reading about the tools she would need made Margret feel faint. Pliers and scalpels, nippers and hooks, glove maker's needles, and most chilling of all, the brain scoop, also used for eyes. Browne, with great brio, provided a black-and-white photograph of thirty-nine tools laid out on a table. They looked like instruments of torture or the crude tools of a frontier doctor, which was sort of the same thing. Hasluck humbly said that you could do the job with only a penknife and a pair of scissors. The brain scoop, he added, could be made by hammering the end of a knitting needle into a tiny spoon.

Over and over Margret read the bird chapters in these books, trying to get straight the correct sequence of skinning and where the danger zones were. Oil glands, crop and bowels, eye sockets. It was like trying to learn a complicated dance by looking at diagrams. "Seize the foot with the right hand and push upwards, at the same time pushing the skin down with the left hand." Such sentences left her brain in a tangle. And yet, reading Browne and Hasluck, both of them obsessed with skinning properly and setting up a lifelike mount, she felt less alone, as if she too were a member of their strange coterie, a throwback to another century where this desire, or maybe it was a compulsion, once had a powerful place in the world.

It was something in her, she'd since thought, a predisposition. She remembered a Met exhibition of Victorian jewelry she'd gone to, back when she was researching her "Sensitive Plant" thesis. She'd been entranced by the accessories of mourning. In one vitrine: rings with tiny graveside scenes of weeping willows and crying cupids;

parures of onyx and necklaces of jet. In another: lacelike earrings and bracelets made of . . . well, you couldn't tell what they were made of unless you read the placard. It was human hair. Ash blond, mouse brown. The loved one's locks had been clipped from the deathbed and minutely plaited, then coiled, into forms. Margret had practically taken root before this case, thinking how hair grows slowly, imperceptibly, like plants and the people in her thesis. Hair and nails grew beyond the grave. And here were the Victorians latching it to their throats, braiding it into their lives.

Margret was afraid to make a first cut on the basis of Browne's and Hasluck's books. She didn't want to waste any birds. So she went online and ordered Russell Tinsley's *Taxidermy Guide*, third edition, first published in 1967, and quite possibly a classic of its kind. It was a big paperback how-to with big, amateurish, black-and-white photos. It was obviously aimed at men and boys who hunted, who wanted to go the whole nine yards with their kill, and it conjured an America of wood-paneled dens and garages with workbenches. Tinsley wrote, "Anyone who can build a miniature scale model from a kit has the dexterity needed to create a mount from a dead animal, fish, or bird." Which struck Margret as wrong, so wrong, this blasé leap from wood and plastic to blood and bone. And yet, Tinsley too thought taxidermy was an art. He too wrote of its need for keen observation and the flash of imagination. His one caveat was, "Never stuff a pet."

But even the big pictures in Tinsley didn't help. In his chapter on birds, he skinned and stuffed a pheasant—a big bird, yes—but in the photos it was a mess of feathers with scaly legs hanging down. Margret went back online and ordered *How to Mount a Flying Duck*, a video from a company called Van Dyke's, "A Taxidermy Tradition Since 1949." Monty Python title aside, it was the closest she could get to warblers and the like, given that the other subject choices were

Canada goose, wild turkey, and pheasant, game birds you could still legally shoot and stuff. The video was homemade, earnest. The man who appeared in it looked more like the local butcher than like an artist. He had two mantras: "If you don't know what you're doing, don't cut," and "Forget to borax your bird, and you're going to get bugs." He spent a lot of time degreasing the duck, which wouldn't be a big concern with the small perching birds Margret had collected. The video helped. Suddenly she could see what Browne and Hasluck and Tinsley were talking about. In the books, taxidermy seemed an endless operation, but here on tape a whole duck was skinned and mounted in an hour.

Along with the video, Van Dyke's sent a catalog. It was bursting with products. Mammals made up most of it—squirrels, deer, fox, bobcat, even antelopes, hyenas, and lions. It made you wonder just what was going on in garages across America. Toward the back, where the bird things were, Margret found the contemporary versions of everything she needed. Borax, Preservz-It, degreaser, wood wool, twine, glover needles, scalpel, forceps, spoon tool, probe, hook and chain, cotton batting, syringes (set of three), multipurpose cutter, latex gloves, and glass eyes, sizes three to nine millimeters. The total came to $130. When the brown box arrived, there was nothing left to do but start.

But she didn't start.

She decided she'd better reread the chapters on birds and watch the video again. She was overstudying, the way she often had in school, shoring up against the unknown, questions that couldn't be guessed, answers that had never been given. It was like the deep breath before a closed door. She said she'd start tomorrow. And then again tomorrow. And then she found the cardinal. Claudia. It's what they always called the females. Claudia Cardinale. Charles loved her in *The Leopard*.

Margret had a freezer full of migratory birds, but it was Claudia—found in Riverside Park near the bird feeder at 120th, probably killed by a feral cat—it was Claudia who would accompany her. Because she was afraid to go alone.

Fifteen

"FINALLY YOU PICK UP the phone."

"Oh, Mom, I'm sorry I haven't called back. You know things get hairy midsummer."

"They do?"

"Why do I have to explain this to you every year? Because of the Christmas windows."

"But I thought you said they were done by summer."

"Just the mechanical stuff, not everything else. We have to prepare those while we're still doing the weekly windows up until mid-November. It's a marathon."

A sigh of fatigue on the other end.

"I'm so tired of your career and I'm not even doing it."

"Mom."

"Well, I'm just saying . . . I still don't see why you don't go back and finish your doctorate. Think of what you could do then. You have the money."

She meant the life insurance, a sum that had come to Margret six months after Charles's accident, because even though the plane was deep in rough water, pieces of it had come to the surface.

"Can we not discuss this now? I can't talk that long. How's Dad?"

"He's fine. Nothing much has changed at the office, but since he was called to consult on Fallingwater, he's been happy as a clam. He goes to Pittsburgh next week."

"Wow. That's fantastic. What's he consulting on?"

"Something to do with the windows."

"And how are you? Is your ankle better?"

"You make me sound so old."

"Noooo. It's just that I know ankles take a long time."

Charles once sprained his ankle running in Riverside Park, and it was months before he ran again.

"I'm getting around just fine. Now listen, honey, in case you should call Charlotte, which I doubt you'd do seeing you hardly call us, but if you do talk to her I want to warn you she's getting a little forgetful."

"Is it just natural aging or something more serious?"

"We're not sure. She's eighty-one, after all. Anyway, Bett's looking into it. But maybe next time I go up for a visit, you could come up from New York. It would be a nice gesture."

"I will if I can."

"I think you can if you want to."

"I've gotta go. Give Dad a hug for me."

"Why don't you come out and give him one yourself?"

"I will at Christmas. . . . Let me know about Boston."

"Okay. Love you."

"I love you too," Margret said, a little too mechanically. Why couldn't she make her voice warmer when she said it? But she hated when her mother threw around the money, as if forgetting where it came from, as if it were merely one side of a simple equation: money equals a more prestigious job. It was just such simple equations that made up her mother's worldview and whipped around you like a high wind.

Margret hadn't even known Charles had a policy, but their accountant did. Purchased in the eighties, it named Yulia Ashur, his widowed mother, as the beneficiary. She'd lived in Cincinnati with her Assyrian cousin, and Margret had gone there with Charles to meet her, a gaunt woman with thin white hair parted in the middle and combed close to her head in waves. The breadth of her hairline, the subtle indent in her chin—Charles. Despite Margret's presence, mother and son kept slipping into Aramaic. Their eyes shone as the language jumped and crackled, a flame between them, syllables sloping like the sides of tents, *L*'s lamby on the tongue and gutterals rising on the ridge. Yulia's gaze had trailed over Margret but held on her son, her only child, as if storing up the sight of him til the next month's visit. She came to the wedding bearing a small rug long promised to Charles, an old embery Turkmen woven so fine it could fold into a tote bag. This woman was herself woven in another world, stirred with a stripped branch, and her embrace of Margret was suddenly fierce. When she died of a stroke two months later, Charles changed the name on the policy to Margret Snow. It was nothing like the sum that went to the wife and ex-wife of the pilot, gung-ho George Fenner, with whom Charles had birded for years. But George was a wealthy Columbia surgeon from a prominent New York family, and he had two sets of children. Not one but two wives-and-mothers let him fly that Cessna.

The insurance money was sitting in the bank untouched. The interest on it was paying the New York mortgage, which Charles had always paid and which for a time Margret had paid out of savings. The pink house at the Point was bought outright in 1990 for sixty thousand dollars. Charles used to crow about that. The property value had quadrupled in ten years, though the house was bare-bones and the few people who visited found it spartan. But she and Charles loved the bareness, the wood floors whitewashed, the living-room walls painted gray like the sea, and the windows hung with white linen, lifting like sheets on the line with every ocean breeze.

Sixteen

FOR SOME REASON Joe had started calling her Marge. He didn't do it when anyone else could hear, only when no one was nearby, or they were alone in a window. The first time he did it Margret was holding the door of the freight elevator for him. "Thanks, Marge." She said nothing because she thought she'd heard wrong. The next time, she was at the nearby Starbucks getting an iced coffee, and Joe, having just come in, said, "Hey, Marge." She looked around for someone else he might be talking to, then turned back to him and said, *"Marge?"*

He just smiled.

"It's Margret."

"I know it is. Marge is a pet name."

"It's not a pet name; it's another name."

"People don't get to pick their pet names," he said, then went to stand in line, leaving her flummoxed. Joe. Sexy, jerky Joe, probably the most hetero-sexy homosexual she'd ever met. He hated her. He was calling her Marge, which rhymed with large and barge, and of course conjured images of Marge Simpson with her absurd cone of blue hair. It was Joe's way of calling her a cow, of implying she was nothing but hair and udder and . . . cunt; she could hear the word coming out of his mouth. To Charles she was Mar, graceful and smart, and now this guy was calling her Marge, and she felt the insult like a blush, and knew he knew she felt it. But it was so stupid, she couldn't even bring it up with Tom. "Joe is calling me Marge when no one else is around." She couldn't say it was sexual harassment. Legally, she couldn't say it was anything except obnoxious.

"It's a taunt," Emily said, when Margret told her about it. "Are you sure he's gay? Maybe he's bi and he's attracted to you. Maybe he's pissed off that he's attracted to you, and it feels good to put you down."

"I suppose he was bi for a while, because Sasha told me Joe didn't switch to guys until his twenties, so obviously he must have had girlfriends. But he's been mean almost from the start, and I never thought he was attracted to me. Anyway it's not fun having to pretend I don't hear Marge, which is really irritating."

"He couldn't have picked a name that is more not you. Which is obviously why he picked it. He wants to erase you in a way. He wants to un-you."

"But why?"

"Well, you said, 'almost from the start,' so try and think what happened or what was said around the time he changed. That might be the key."

But Margret couldn't remember. It was a creeping thing. The way she'd noticed him looking at her in meetings, slitting his eyes just the littlest bit or leaning back when she talked. And then the comments under his breath. Tom had spoken to Joe; she knew that. But Tom could only do so much. He couldn't fire one employee for not liking another. Stephen was scared of Joe, and also a little infatuated with him. Sasha was neither, and when Sasha was around, Joe was okay. Unfortunately Sasha wasn't around all that much. When the heat hit in July he pulled his Oblomov routine, staying put in his white studio with the slanting floorboards. The Saint Petersburger in Sasha longed for a frozen river and greatcoats trimmed in fur. He made due with a Friedrich air conditioner that filled his window. He called it Friedrich the Great.

When she got Sasha on the phone that morning, at first all she heard was his broad low laugh, hoarse from cigarettes. "*Diabolique*," he finally said, enjoying the word. "It's like Elisabeth of Austria, assassinated with a nail file."

"I'm not assassinated, because I'm just ignoring it."

"*Are* you ignoring it?"

"I just want to know why he's doing this. Don't you have some Old World wisdom? You know him better than anyone. Has he ever said *why* he hates me?"

"You Americans. Always wanting to be liked."

"I'm just trying to understand."

"So? If you understand, then you won't mind being called Marge?"

She didn't answer. She heard him take a long drag.

"Daaaling," he exhaled, "this isn't hates-me or likes-me. This is energy, veeery complicated energy."

"Negative energy."

"Not necessarily. It might be more . . . mixed up. It might be . . . *affinité*."

When he said that, Margret was looking at the insect collection she'd made during one of her Augusts in Boston, the two to three weeks she used to spend with her grandparents every year. She'd removed it from a shelf in the library and had it on her lap, studying it for a window idea she was trying to hatch, to showcase the new Hermès boutique Saks was putting in. The orange of the orange sulfur butterfly, she suddenly realized, was the exact same Creamsicle orange as the throat of the Blackburnian warbler she'd found in April. Both oranges were set off by black. Affinity, she thought, but Joe and I have nothing in common but windows.

"All we have in common is windows, and hardly even that, considering how snotty he can be about work."

"Sweetie, it's like magnets."

"What do you mean?"

"You know, those things that stick to metal."

"I know what magnets are. How are we like magnets?"

"Turned one way they stick together; the other way they push."

She was silent.

"Just keep it in mind."

"I'll try. So can you be in this week?"

"I have a deadline with one of those idiotic magazines."

"Which one?"

"*Nylon*."

"Pretty hip. What are you doing?"

"Galliano, Gautier, Lacroix."

"You love Lacroix."

"That's why I said yes, and maybe they will only get Lacroix. We shall see."

They hung up and she pulled the collection onto her lap, a ten-by-twelve-inch rectangle. "My pièce de résistance," she said the first time

Charles saw it, which was the first time he came to her apartment. She'd found him standing in front of it when she emerged from the bedroom, having changed her shoes at the last minute because it was misting outside, pale coronas sweating around streetlights.

"You made this?"

She nodded, then went over and stood next to him to look at it too. Insects of the Goldenrod. On a summer afternoon when she was sixteen, Margret had lettered that title again and again because she couldn't get the *I* right, though it would never look as beautiful as the *G*, which was admittedly flamboyant.

She remembered so well standing next to Charles, her lover of one week, remembered being close to that shoulder clothed in sea-green Harris tweed, his bare hand emerging from the sleeve, a hand that was now hers but still strange. She told him how she'd made the collection with her grandfather's guidance, that he was an amateur entomologist, and how they'd bird in the morning and look for insects in the afternoon, catching them if it was sunny, pinning them if it rained. Since his hands were getting old and she had steady fingers, it was her job to paper the wings and arrange the antennae.

"Like Milton's daughters," Charles said.

Margret was stunned. She'd never thought that before.

"His name was Milton," she said.

And though he wasn't blind, her grandfather did have a problem with one eye, which was sometimes teary, having been sprayed by a wheel bug in the days when no one knew wheel bugs could project their venom. *Arilus cristatus*. He published a paper on it, and it was big news among naturalists. But Margret didn't mention it then, because she didn't want to distract from the collection. She wanted to see how long Charles would talk about it.

"You weren't afraid of these?" he asked. "They're mostly wasps."

"August is when they're hunting and harvesting. You get used to them."

"Were you stung?"

"Once, by a yellow jacket. You know how when you close your eyes, you see a vibrating pattern? That's what a sting feels like at first, a sort of op-art tingling. It takes about a minute to focus into pain. But you must have been stung . . . haven't you?"

"Not by bees." He again leaned into the collection. "Which is your favorite insect of the goldenrod?"

No one had ever asked her that. The collection had been at her grandparents' house until Milton died. Margret brought it home after the memorial service, and it stayed there during her college years at Vanderbilt. But when she was leaving for Columbia, her mother had said, "Why don't you take it with you? It's a conversation piece. It will give you a chance to go on about your grandfather."

Go on . . .

That's what her mother did. Out of nowhere, a stinger in the honey. She did it to Margret's father too. "And where did that come from?" he would ask, glancing emphatically around the room. Margret's mother would answer . . . well, she had a whole repertoire of answers. Mock helplessness, like it wasn't her fault everyone was so oversensitive. Or imperious pain, falsely accused yet again. Or on a good day, genuine regret. "I don't know why I put it that way. Forgive me?" They always did because she asked, and they loved her. Margret knew her mother didn't set out to be mean, but it still took the wind out of her sails. So what if Margret had grown to love her Augusts in Gloucester and Cambridge, those weeks with all the cousins around and her grandfather mostly off work? She never asked to be sent away ("so your mom can have a rest from you" was how one cousin put it).

Then to have it turned on her as she was packing for grad school. Go on. Sometimes Margret and her father discussed it, but he would end up saying, "She's fragile," as if that excused everything. The fact was, he was fragile too, so they were well matched, like butterfly wings. "How did two fragile people produce unfragile me?" Margret once asked Emily, who replied, "It's math: two negatives produce a positive." She was probably right, but who wants to think of their parents as two negatives? To Margret, it often seemed that their fragility was the sum of their fineness, their erudite tastes, their endless intellectual calibrations about class, architecture, art—saltbox or cape, Updike or Cheever, Solti's Mahler or Tennstedt's, Matisse or Soutine—which were all somehow the same thing.

No, it was the Augusts, how she had settled right into them, the mornings so crisp and full of plans, the noons a reconnoitering, the nights tired yet taut with cricket song. And the clapboard shore house unchanging, its ground floor bleached and chintzed; the second floor clean and creaking, each bedstead with a thin old quilt folded at the foot; the third floor, her little room up in the trees, and that bathroom with the pull-chain toilet that coughed and gurgled. It was a house you didn't worry in, its life as steady as the seasons. No whispered wrestling over money and the neighborhood and what was promised if never said. No sudden sliver of light invading from the hall as her father made his way to the living room where he could soak his stings in scotch. Margret would fold the pillow around her head, terrified her parents would divorce and the earth would open its craggy maws like in the movies and she would disappear like the dinosaurs. Her father went down the hall and eventually Mom would go after him, and it was like they were in their own dark maw, no one but them, and that's what bound them, their need for each other between the narrow walls of the world.

No one talks about grandfathers at grad school, Margret had told her mother. But Mom insisted she take the collection.

It wasn't a conversation piece. Or rather, it was the wrong conversation. At Columbia, female friends would come into the apartment, and if they noticed the insects, which most didn't, they would just say, *Ick.* As for men, they would think it cool, though some changed their tone when they learned Margret had made it. One date looked alarmed. Another eyed her amorously, saying, "So will you catch me in your net?"

Now Charles was asking about her favorite. Margret and Milton had never talked about favorites. They spoke of beauty, the secret beauty that emerged under a magnifying glass. The feet of the bumblebee, little *U*'s, tiny two-pronged pitchforks, pitch black, pitching pollen into golden baskets on their back legs. The furry hair of the great golden digger wasp, like molten gold brushed on brown velvet. Which was her favorite? Margret loved the snowy tree cricket, its translucence, and the tiger stripes on the eastern sand wasp. She loved the two green metallic bees, so Emerald City, and had placed them just under the sand wasp, like twin cops in a motorcade. "It's not scientific," her grandfather said when he noticed there were two. And he'd looked a long time at the bed of drying goldenrod, already going ochre, resting along the bottom of the collection. "A bit scenic," he judged, "but appealing."

"It's irrational," she'd said to Charles. "Favorites. I love the little green bees. But my favorite is the paper wasp. The yellow spots on each hip, the scallop patterns circling the abdomen . . . the proportions are perfect, like a picture I once saw of a Dior suit."

They peered in closer.

"Have the colors faded?" he asked.

"They were all more vivid when I caught them. The digger wasp . . .

its legs were tangerine. The colors dim though, in just a day. It always made me a little sick."

The cricket hunter. She felt especially sick about that one. It was huge and she didn't want it; she already had a perfectly good cricket hunter for the collection. But that day every time she went to the far stand of goldenrod, the wasp was there, an irradiated blue-black, so huge and beautiful on the noon-drenched boughs, it was almost taunting. She dropped her net over it casually because she didn't care, and of course she caught the thing. It was furious, an angry energy pressed in netting to the ground. Even then she could have let it go, could have heeded her grandfather's oft-repeated words, "Never take more than you need." She could still see Milton's face the day he'd looked into her killing jar—she was eleven then—and saw ten honeybees curled in death. Ten. Then a pause she could still count out. *Why in God's name did you take ten?* He'd never cursed at her before. She remembered focusing on the jar in his hand, the glassy blur behind his waxy fingers. *What were you thinking?* How nothing could get away from her that day. How if Gene Delaney, the boy she loved, were to appear—he couldn't, he was back in Chicago—he would see how quick she was, queen of the field, and he would ask her to go steady and they'd hold hands. She'd been picturing her quiet possession of Gene. So, no, she couldn't tell Milton what she was thinking.

With the cricket hunter, though, it was almost the opposite, a powerlessness that effaced her. It reminded her of a day when she was twelve. She was birding into a late September dusk, the light going. She was by the lilac bushes in the park, a shadowy spot. A beautiful young man emerged, nineteen, twenty, with pale skin and full pale lips and the pale curls of an Italian angel. Bathed in failing light, he softly asked, *Are you wearing underwear?* Knowing she should run, Margret answered yes, unable to run, unable to break the spell of his soft voice;

it was like amber. *Panties or bikinis?* Frightened that only a few feet stood between her and his insinuating softness, she answered, "Panties," a word she never said because in her family they said underpants. The feel of the word in her mouth made her think of panting, the pink softness in a dog's mouth. *Do you wear a bra?* Blood rushed to her face because she wore one a year before her friends, another softness, as if nature had singled her out for something and here it was. She said yes because she couldn't lie, not even in this dusk. And then he was gone, absorbed by the lilacs, and she ran the blocks home to escape his words, and never mentioned him to anyone. It was almost as if the cricket hunter was that man in another form, beautiful, insinuating, smug. She didn't think this then. She thought it later, when she looked at the collection and wondered why, when it was scaling the sides of the jar frantic to get out, the poison having thinned, why didn't she unscrew the lid and let it go? Instead she put the jar into her backpack so she wouldn't have to see that energy, which scared her. But why should something wanting to live make you afraid of it? Or were you afraid of yourself for killing it?

"The cricket hunter was the blue of an electric guitar. But within hours of dying it went brown."

"Blue is a law unto itself," Charles said. "It's like the feathers of blue jays, prismatic. It's all about the play of light, the gases in the air." He ponytailed her hair with his hand and said, "But last Friday I was telling you about cochineal bugs, and you were all wide-eyed and innocent. And now I see you know all about insects. More than me."

"I liked hearing you say cochineal. And I really don't know much about them, except their being red."

He wound her hair around his hand for the first time, which brought it tight to the nape of her neck, and he whispered in her ear, *cochineal.*

. . .

Margret stared at the collection. How had she not noticed this before? The splash of yellow in the lower left corner was gone. The clouded sulfur she had placed down there after much deliberation, finally deciding the clear color, like yellow Kool-Aid, would give the collection a lift if placed low, was gone. All that remained were a head and thorax on a pin, two antennae standing exactly as Margret had positioned them, at eleven and one o'clock, and bits of brown powder at the base of the pin. Next to it a cabbage white was missing its left hind wing.

Margret took the collection to the window, which was full of morning sun. Peering in, she saw nothing moving, just those tiny piles of powder. She could be looking right at the culprit, whatever it was, mites or mold, probably mites, and not see it. They were in there, right here in her hands; they had got under glass on a bookshelf ten floors up on Riverside Drive, right under her nose. They would eat everything on pins if she didn't stop them.

Cyanide, formaldehyde, carbon tetrachloride. She didn't have access to the chemicals of her grandfather's day. She'd buy mothballs and stick them in tonight and stop it, whatever it was. She turned the box straight to the sun, and it just lit up. Yellow stripes, copper scales, ultraviolet wing spots, topaz eyes. The green metallic bees were like twins from Oz. Then she angled the box so the insects would cast shadows within, exquisite replicas of themselves in ghost gray, barbed legs trailing, antennae curled like ram's horns, pedicels thin as thread. The shadows had a stillness apart from death, like delicate statuary. When Margret tipped the box a little more, the stillness lengthened. This moved her. She loved these shadows cast behind glass, how captured they were, and how you could let them go into nowhere by just tipping the box.

Were you stung?

She could hear him asking the simple question that Friday night, could hear the curiosity in his older-man's voice, the rise on "stung" that made her think he must have had a protected childhood. Because who doesn't get stung? She returned the box to its place on the shelf, the insects like old friends in a yearbook. Each one . . . I remember catching each one. But more than that, Margret remembered the feeling of being with them, being one of them.

It was a feeling she'd told Charles about months after their first two Fridays, when they were falling asleep one night and he asked what she was thinking and she said, "I can't think, I'm in a bliss state," her phrase for that heavy happiness after sex. So she told him about the goldenrods. The old empty lot, a half acre deep in bugleweed, wood aster, sunflowers, pigwort, purple thistle, but mostly goldenrod by the armful, much of it shoulder high. She told him how time stopped as she stood among the growth, bees and wasps floating inches from her face, her forearms. She described how, to catch them, you had to watch them, and watching creatures with stingers laze and drift and drink was seductive, and slow. So it was a slowed-down, sun-heated drone, hum, thrum of vibration all around—a bee, a wasp, a hornet, a hunter.

It wasn't like birding, where observation was made from far away and the whole thing was hands-off, a story already forming about what the bird was or wasn't, and why you made the call or couldn't, and the song you heard or didn't. This was storyless, wordless, close-up, and mortal, the voyeur sun quiet in the sky, baking you in the grasses, as the honeybees, hoverflies, drone flies alighted on tiny blossoms with the same plummy land and droop, land and droop. And everywhere *Polistes*, busybody paper wasps, drunk on sun and spatting like territorial kittens. Her grandfather loved the irritable play of paper wasps. And the bumblebees minding their own business, like accountants in Dickens, going dutifully from cupola to cupola, big bodies disappearing into wilting morning glories, pink and blue. Perhaps Margret had learned from the bees, had learned to go from book to book in the same steady rhythm. She'd been famously productive in the stacks. But that wasn't bliss. Bliss was in the weeds, in the hum and drone of honeyed abdomens and legs laden with pollen, boughs of goldenrod bouncing, crawling, with life. It was a world, she said to Charles in the dark, where all that mattered was nectar and the sun.

"It sounds like paradise," he said, his voice small with sleep. She remembered that, the smallness.

Seventeen

MARGRET WAS OVERWHELMED. Tina was out for at least three weeks, with a wrecked knee, and Margret was suddenly in charge.

"Those damn kids," Tina said on the phone, "wandering over the green line into the path for bikes and blades. You should have seen my knee when I landed; it was twisted like a swastika. Strangely, it didn't even hurt, just felt like Styrofoam. Long story short, I tore cartilage and ruptured my ACL, which means surgery, which I can't have til I've done therapy to build up the muscles around the knee. So I'm taking a couple of days off and then I'll be in part-time."

"Oh, Tina."

"You know what really pisses me off? I could've killed that kid. I mean, I was really truckin'. So I blow out my knee to save his life and I'm on the grass in a swastika, and the mother just grabs his hand

and keeps walking. Doesn't come over. Doesn't say sorry. Not even thanks."

It happened on the Cherry Walk, where Charles used to run. For him it was the reverse. He was always complaining about the cyclists, how they weaved from lane to lane.

"So you're gonna have to be me while I'm out," Tina said.

"You know, Tina, some of the guys aren't going to be happy about me being you. Sasha won't mind, but I don't have seniority over Stephen. And do you think Joe's going to listen to me?"

"First of all, you have brain seniority over Stephen. Second, you need to step up to the plate. You're getting like a ghost down there, floating around. Just be firm with Joe. Look him in the eye and tell him what you need."

"Does Tom know about all this?"

"Oh, yeah. We spoke last night. Isn't he there yet?"

"He's over at corporate."

Margret should have wanted this. She should have wanted to be the boss. But it meant she had to come in every day. It meant she had to engage all those egos, had to be the first one in and the last one to leave and would lose time with her birds. On top of that she had to create a window for Emily's September show, which was opening in three weeks. She brought her sketches for the Hermès windows to the big white table for the meeting she now had to run. Joe walked in and said, "Hi, Marge."

"Joseph."

He gave her a funny look.

"So now you're my mom?"

"No, I'm Tina."

He guffawed.

"She injured her knee Rollerblading and asked me to fill in, which means you and I have to communicate. If you want to call me Marge, fine, shout it out. Just let's get the work done."

"Brava," he said blandly, and then went to his office.

Holt came in. With his stick body, spiky blond hair, and those eyeglasses the shape of sugar wafers, he always looked to Margret like a hip robot.

"Tom said for us to start without him," he said. "He's hung up at Corporate."

"Did Tom tell you about Tina?"

"Yeah . . . her knee. What a drag."

"Tina asked me to fill in when she's not here."

"Cool." He leaned back in his chair and yelled, "Joe, you wanna get started?" Then he tipped forward and said, "So it's the Hermès launch? Gallery windows or Fifth Avenue?"

"Fifth."

"What's in Gallery and Men's?"

"Marc Jacobs schoolgirl look and blue blazers."

Joe pulled up a chair.

"I went and looked at the scarves," Margret began, "and the colorways this season are very insectlike—bright greens, purply blues, orangey reds. So I thought since we're behind, something fast would be to use matte-black board at full height and about three-fifths the width of each window. At the center we cut out the wings of the insect in one piece, huge, and lay scarves over the cutout piece and then push it back into the board. Float this mid-window. Then behind it, for visual punch, fill out the sides with board that pulls a color from the scarf. Here's a small version."

She held up a black board on which she'd done a cutout of monarch butterfly wings, and had pushed through a red-and-brown scarf of her own.

"See how the colors pop against black?"

"Nice," Holt said.

"You just pouf out the silk at the edges to give it dimension and hide the edges. And the other parts—antennae, thorax, abdomen—can be painted with white or gold."

Tom had returned. He threw his keys on his desk and came to the table, picked up the board, and studied it.

"Here are sketches of the other five cutouts based on the scarf colors we have: a ladybug for reds, a dragonfly for purples, a swallowtail for yellows and blacks, a luna moth for pale greens, a june bug for bright greens."

"I like it," Tom said. "How many scarves per bug?"

"They're thirty-six-inch squares, so two to four."

"Didn't Bergdorf just do something with bugs?" Joe wondered aloud.

"Not like this," Holt said. "They did black beetle shapes on a white board, and it was a backdrop to . . . I can't remember what. It was sort of stopgap."

"The beauty is," Margret continued, "the scarves won't be damaged in any way. No tape, pins, or anything."

"Joe . . . if Margret draws the cutouts, will you have any problem getting them out in one piece, without bending the board? Wood might be less flimsy."

"Thick board is better," Joe said.

"And the title in every window would be 'Field Guide: Hermès,'" Margret concluded.

"Clever," Tom said. "Next."

They went on to blue blazers and schoolgirls, and Joe was fine, not nice but not hostile. When they all went off with their to-do lists, Tom pulled Margret aside and said, "Good job." She was pleased. Before she began on this, though, she wanted to get the window agenda straight for the week after. There was going to be a Ralph Rucci trunk show, the Holland & Holland line in Men's, and a Juicy Couture catalog tie-in. She should call the buyers now. And Rucci . . . the gowns in the look book were so Renaissance: sleeveless columns, slightly empire, some deeply cowled in back, in garnet, aubergine, amethyst. She was thinking Arthur Rackham, hills and castles in the distance, the use of silhouette. She'd get Sasha to work on that, do something eerie with the mannequins' faces. Stephen could have fun with Juicy Couture, do something cute-camp with all that pink. Margret looked at the schedule she'd drawn up and thought, Okay, I can do this. She segued to Emily's window.

The exhibition was called World, and it was the work of a man who painted watercolor maps on parchment. The maps were hemispheres, circles filled with lands and seas, and the colors were gorgeous, those eggy pastels one saw in the frescoes of Giotto, as if a baby had breathed them. Some were stern, continents caged in longitudes and latitudes, with relief lines that showed depths and dangers. Others were fanciful, with curling winds and sea serpents like green clouds. Margret had asked Emily if the artist might paint one that could be formed into a globe, around twelve inches in diameter. Emily was getting him to do it. Margret wanted to suspend it in the window, which she planned to line in a mosaic of iridescent blues, greens, and golds cut from paper, very pale and shimmery, a sort of Byzantium, she hoped. During gallery hours, she was going to have dry ice in the window, to make vaporous clouds. She'd never tried dry ice before. And suspended near the globe, as if in migration, would be one of her birds. Why not? She could tell Emily she found in it a prop shop. No one would be the wiser.

She had just the right bird, a white-throated sparrow that she'd mounted in a position of flight. It was the species with the highest kill rate in spring migration, felled on the way to its northern nesting grounds. Usually seen in bunches scratching food from the grass, this little brown bird with the clean white bib was distinguished by its dropping song of simple whistles—notes so thin, so full, they seemed to capture the poignance of existence, the endless scratching for invisible seeds. *There's a special providence in the fall of a sparrow.* The grandeur of the earth and the humility of the white-throated, both of them suspended. Margret thought it would be enough.

FALLOUT

Eighteen

WHEN TINA CAME BACK at the end of September, Margret's momentum sagged. She'd done a good job subbing. She'd kept things buttoned up. The Hermès windows had been a hit, which was a good way to start. And the Rucci windows were even more popular. Joe's miniature cutout castles were so cute that everyone wanted to take one home, and Sasha had outdone himself, turning the mannequins into drifting princesses with pearlescent gauze pulled tight over their heads, just a memory of a mouth brushed on, and the gauze gathered into phantom sprays in back. In fact, Sasha got a call from Bergdorf's after that, which he didn't return, but it was high compliment anyway. As for Joe: "We're ships passing in the night," Margret told Emily, "speaking in semaphore when we speak at all."

"I guess that's better than 'Hey, Marge.'"

"I suppose."

When Tina came back, Tom rewarded Margret by making her responsible for the Christmas snow. It was a job he always did himself because he had such a high standard for how snow should look. If Tom said it once, he said it ten times: "I stress about snow." It was not an easy job. Besides salt, there were umpteen grades of snow, from biggish pieces of plasticine to really artificial soft powder. Then there was the Crystalina that had to be ordered separately, for the sparkle on top. And should the Crystalina be clear, iridescent, or multicolor? Well, not multi. It could make the snow look dirty.

Margret should have been flattered by the assignment, but she just couldn't get into it. By October they were all sick of the Christmas windows, having begun them in January. As Tom said every year, "These windows are a Christmas card to the city, and it can't be a flimsy little card." This year's theme was the Little Match Girl. Each time she lit a match, she would see a vision of holiday happiness through a window: cakes in a store, tree getting decorated, gifts being opened. Obviously, they had to stick a happy ending on it. So instead of freezing to death in an alley she would be rescued, à la Oliver Twist, by a rich aunt and uncle. Well, it was different from the overused *Christmas Carol* and Santa Claus, and it wasn't some dumb made-up story. They all loved the idea of windows within windows. And there would be neat lighting effects, the match flaming and the windows brightening, though Holt would have to grade it carefully. Margret had to come up with snow that would read in both a nineteenth-century twilight and golden warmth. Not too sooty, not too blue. She was gathering samples, playing with combinations at her desk. Soon, she kept saying to herself, soon I'll have something to show Tom.

But she felt like a dog on a leash, pulling to get home. It wasn't just that her window for World was perfect, the dry ice a total breakthrough; really, she'd never before seen it used in a window. Yes, it was a pain for the staff to have to set it smoking in a dish every day at ten and two, but the effect of cloud vapor was so wonderful that even Emily didn't complain. Then there was the sparrow. No one said boo about where she'd gotten it, so fresh, so alive-looking, flying in the stratosphere over South America or the Atlantic or Africa, depending on which way the globe had turned on its fishline. She'd worked hard to get the position of the wings and the way a white-throated holds its head in flight—the jizz, almost kinetic—and her success with it fired her up.

She was racing home to her guides and photography books—well, to Charles's. He'd collected field guides and would pore over them after a day's birding, going back and forth between them, harumphing over contradictions. The transliterations of songs and chips really got him going. "Is it *zee* or *tsee* or *tzee*?" he'd thunder from the other room. It was such fun to be with him at Higbee's at dawn. Such fun to be waiting in the mist on those big Cape May days when the warblers came through, zooming ravenous out of the sky, hundreds skiffing along the treetops, dropping into the boughs, popping in and out, here and gone, and everybody lined up on the path, calling out the really good stuff—worm-eating, bay-breasted, golden-winged. She'd be standing near Charles, feel him swinging his bins from bird to bird, his lips moving under the black barrels—parula, redstart, blue-winged—the darting birds caught in words like notes, branch to branch like Glenn Gould playing Bach, a fugue state. The amazing thing was he always knew how many species he'd seen without writing it down or doing a quick flick through the guide. It was why he was good at bridge, a game Margret found baffling when he tried to teach it to her.

She had the birds in her head after a lifetime of watching, but was still checking the guides before she stuffed and positioned a mount. *Birds of America* was inspiring, a mansion full of endless rooms, and in each room a different pair of lovers. But Audubon's bird postures, so often acrobatic and alarmed, she couldn't quite trust. His Blackburnian was terrible, no help at all when Margret was trying to decide how to position her male. Roger Tory Peterson's was the guide she'd grown up with, but the drawing was static. And though she loved the charming *Golden Guide*, its Blackburnian looked like a dutiful student. *National Geo*'s male was gorgeously colored but forlorn. Kaufman, the new guide with photos, was invaluable for jizz, but it was Pough, a guide from the forties, that got the character. Pough's Blackburnian—actually, Don Eckelberry's; he did the drawings—was singing just like the one Margret had seen from ten feet away in Riverside Park, near the little turret at 120th. She'd watched it for twenty minutes. The way it threw back its head to let loose those high-wire notes. The way the chest puffed up. She wanted to position her male singing, but she also wanted him blazing. She saw him as a force of nature. A Vesuvius, a Prometheus, an Apollo. She positioned him in a short flight, wings pulled in for a dive.

Skinning had its sticky, gloppy problems, but the stuffing possessed her. She did it as soon as the skin was clean, boraxed, and the legs and wings injected with Preservz-It, because the books warned about letting the skin stiffen. Margret took tips wherever she read them. When she removed the carapace of flesh from inside the bird, she placed it on white paper and traced around it, sideways and dorsal. That way you didn't make the excelsior stuffing too big, which would strain the skin and keep the feathers from lying flat. On the same white paper she'd jot down the eye color—brandy, blackberry—so she could accurately paint the back of the glass eye.

Wiring the wings, legs, and head was tricky: each wing and leg wire had to enter the tow body at just the right angle and then be pulled very tight; otherwise you'd have a bird "all shaking and trembling." Margret tried to use wire in heavier guages—no. 23 and no. 24—but wingbones and legs were so fine, she frequently had to go higher. Hasluck warned that the legs on passerines were never straight, and that the heels were closer together than the feet. Also, the tail of a bird in flight is spread in line with its body, and the feet are close to its breast, claws shut.

She developed her own tricks, like using a toothpick to slide the eyelid over the glass eye once it was pushed into clay in the socket. For finish on tiny bills and horny legs, she used nail-polish bases and topcoats. There were sheer pink polishes that worked for pink-legged birds, and in a goth shop she found black polish, easily thinned for transparency. She'd never forgotten the black skimmer at the Peabody Museum, the horrible highway orange someone had painted on its homely old bill. It looked so sad.

Margret loved the humble prick and pull of needle and thread as she stitched the bird up under the wing. "Who'll make his shroud?" she sometimes recited to herself, "I, said the beetle, with my thread and needle. I'll make his shroud." She loved the magic of it, making the bird airtight once more. They were far away from the first moment, when she held the bird in her hand and felt its weightless weight; when the wings fanned out easily, geisha-like, and sprang slowly closed when released; when she drew open the talons, reptilian really, then let them curl over a finger. The spring and the curl were gone. But the delicacy, the beauty, remained. She just had to make a home for it. A space where it could breathe.

Nineteen

MARGRET WAS THE FIRST one there. She was sitting on a stool in the crowded bar at Ouest, waiting for her favorite cousin, Jack. He'd called that afternoon and said, "I'm in town for the night. Pick a place." Amazingly, Ouest had a table.

It was a nice perch, this stool, and a good spot to watch the whoosh of the burgundy curtains near the door, hung there to catch and hold cold November, and then to see who emerged from between the curtains. Jack wasn't known for on-the-dot punctuality, but he was never more than a half hour late. It was the in-between. She always felt he was in Timbuktu those thirty minutes.

The last time she'd seen him had been four years ago, when she and Charles went up for her cousin Stu's second marriage. Jack was his brother's best man for the second time, and he had, under pressure from the family, shaved off his beard the night before, which he couldn't stop mentioning in a very funny toast. Jack is six years older than I am, Margret thought, so he's now thirty-seven. Then *whoosh,* the velvet curtains parted, and there he was, a shock as always at six foot two, with a beard as black as his blue-black hair.

"Mar," he roared, then grabbed her in a big hug, pulling her up off the stool.

"Jack."

She kissed the plane of cold cheek above his short beard. He was a head above everyone else in this small sea of heads, some of them turning to take him in, a face made for a sailboat. She led him through the crowd and gave her name to the maître d', who handed their coats and Jack's canvas backpack to a pretty young thing and then took them to a corner table in the main room. Once seated, menus in hand, Margret leaned in.

"So what are you in town for?" she asked. "No, before answering that, I need to know what you are."

"Scorpio?"

"No. Your major. Mom and I were arguing about it the other day. She said botany, and I said biology."

"Both wrong. Biochemistry. And I did some follow-up work in neurotoxins."

"Okay. In town for?"

"An East Coast shareholders' meeting. I give talks now . . . lectures. I gave one today down on Wall Street."

"About what?"

The waiter was standing over them.

"Two martinis up, Boodles, olives. Okay, Mar?"

She nodded, noticing how young he still looked, how thin he'd stayed, and how un–New York he was in his starched, now wrinkled, white shirt. Pure Cambridge, Massachusetts.

"The talk was on drugs in development, biochemical discoveries in Amazonian flora."

"And you didn't need a jacket?"

"It's rolled up in my backpack."

Charles would faint at the thought. He was so careful about his clothing.

"Now when did all this start?"

"Genentech made me an offer I couldn't refuse. I'm the company's token wild-child field guy. I do corporate functions, conferences, outreach, and in return I get two months a year in the field, which is basically a two-month vacation. I even get to keep my beard"—he stroked it—"as you can see."

"And you travel around the country giving speeches?"

"Europe too."

"Wow."

"Look, I couldn't do it if I didn't believe in the research. The pharms are monsters when it comes to their profit margins. But the drugs not only save lives, they also make them livable."

"So why doesn't anyone ever know what you're up to when I ask?"

"Because no one ever listens when I tell them."

They looked at their menus, and Jack decided they'd share six appetizers, starting with two different salads, which was fine with Margret.

"I like a lot of different tastes," he said. "That's why I'm such a half-assed vegetarian. It's too boring without fish and chicken. Now what's up with you? How's Saks?"

She told him about Tina's knee and being fashion manager for six weeks, about her World window at Flow, the success of the clouds, and her current problems with the snow, "which sounds so unimportant after hearing about your miracle drugs."

"You shouldn't make that kind of comparison. Those Christmas windows give joy. They become memories. Now where's Flow again? I'm gonna shoot down there after dinner and look at your window."

"But that show's over and the clouds are gone."

She wanted to tell him about the white-throated sparrow, but couldn't figure out how without sounding weird, so she didn't.

Their salads came and instead of ordering wine they agreed to have two more martinis. "It's so good to be bad with a cousin," he said, eyes bright.

"Ja-ack," she said.

"I didn't mean that kind of bad!"

"Seriously, the question everyone in the family asks when the subject is you is when will you marry."

He groaned.

"There's someone in Seattle, semiserious. And later tonight I'm meeting an ex for a drink. She works at the UN. But the whole setup . . . I'm not compelled. You have to be there all the time, and if you're not, it's 'you weren't there for me.' And the tyranny of 'there for me' . . . it doesn't interest me."

"You're like Milton then?"

He was taking a bite of the truffle soufflé, half of their second course. She was starting on the gravlax.

"Oh my god," he exclaimed, "you've got to taste this now, while it's hot." He reached a spoonful into her mouth. Butter, eggs, truffles, mushrooms.

"Straight to the heart," she said. "What I mean is, Milton always seemed a reluctant family man."

"You think?"

"I always thought Charlotte had somehow trapped him into marriage. That he really didn't want to run the bank—he wanted to be free, like you. You know the globe in his study? Did you ever notice he always had Africa facing the room? I turned it once, to the Americas, and the next day it was back on Africa. So I always thought he wanted to go there, to study insects."

"With his table at Locke Ober? His seats at the symphony? Mar"—he said it like she was six again—"Charlotte didn't trap him. Don't you know the history?"

Margret shook her head.

"Charlotte was married to Ned, Milton's older brother. It was during the war. He was a bombardier and his patrol was stationed in Ireland. He wrote the most moving letters home; I read them once. Anyway, they flew raids into Germany, and coming back from one the plane was hit and went down in the English Channel."

He paused, watching her.

"Milton never mentioned him to me ever," Margret said, "except to say about that Baltimore oriole in his study, My brother Ned made that. I knew he died . . . you know, killed in the war . . . but not anything about Charlotte."

"Milton didn't talk about his brother, because it was too painful. That was the thing. Everyone was devastated. Milton was in the war too, but they brought him home. The surviving son. And Charlotte and Milton, in mourning for Ned, fell in love. So it went deep with them."

"How could I not see it?"

"Well, they weren't lovey-dovey. That generation wasn't."

Their last course arrived. Sturgeon sashimi and a lobster ravioli.

They began to reminisce. The beaches of Gloucester. Milton's wheel bugs. The day Jack finally took the dare and jumped from the third-floor window to the limb of an old oak that begged you to jump even as it willed you to fall.

"I was terrified," Margret said. "I was like seven, and I thought you were going to die."

"I remember you shouting, *Noooo!*"

"'Cause the cousins were shouting, Jump, jump, jump! And then you fell and it was like slow motion."

"Because I had the branch. It's just that it came down with me."

"We thought you were dead. And then you started writhing."

He was laughing.

"A measly broken ankle. God, I was lucky. But Milton was furious. He called me an idiot. I think I'd been reading Tolkien. Anyway, that oak was sentient, a real Treebeard. I thought it might take me for a ride."

"Yeah. To the emergency room."

"And I remember you were always in the study."

"I know. He let me in there."

Milton told Margret he could trust her there because she was respectful, didn't roughhouse like the boys.

"You were always talking about that heron," he said, "which was strange for a girl."

"Lord Heron." A black-crowned night heron in a huge Victorian bell jar. "I loved that little piece of mercury glass down at the bottom. The suggestion of a swamp, with all those dried reeds around it. You have to admit, it was an imaginative mount."

He nodded, waving for the waiter.

"I'd like an espresso. Mar, do you want coffee or dessert?"

"Just a cappuccino."

"By the way, how's Emily doing? Is she with anyone yet?"

"No. She dates, but never one guy for more than two or three times. She still hasn't met the right man. And she's going to be furious she didn't get to see you. She loves that your hair is even blacker than hers. And you know she's had a crush on you forever, which is probably why you asked."

"I like crushes. There's something innocent about them. But they seem to have gone out of style, like the ingenue. I remember Charles had a name for Emily, but I don't remember what it was."

"The unicorn."

"Yes," he said. "It's so good, and I can't even say why. But she *is* a unicorn."

His brown eyes softened.

"And what did he call you?"

He was giving her an opening to talk about him.

"Mar," she said. "Just Mar."

"Like we do."

Twenty

HE CALLED EMILY the unicorn because she was so pure in her way, so pointed and alone. And he called Margret moonstone because of her gray eyes. Sometimes he called her Miss Snow, because he thought there was something governessy about her spells of silence, though once he said, "But you're too busty to be a governess." He called her Mar. And because she liked to take long baths, like Bonnard's wife, long soaks in lavender scent, her skin pink from the heat, and her hair black like wet branches though it was really dark brown—seal brown her mother always called it, which Margret had never liked because seals are fat and she'd always had curves, had never been bony—because she was in there for such long stretches, with Charles talking loud to her from the study while she smiled or laughed or made sloshing sounds reaching for the soap, he called her Marmaid, his Marmaid with the dark hair and naked breasts, or Murrmaid, because of King and Queen Murr.

Twenty-one

AZAM CALLED MARGRET out of the blue about a Martha Graham gala at the New York State Theater—seven o'clock curtain, then a party on the promenade. He called Emily too, who immediately called Margret to say, "Rich patrons. We have to go."

"But I don't want to hobnob with rich patrons. They're from another planet."

"You're not going for them; you're going for me. For the umpteenth time. I have to hobnob."

So here they were in a typical New York crush, the perfumes too strong, heels too high, men too close, women too thin, arms too bare, chat too fast, champagne too dry, and everyone a little too hungry, having skipped dinner for an early performance of two Graham classics. The food was arranged on silver trays laid out on a very long table. Slim rectangles of salmon on beds of dill. Beef tenderloin medallions, pink as cheeks in Frans Hals. Baby vegetables stripped and shivering in rows. And a huge plate of grapes tucked between French cheeses oozing like old whores. Old whores? Margret wondered. Why would I think that? I love runny cheeses.

Emily was working the room. She was near the north wall of windows, dressed elegantly and sensibly in a red-satin strapless Beene, fitted like a bandage across the bust but floating out at the ankles. My best friend, Margret thought, a postmodern infanta. Azam, meanwhile, in a loose-fitting white silk shirt and skinny tuxedo pants, was surrounded by slim Pilates blondes, the wives of the wealthy, their core strength radiating to their fingertips and toes. They were like arrows from a quiver, and Azam, it appeared, was the bow. He'd danced the Minotaur in *Errand Into the Maze*, and his costume left little to the imagination.

Margret finished her manhattan. She didn't drink bourbon, but for some reason she couldn't decide what to order so Emily had said, "Two manhattans up." Margret was in her sleeveless vintage sheath of ivory eyelet, a sort of lineny silk, high in front with a low button-down back. It was a dangerous dress to wear in a crowd, where food or drink could be bumped right on you, so she was standing somewhat apart and eating only baby carrots. Anyway, she'd escape soon and eat more when she got home.

"I saw you were getting low so I brought you another manhattan."

It was the cute blue-eyed waiter. He took her empty glass and handed her a full one—so full, she took it right to her lips and sipped. It was smoky sweet, with a brewing undercurrent.

"You've got a great memory. Thank you."

"I always remember what the pretty girls drink."

"I don't really drink these, but my friend Emily—she's around here somewhere—she thought it was a night for manhattans."

"Well, go easy. Bourbon sneaks up on you. Ciao."

She was alone again, but she felt less ignored. She could have gone over to Emily, but Emily was in a zone, spinning her web as Mr. Emmerich used to say. Azam was also spinning to some degree. This was a fund-raiser after all. Because Margret didn't know anyone else, the high spirits around her seemed to be on the other side of a window. Too bad Lee Grovenor wasn't here. They could have found a nice corner and had a chat. She'd thought about him from time to time since the dinner party—his quietness, his intensity, the way he heard you without appearing to listen. She liked that. Marriages were so mysterious. Each one a world. Each with its own suns and moons, oceans and inlets. Charles said you couldn't judge other people's relationships because warmth to this person is smothering to that one, coolness here is freedom there. His relationship with Susan Baughman, a perfect example, had gone into eclipse a year before Margret left Columbia; there was a difference over children, not when they should have them but if.

"Come on, Margret, finish that drink and let's dance."

Azam waited for her to gulp down the manhattan, then led her to the dark circle that had opened in the crowd. Oh, god, I have to dance with a dancer. But the music was "Love Child," the Supremes, an easy beat, and Azam was a master, careful as he guided her under his arm, twirled her, pushed her away with one big hand and pulled her back with the other. It was fun dancing, fun being with beautiful him and seeing envy in the eyes of those other women, glittering eyes in the blur outside the circle. With his big hands, he was like a Great Dane, though his nose was more aristocratic, a borzoi. She let her head fall back, her hair flying out, let down for the gala. As the song ended, he pulled her into his arms laughing, and kissed the top of her head. "Not bad," he said, then whispered into her ear, "Get another drink. I have some dances I have to do, if you know what I mean."

Why not have another? But not from the blue-eyed boy.

She went to the bar on the far side of the floor. Then she went looking for Emily, who didn't seem to be anywhere. Not by the windows, or the bar, or at one of the tables. Margret stood outside the ladies' room for a while, not wanting to take her drink in there, but Emily never emerged. Did she leave without saying goodbye? That wasn't like Emily.

Margret went to sit on the bench by the stairs, and hit down with a bump. The seat was a lot lower than she'd thought, or maybe the problem was things were starting to tilt. The room looked as if she were still turning in Azam's arms. She put her glass on the floor and both palms on the bench, for steadiness. Closing her eyes didn't help, just made her feel she was spinning in outer space, vaguely nauseated. She squinted her eyes, a kind of halfway state, and concentrated on breathing. Azam was standing over her.

"Are you okay?"

"The room is spinning, and I can't find Emily."

"She couldn't find you and told me to say she was going with the Spades. For a night hat."

Nightcap, she thought; he must mean nightcap. Which would have been cute if she wasn't feeling like the *Titanic* after the iceberg. Sneak up? She was sinking. And she'd hardly had any of that third drink.

"Stay here while I get our coats. Where's your ticket?"

She reached into her woozy little purse and pulled number seventy-five from the pocket.

"Ha," he said. "The year I was born."

Four years younger than me and Emily.

Azam came back with their coats, helped her into hers, and then they went down the stairs to find a jam of people standing at the glass doors, looking out, looking glum. It was snowing those big white plasticine flakes, and there was a good two inches on the ground. Because it was Sunday night and Lincoln Center was dark, there were no cabs at the stand. Jimmy Choos and Manolo Blahniks would be ruined. The hems of gowns were in danger too.

"I can take the subway," Margret said.

"No you can't. You're coming to my place. I'm only two blocks away."

Life was starting to feel better with her eyes more closed than open, so she just nodded and let him lead her out into the cold white night. He walked ahead of her, clearing a path in the snow so her fawn suede slingbacks wouldn't get too wet, and she held on to the back of his coat so she wouldn't fall. Like a little two-car train they passed the old church south of Lincoln Center and then turned west toward the river. They went into a factory-type building and up about five floors. He unlocked one of those old industrial doors and led her into his apartment. She stepped out of her cold shoes.

"What time is it?" she asked.

"Not late . . . about eleven."

After Azam took her coat, he pointed to where the bathroom was. Before she came out, she splashed her face and drank water from the faucet, bending over sideways. She almost fell as she went to stand up. He led her to his bed, which was positioned against a brick wall and was low like that bench in the theater, but at least not on the floor. She sat down and he brought her a cold cloth for her head and a glass of water, and then put a bowl next to the bed. "In case of throw-up. Now just close your eyes and sleep." Then he turned out the light next to the bed, a Turkish lantern with an intense gold glow. He pulled a curtain—a Suzani, she thought—to close off the rest of the room, and left her there.

• • •

Margret's eyes opened. Where was she? In shades of gray she saw the Suzani and remembered. She was at Azam's. She was in his bed. The apartment was dark. She looked down at herself. Her dress was all unbuttoned but still on her, over her, like a blanket with two holes for the arms. She thought of the play *Yentl*, how the characters had sex through a hole in the sheet. She heard a sigh and there to her left was Azam, a shape under the covers. Her mouth was dust, but at least she wasn't spinning anymore. She remembered the glass of water and lifted herself to take a sip. She saw a little travel clock. It was two A.M.

"How do you feel?" he murmured, pulling up onto one elbow.

She looked back at him in the dark, the outline of him coalescing into bare shoulders.

"Better."

The city was silent because of the snow. Under the white blanket of her dress she felt doubly snowed in.

"I unbuttoned you. I hope it's okay. You didn't look comfortable."

She nodded. She felt safe with him.

"But maybe now I should see what's under this dress. . . ."

She could tell he was smiling by his tone, which was teasing. His hand went under the eyelet and found her stomach, his fingers flattening on it, a diplomatic pause like the tip of a chess piece before the glide; then he moved up to her breast. Margret didn't take her eyes from his face. She was letting his hand go under her smoothie one-piece, letting his thumb caress her nipple, so lightly, her nipple stiffening, and a cascade of sensation below her navel, like snow sliding off a branch.

He removed her dress from her arms and the straps of her smoothie as well, which he pushed down to her waist. He put his mouth on her nipple, and his tongue was soft, little kitten licks at the teat. She didn't make a sound; if she didn't make any sound, this wasn't really happening, this wet mouth lapping and sucking softly and that feeling of warm melted snow between her legs. Even when his hand moved downward from her breast, when he found the little hook-and-eyes in the crotch of her smoothie and undid them, and slid his long middle finger into her, she made no sound. His hair had a sharp smell of sweat and lemon. A low rhythmic *hmmmm* was coming from his throat. The slick and soundless in and out of his finger was filling her, softening her. She closed her eyes to see her husband better. His black hair, his burning brow, his cock she missed so much . . . she was trying to think of all these things but could think only of this finger and the climax that caught her like a dog and shook her. Still she didn't make a sound, only opened her mouth to the darkness, panting silently as he kept his finger in to the knuckle, pressing like a second pulse.

She wanted to go. To go home now. She needed to tell him. She was turning to tell him and he put his mouth on hers, his tongue on hers, a kiss that seemed to have begun long ago and didn't seem to end; it just held and drifted. He took her in his arms, continuing the kiss that was deep then shallow, deep then shallow, and it felt so simple and innocent and flowing, like a brook in the dark, that she found her arms sliding up around his back and tightening. He reached his left arm to the side table, then pulled up a bit and tore open a condom wrapper with his mouth. He was sitting up, rolling it on, and she could stop him now. There was time. It wouldn't be nice for him but she could do it, she had a right to, even if it wouldn't be fair that she hadn't reciprocated.

But she couldn't move. Or she didn't move. The current was too strong. She wanted a cock, her body wanted it, and though the wife in her didn't want it, her body was stronger, adamantly aroused, the kind of desire you have to fuck your way out of. Azam lowered his hips between her legs, and she let them fall open. He was moving his dick in its rubber against her, then pushed it down and in. She could see herself under him, like that butterflied quail the night they met. He, with his long-muscled body like a river. She, white skin opening on rose pinks and deep magentas, tissues driven and swollen. She was ignoble laid out under his body, ignoble and still drunk and thinking if Charles could see this . . . Oh, why was she doing this to him? But god, he was good, both hands holding her head as he pumped his cock into her, graceful and careful. He whispered, "Find your spot," and then started that kiss again. She closed her eyes and braced her legs, pressing for pleasure against the thick hair at the base of his shaft. She was the kidnapped princess in Ali Baba's cave, bound in cavernous flesh, arching bliss, this screwing surrounded by snow and sand and sleep.

Twenty-two

MARGRET GOT HOME at seven A.M., having caught a cab at first light, the snow already slushy on the sidewalk though she no longer cared about her shoes. She bathed herself kneeling in the tub and sudsing from the tap, then got into bed where sleep was empty and fitful. Headache, hunger, and soon a bright winter sun glaring through the curtains gnawed at her. Even with the covers pulled over her eyes, light pressed against her lids. Hiding from the sun was like hiding from yourself, impossible really, unless you went underground. She wanted to go to the bathroom to get an aspirin for her head, to the kitchen for some crackers for her stomach, but she'd didn't want to move. She couldn't go to Saks; she felt too sick. She *was* sick. Like a mollusk pulled out of its shell. Flooded with regret. Stung with self-loathing. Her heart so hollow, she couldn't even cry. She'd betrayed her husband. His memory. Their bed. She wasn't his Mar anymore. She wasn't anyone's.

"Hey, Mar. So last night was kind of fun after all. I'm sorry I had to leave without saying goodbye. I couldn't find you and I really needed to continue with the Spades. And Azam said he'd make sure you got home okay. Where are you anyway? You're usually still there at nine. So call me."

Margret erased the message, a call from Emily at eight forty-five that morning. It was five o'clock in the afternoon and this was the first of many calls she hadn't picked up. The next was a hang-up. And then after that, at eleven: "Margret, this is Tom. Where are you? I put you in charge of the snow and we need the snow, and I don't know where it is. Maybe you're on your way in. I hope so. If not, if something's wrong, call me ASAP."

Then at twelve: "Tom again. I'm going through the snow file on your desk, and I don't see any orders or receipts. Is it possible that with ten days until the Christmas windows go up, we don't have any snow in the house? That can't be possible. Where are you? Call me."

It *was* possible. She'd been trying to locate Crystalina with a lavender tint, to go blue in the twilight and pink in the golden light, and the sample should have arrived today, when she could get a consensus. So, yes . . . no . . . she hadn't ordered it yet.

At three Stephen called, wanting to know if she knew where his purple scissors were. And then at four, Tom again, his tone tired. There was anger underneath, she could hear it because she knew him so well, but a controlling reason on top, because he was deeply reasonable.

"It's Tom. I don't know what happened to you today. I wish you could have called to fill me in on the snow. At any rate, Stephen showed me the FedEx that came in with a sample. He's going to finish the job. I know I should wait to discuss this with you in person, but your absence feels like a long time coming. Since the accident you've been erratic. You did a great job filling in for Tina. But lately you seem to drag through work, leaving as early as possible, coming in late, zoning out. Now this. I'm not firing you. Let's call it tough love. I don't want you here til you can prove you want to be here. You can call me, we can talk, but at least until spring you're suspended."

One by one Margret erased the messages. She walked to the living-room window and looked out. The dusk was gloomy, the snow on the rooftops completely gone. If she left to get the car now, she'd hit rush-hour traffic. If she waited an hour, she'd be on the road closer to seven, and she'd get to the Point by ten, ten thirty. But that hour of doing nothing, waiting in silence, with the dust, looked unbearable to her. She'd rather sit in traffic than sit here. She went to the closet for her coat.

Twenty-three

THERE WAS NOTHING as black as the ocean at night. Nothing as silent as the bat-brown scrub going up the dunes, the ocean sawing and sighing on the other side, or as furred as the pines against the gray-black, blue-black sky—the lampblack colors of Old World shutters and doors. And the lighthouse just blocks away, sweeping the darkness every ten seconds. Once they'd counted it out. One-thousand-one, one-thousand-two . . . Night on a beach was a world before light.

Was the ocean really blacker than the shadows their bodies cast walking to the dunes to see the stars, to take the sea air like a night-cap? It felt blacker. Its depths, its reach, its cold blind hold, the vault of all life crawling endlessly up the sand, taking back into itself anything not strong enough to stay. Margret didn't go into the water during the day, hadn't for two years. But night was different.

She took her shoes off at the end of the path and rolled up her pants. On cold hard sand she walked barefoot down to the water, a long walk, the tide out. She inched in to her ankles, feeling the sharp coldness on her skin, the freezy prickles eventually dissolving into a dullness not warm but temperatureless. And then the lurches of fresh cold as waves swelled higher on her untouched leg. And the tug of the undertow, a low hug and release, hug and release, a rhythm like the long slow breathing of someone sleeping, sleeping in the water far away.

She walked into the ocean up to her knees, the freeze of it angry. It was painful, the ocean in November. Her lower legs were turning into ice. She closed her eyes so that all she heard was the tide and all she felt was the cold, and in the swaying darkness inside her head she said, I'm sorry, I'm sorry, I'm sorry.

THE BIRDS

Twenty-four

MARGRET CALLED JAY MARTI a week after Tom fired her. It was the Monday before Thanksgiving, not the best time to call; he was probably deep in his own Christmas windows. But she needed a paycheck, and she wanted to get the call in before it was officially the holidays, when nothing got done. She'd spent the whole week working at the Point and hoped to go down again over Thanksgiving, but if she had to, if Marti asked her to, she'd stay in the city and work at Lord & Taylor to prove her commitment to the job. Anyway, Margret had told her parents and Emily that she was going to Tina's for Thanksgiving, to keep them out of her hair. Why did every holiday have to be spent in food and drink, clinking glasses and stuffing yourself? Holidays were pointless.

Marti returned her call later that day. He wanted her to come in the following Monday; he had some work for her, and he'd tell her about it then. Which meant she needed to get her things from her desk at Saks, where she hadn't been since . . . Margret closed her eyes and shook her head, crushing the memory in the blackness behind her eyelids.

Margret called Tom about getting her things, and he was very nice and said to come in on the weekend. She still had her key, but she should leave it behind when she left. She could tell he didn't have time to deal with her, and she was glad. She didn't want to discuss her failure. And she didn't want to risk seeing anyone, so she waited until Sunday and went in at seven, the store still buzzing with holiday shoppers but the Boiler Room locked and dark. She let herself in, switched on the light, and went to her desk. Tom had said her stuff was still in her drawers, but other people had parked there. Other people clearly being Stephen. His pencil with the Barbie Doll eraser had pride of place in a crystal cup, which also held his purple-handled scissors. Margret pulled some stationery out of a drawer and wrote a quick note.

Dear Tom,
Congratulations on the Match Girl windows. They're terrific. The crowd outside was captivated.

Should she say how great the snow looked? Better not go there. She added:

I also want to say, thank you for being so kind.
With love, Margret

Then she took the note and her key, put them in an envelope, and propped it against Tom's office door. Back at her desk she began emptying the drawers into a Saks shopping bag. Alone in the eerie quiet, she had to admit she didn't miss the place. It had the feeling of an empty classroom.

In her top drawer was paper, pencils, scissors, and the month-at-a-glance she used for the window schedules. The middle drawer was a jumble. Lip glosses she hadn't used in years, some old eye cream, a hairbrush, a box of tampons at the back of the drawer, a really nice leather-covered diary in which she hadn't written a single word, and oh, her copy of Frost's poems; she'd wondered where that went. Her stuff was mainly in the deep third drawer: folders and big envelopes full of magazine clippings, window sketches, fabric swatches, foil trim, and flattened maquettes. She lifted them one at a time and flipped through them, then stopped when she realized she was hearing steps on the stairs. Joe was in the doorway, hands on the jambs and his body leaning in.

"She's baaa-aack."

Margret concentrated on her files.

"Let it snow, let it snow, let it snow," Joe sang as he went to his office, knocking a little against the big meeting table and futzing about in there. Then he came out, crossed over to her side of the room, and sat himself on the table, legs hanging, facing her. She'd never seen such looseness in his movement, from the way he leaned back on his hands to the small act of putting a cigarette to his lips and reaching into his pocket for a lighter.

"You'll set off the smoke detector," she said. She didn't want to get in trouble down here.

He flicked up a flame, waved it in the air, then snapped the lighter shut. He put the cigarette in his pocket.

"What are you doing here, Marge?"

She threw some old colored pencils she'd never liked back into the drawer.

"You know," he said, "I used to screw a lot of girls like you."

He was drunk.

"I'd woo 'em, screw 'em, and then not call 'em. It was fun. All that hurt pride when they passed me on the quad."

"You're a regular Valmont."

"Ohhhh, literary allusions from our Miss Widow. Or should we go back to Marge? Since you don't work here anymore, I don't have to be nice to you anymore."

You were never nice.

"No more homage to your great loss. What a fucking relief. No more pussyfooting around."

Margret was stunned. But she forced herself to say, "I thought I was pussyfooting around you. Though who knows why?"

She turned back to the drawer.

"Don't you turn away from me. Don't you get on your high horse with me. All you need is a dick. I'd give you one just to get that look off your face."

She continued staring into the drawer. And then Joe was standing over her, smelling of scotch. His face was so white, yet with a blush across each cheek that looked like the swipe of a paintbrush. His blue eyes were dilated, dark and hard. He moved toward her and she shrank against her desk. He grabbed the back of her head and was bringing his face to hers, but she squirmed out from under him and ran to the bank of mannequins.

"So it's just an act," he jeered. "You don't really want to go."

"What are you talking about?"

"God!" he swore at the floor. Then he glared at her. "I lost someone too. And it could've been me who made him sick."

He dropped down into her desk chair. Margret remained standing, backed by the troop of white plastic mannequins.

"And everything's for you," he said.

Had Sasha tried to tell her this? Is this what he'd meant by affinity? And when did it happen? Before Saks, obviously. Did only Sasha know, or did everyone know but her?

Joe was staring at Stephen's Barbie Doll eraser. Margret knew there was nothing to say.

"We should go," she murmured.

She picked up her bag and walked to just outside the door, her hand inside on the light switch, waiting. He heaved himself up and came slowly across the room. When he got to the door, just as she turned off the light, he reached for her and pulled her from the light in the hall back into the darkness, crushing her against the wall, his collar in her face, his belt buckle sharp against her hip. She didn't fight, because she wasn't afraid. She went slack in his grip, dropping the bag, giving in to the strangeness of his chest, their bodies, so close, the smell of cigarettes and liquor, him breathing above her head, holding her like prey he didn't want. Then he backed away.

He leaned down precariously and picked up her bag. He started for the stairs; she followed. When they pushed out of the employee exit into the cold night air, they stopped and looked at each other, a silence neither tried to fill. Then, as if it were a gift, he handed her the shopping bag and turned east toward the silver stars.

Twenty-five

MARGRET STIRRED THE SOUP. It was her grandmother Anna's recipe, a chicken soup she'd loved stirring as a child. It was the day after Christmas, and she would fly back to New York in two days. Her parents were both out, her dad gone to the University of Chicago bookstore, and her mom off to Marshall Field's for the sales. Mom was definitely brighter this Christmas, and there was no doubt about why. On Margret's first night there, at dinner, she told her parents she'd left Saks. Her mother broke into a big grin. "Honey," she beamed, "that's the best gift you could have given me."

The apartment was as beautiful as ever, with a Scotch pine, tall and tinseled, in the living room, and pine garlands hung over the leaded glass windows. Margret had grown up in this apartment, one of those Arts and Crafts relics that no one wanted in the seventies, the oak wainscoting and mosaic tiling momentarily deemed passé.

Her parents had bought the place as a starter for a song, a three-bedroom with a butler's pantry, a maid's room, and a sunroom, which her father had restored bit by bit. Now it was a showplace, and the Hyde Park address was enviable, prestigious. Though still her mother sighed for the house they'd never owned.

For years her father had said, When we have a second child, we'll move to a house. But the second child never came. Bonnie Snow miscarried one pregnancy after another, which explained the oppressive descent of tiptoeing silence once or twice a year. Margret began to know what was what when she was six and returned from school to find her mother kneeling on the bathroom floor, choking with tears, her arms atop a toilet bowl full of blood. Margret reached over to flush it, and her mother grabbed her wrist hard. "No," she cried, and said something about "your brother" before pushing Margret out the door and pulling it shut.

Margret loved the apartment, had loved helping her father mix plaster and grout, handing him tools, and going with him to the store for tiles and paint chips. He was trying to make it beautiful for Mom. He even set up the sunroom as an art studio for her. There's more light here, he would say, than in any upstairs room in any house. And it was true. Because they were on the fourth floor, the treetops were just under the windows, which meant lots of sun and birds, and also a floating field of green you felt you could touch like grass. And Mom in her painter's smock—what a metaphor. It looked like a maternity top. As a child, Margret had loved seeing her in that smock, a brush in her hand, the way she hummed as she stirred the brush in turpentine, puffs of color storming the clear liquid, then turning flaky, solid, settling on the bottom of the jar. But little had come from that room lined with windows, because Bonnie went into it less and less; she said she felt too exposed. Eventually the easel was out, and one of her mother's finds, an antique suite of ornate Anglo-Indian wicker, was in. Dad painted the set gray, and in one of those woven chairs from another world her mom would read novels and *New Yorkers* in a cloud forest of orchids, purples and whites blooming biannually as if nourished by her afternoon naps, the dreams she exhaled into spidery roots.

Margret didn't go to Field's, because she'd had enough of stores at Christmas. She knew her dad would be home soon, and it would be nice to be alone for a while, and then alone with him. They were going to see one of his colleagues for cocktails, and she thought chicken soup with French bread and a salad would be a nice light dinner when they got home.

The soup had been on for about fifteen minutes, just a whole chicken in water. The key was not to let it come to a rolling boil. You had to be there in the beginning, to watch for when the surface wavered, like someone about to cry. During this time you cut up carrots, celery, and onions, and when small bubbles erupted you turned down the heat and threw in the veggies. At this point you covered the pot—lid slightly askew—and let it simmer and simmer some more. The simmering is what she remembered from regular trips to Escanaba Street with her dad, the way his mother kept things on the stove all day, soups and stews ladled steaming into bowls for whoever came in the door, the house smelling of stuffed cabbage leaves and chicken paprikash. When Margret asked to stir the soup, Anna Snow would pull over a chair and lift her up, smoothing her granddaughter's hair away from the heat.

It became a ritual, Margret stirring the soup, watching the circles of fat that lay razor thin on the surface, like something on a slide, twirling and separating. Deeper down in the staw-colored broth, bits of carrot and white meat would surge and sink. And somewhere in there, the gizzard and the heart. Margret always looked for these grayish nuggets, as if it were a game. She liked the gizzard well enough, taken out and salted on a plate, and then the crunchiness of it, a consistency that made her mother groan; but then Mom couldn't stand the feel of peach fuzz either, or dry dirt on her feet. So Margret would try not to crunch too loud, or would wait til her mother left the kitchen. The heart was the prize, partly because it was so hard to find, bouncing weightless off the spoon as if in outer space. But also because it was velvety, not crunchy. Finally catching it felt like something from a folktale, as if the one who found the heart would win the hand in marriage. It didn't really make sense. A chicken heart simmered in a pot; it wasn't the stuff of French fairy tales.

Each family makes its own fables, Margret thought, and that simmered heart . . . well, maybe it was because her father loved hearts too. Mom wouldn't eat them. Organ meat wasn't what she was used to. Dad once described the glory of blood sausage, and Bonnie nearly fainted. But they seemed to enjoy these roles, the princess and the peasant, the Wasp and the Croat, the beauty and the brain, at least when Mom was on an even keel. If only she'd had something to engage her through the years, to pour her yearning into. "She's like a woman with empty-nest syndrome," Aunt Bett once said, not very nicely, "except the nest was never full." The apartment itself was testament to Bonnie's decorating skills, a period sensibility with a light touch. Her last paintings, a series of small oils done outdoors, standing on the rocky edge of Lake Michigan, hung in the dining room. People spent a long time looking at them, said they had something. It's just that Mom didn't want an indefinable something; she wanted what everyone else had, more children. Painting wasn't enough for her. Or Margret wasn't enough.

Cleaning the chicken, Margret had reached inside for the livers and out slid the slippery, glistening lobes, more liver than belonged to any one bird. And not one heart came out between her fingers, but three. How did that happen? Three in one chicken? She'd once bought a pack of chicken hearts. It was in those first days, when she'd begun shopping again for just herself, everything suddenly random. She remembered how at the checkout she'd looked at her choices on the conveyer belt, and they were like items in one of those TV game shows, where you had to guess the connection between things. She still remembered what she'd bought. Potato chips with sea salt and vinegar, because her mouth had watered when she read the word "vinegar." A pricey tub of mesclun salad. Ale in a squat brown bottle, made by Trappist monks. It looked like a little monk. And chicken hearts, about thirty for a dollar, which embarrassed her, not only because they were food for poor people, but because of the way the hearts pressed against the saran wrap, crowded together in various sizes, a color between pink and brown, with little blushes of mauve. The shape and color reminded her of the glans of a penis. There was something obscene about raw chicken hearts, and she'd wondered if the cashier and the woman in line behind her were thinking it too. At home she'd thrown them into a Pyrex dish with a little olive oil and salt and baked them at 350 degrees. But when she cut into one, the smooth muscle was like that of a squid, and when she put it in her mouth, she couldn't eat it. She threw them all away.

Margret prodded the chicken with a big spoon to see if it was coming apart yet. It wasn't. She spooned up some broth, blew on it, and tasted. It was still pale.

"Something smells good."

Her father was back.

"I'm in the kitchen," she called.

He came in, his cheeks red from the cold, his gray eyes watery. He was still handsome, but in a threadbare intellectual way. He looked into the soup and smiled that warm smile of his.

"Did you get your book?" Margret asked.

"I ordered it," he said. "Let's have a glass of wine."

He pulled a bottle of white from the fridge.

"Mar, I know we talked about this already, but are you sure your pay at Lord and Taylor will be enough to live on?"

"It's a little less money but a way more focused job, just eight little windows that can be done in three days or less. Just accessories. So I'll have time to find more interesting and lucrative freelance work. And also to think about what I want to do next."

She watched her dad's large hands turn the corkscrew and pull the cork from the bottle. Then he poured a glass and handed it to her.

"Still, it's an odd time to leave Saks, just when you have the holiday slowdown."

Her father always knew when something was off with her.

"Well, I . . . the truth is, I was let go from Saks. I screwed up ordering the snow."

"How does one screw up ordering the snow?"

"I didn't order it on schedule. And Tom's a nut about the snow. So he suspended me until spring."

"That isn't like you. Do you think you wanted to be suspended? Instead of having to quit and leave your friends?"

It was a nice interpretation.

"I don't know. Maybe. I don't feel real interested in long-term stuff, schedules reaching months in advance. I feel exhausted just looking at a calendar. If I were still at Saks, we'd already be talking about next year's Christmas windows. Short-term is all I'm up for."

"So concentration's a problem?"

She knew what he was thinking, that she had phased into depression.

"It's just been a long hard fall and I'm tired. When I'm doing my own work, I'm totally concentrated."

"You mean freelance windows?"

"Yeah. And a project I'm playing with."

"Tell me about it."

"I can't yet. It's still just mine. By the way, this wine is delicious."

"Another one from your mom's wine-tasting class. She's really into it. I think she has a natural palate, and she says she's teacher's pet. Now, of course, she wants to go to Napa. Or Alsace. She can't decide which. I told her she's the oenophile, so she should plan the trip. Do one this year, one the next."

Margret took another swallow and smiled happily at her dad even as her throat stiffened, seized with a clamoring sadness. She went to the soup and took the cover off, a hot mist rising into her face, rising in her eyes, tonight, tomorrow, next week, next year, all lost. She stirred the soup, focusing on the circles on the surface. Her dad came up behind her, put his hands on her shoulders and squeezed. She still couldn't speak. He whispered into her hair, "I'm so proud of you." She bowed her head, her throat aching, and nodded yes, trying to see past the heat in her eyes, stirring again, to find a heart for him.

Twenty-six

THEY LOOKED AT HER windows from the outside, and Jay Marti was pleased. In each window she'd made a curved space with thick black paper, fixed at the top front of the window and the bottom front. She'd pricked pinpoint stars into the paper and illuminated them with a light from behind. In each of these black spaces she'd hung a bluish moon in one of eight phases, and each moon was wearing a piece of the new Diamanté collection from Kenneth Jay Lane. Earrings, bracelets, necklaces. All Jay wanted was for Margret to move the little plates with the brand name an inch to the left. They came back into the store and went into the dark corridor behind the eight windows. He said he'd do four.

"I'm curious," he said. "What made you leave Saks? Because when I didn't hear from you, I assumed you'd been promoted."

"Jay. It's a small world. You must have heard through the grapevine that I was let go."

He laughed that skiffing laugh of his, full of light.

"I did hear. What gives?"

"I screwed up on the Christmas snow. I didn't order it."

"I heard that too"—he laughed some more—"but the snow in the windows looked fine."

"I was about to order it. The sample came the same day I didn't come in. And the snow in the window looked like my snow. I'm not saying I wasn't in the wrong, but Tom might have overreacted a little."

"I ran into Tina at Tinsel Trading and told her I'd hired you. She said Tom was frantic. They didn't know what kept you from returning his calls. They thought something bad might have happened to you."

Margret hadn't spoken to Tina since the week before Tom called.

"I guess I let her down too."

"No," Jay said. He had turned to look at her. "She loves you. She said, Margret's been acting normal for too long; it's not natural. She said you can't expect normal behavior from someone who's been shattered."

It hung there. Margret focused her attention on getting the black paper back into a symmetrical curve, but her eyes were blurring. What was happening to her? She didn't want to be crying on the job. But everything was turning to tears. That Tina understood. That Tina had been watching. Hovering in a way, making her manager. She felt her throat swell. She tried to freeze herself. Took a deep breath.

Margret hadn't told anyone about that night, not even Emily, but it was like a band on her heart, a black band she was wearing inside, and Jay's Incan eyes seemed to see it, here in this dark corridor. He seemed to see that her heart was a dark corridor. And it came like a wave, her sorrow, doubling her over, words and tears spilling together.

"I slept with someone . . . I didn't mean to. But I miss my husband so much, and this man was like him in some ways. I drank too much and I ended up in bed with him, and I could have left and wanted to . . . but I didn't leave and didn't want to. And I betrayed my . . ."

She couldn't continue, the pain of it choking her.

She turned to the window, tried to close the back of it, then leaned against the wall, wiping her eyes with the heel of her hand. He leaned against the wall too, next to her.

"When I was a child," he said, "our cat caught a mouse, the tiniest mouse I'd ever seen, the size of a nickel. My mother got the mouse away from the cat and threw it in the toilet. I was screaming for her not to, but she flushed anyway. That tiny mouse swam; it swam with a strength that stunned me. The memory haunts me to this day. But I saw something I've never forgotten. Life force. How powerful it is. And how it fights."

She saw Charles in the water in the plane, strapped in, the ocean rising, rushing, sinking, Charles glassed-in, *please please let him not have known, please please have knocked him out and never known . . .*

"The life force inside you said swim. That's why you couldn't leave."

Then he said, "Margret. He wouldn't want this kind of love."

And because she knew it was true, but could see no other kind, her shoulders shook harder with tears. Jay put his hand on her back and said softly, "Go ahead and cry. That's what living things do."

Twenty-seven

IT WAS A BOOK she'd bought him. Margret found it upstairs at Barnes and Noble, seventy-five dollars, and it weighed a ton. It was titled *The Great Auk*, and the cover was Audubon's famous aquatint of an auk standing in profile on a rock, waves pitching all around. The way they stood upright, like penguins, was what made them charming, like little people, and vulnerable. Whoever designed the jacket knew what they were doing. The image was scaled so the auk filled the whole cover, which made it the same size as a newborn baby. And the color sense was so perilously beautiful. The pale blue Atlantic sky, the frigid waters of teal frosted with periwinkle, the bare mountain rising grisaille in the background, and the auk, coal black and snow white, awkward and noble, hunted to death. She couldn't believe Charles didn't already have the book, but he'd never mentioned it, and she knew he would love it. It was October when she found it, so she'd hidden it until December, hoping he wouldn't buy it for himself before then. When he opened it on Christmas, which he celebrated for Margret's sake, he was thrilled. He turned to the inside endpaper, and in his stalking script, the inward curl and hurl of the lefty, he wrote:

From the Murrmaid
December 1999

She could never get him to say why he was obsessed with the auk. He learned of it as a child, way before he was interested in birds, when he was reading *The Water Babies*. "It stood alone on a rock," he explained, "the last of the Gairfowl. And cried tears of pure oil. Because when it was gone, the rock would be all alone. I couldn't sleep some nights, thinking about that auk on the rock. And those tears of oil."

Obviously, a man who specialized in the art of ancient Assyria, an extinct culture, might be attracted to an extinct bird with its own culture, the icy climes of the North Atlantic. On maps he'd shown her the main breeding grounds, off Iceland, Scotland, and east of Newfoundland. On little Lundy Island, in the Bristol Channel, fishermen had called the couples King and Queen Murr, because they were bigger than murres, a related species, and stood up "so bold like." When auks weren't nesting, they lived in the sea, which was the only place they were safe from humans. Their bones, their bills especially, with that strange arrowhead-like chiseling, were totemic. And it was this too: history could pinpoint the last breeding couple that had been killed. In June of 1844.

"It's almost like the two fours in 1844 are the last two auks," Margret had said, when he told her about it.

"Horrible, isn't it? Though debatable, given later sightings. But those may have been nonbreeding birds."

There were other extinct species that obsessed birders. The ivory-billed woodpecker, the Eskimo curlew. Why the auk and not the ivorybill?

Because the ivorybill is a ghost bird, he'd said. Who knew if it was really gone? It just hadn't been seen in those thousand-acre, old-growth forests. And it was never the object of slaughter.

But the auk . . . Auks, like dodoes, were for centuries a food source for sailors, who drove the trusting creatures up gangplanks by the hundreds, and then clubbed them into airless ship's holds. When they weren't killed for food, they were taken for their feathers. This creature that evolution so heartlessly aimed into a niche that left it naked, was finally beaten down to two, Adam and Eve in reverse, King and Queen Murr and a boat full of fourteen men come to get them, collecting them for a rich client. The last ones, her husband said. The end of an existence, a rhythm in the world. The reverberation, he said, was profound.

So it was to the Grande Galerie de l'Évolution that Margret and Charles flew on their last vacation together, a last-minute thing, really; Paris in August was not everyone's idea of fun. But on the spur of the moment he'd decided he had five days free before the term began, and he said, "Let's hop a plane and see the Paris auk." Tom had grumbled, but then said go.

The museum was magnificent. Margret was blown away by the insects, which were perfect, every leg and antenna in place. "Couture pinning," she exclaimed. "If only my grandfather could have seen this." They looked everything over pretty well, building up to the corridor they'd come for, the Gallery of Endangered and Extinct Species. They entered the shadowy room and were alone in it, the only sound an air conditioner humming behind the wood paneling. The auk was to the right of the entrance, so Charles went left to one of the curving wood staircases that led to a mezzanine level; he sat on the second step so he could stare at the bird, contemplating it from a distance of ten feet or so.

Margret left him alone there. She walked the length of that sad hall, taking in the Chinese tiger, the aye-aye, the grande tortue de Rodrigues, and the albatros de Chine, which wasn't extinct, just very rare. She saw a bird she at first thought was a sunbittern, remembered from one of her grandfather's books, but the French name was *Outard barbue* and the Latin name *Otis tarda*. She knew *barbue* meant "bearded" and *otis* meant "bustard." Bearded bustard? But what was *tarda*?

Charles would know. She'd show this to him when he was done with the auk. He was good at languages, having grown up speaking Aramaic and English, learning French in high school and German in college, and taking a year of Latin to boot. At one time he'd investigated the Hebrew word *qippodh*, which was thought to derive from a verb meaning "to roll up," and in common usage meant "hedgehog." It appeared in the Bible variously and inexplicably translated as bittern, bustard, or heron, perhaps because the creature it described was identified with a desolate and watery place—the land that would be left when God broke the Assyrians from it. Isaiah 14:23: "I will also make it a possession for the bittern, and pools of water." Which implied a marsh. Even translations that used bustard, a land bird, referred to "a waste of fen," which was a peaty marsh. Margret wanted it to be bittern because she thought it such a beautiful word. Bittern. Charles told her she was confusing poetry with scholarship.

She returned from her slow round, and he was still just looking, his chin resting on his hand sort of like Rodin's *Thinker*. But what was he thinking? At what angle did this extinct creature intersect with his work, his dreams, his childhood, his eye, the fertile crescent that was his mind? When Margret came to stand by him, she waited for him to talk. He'd glanced up at her and smiled. She said something about how the auk was the most majestic creature in the gallery. He simply nodded.

The Paris auk was certainly splendid. Margret had wanted to say how beautiful it was compared to the auk in the London Museum, so dusty and dumpy, like an old headmaster. Not to mention the London auk was stuck sharing a case with the dodo, a blockhead student, though it did make sense to put them together. Both were extinct because they were flightless, prey to humans because they couldn't outrun them. Charles had been appalled by that mount. He greatly loved London's Natural History Museum, the joie de vivre of its stonework, its interior space something between a cathedral and a greenhouse, those windows at the top. It troubled him that their auk was second-rate. And yet it was funny too, and they'd both laughed. This auk, however, stood up so straight, almost two feet high, and its neck was stretched as if it were looking over the horizon. The vestigial wing was tiny, fetal, positioned far down on the body. A wing fit for ruddering in water but unfit for life on land. And the white patches in front of the eyes, which from a distance gave it a blind look, puffed out a little, like meringues. The bill was fascinating, with those chisel marks. Charles loved the way auks, drawn in profile, were like bas-reliefs.

"Those white eye patches are like floating islands," Margret ventured.

"Yes. Its fate was tied to islands. In the water nothing could touch it."

"Leave it to the French to do such a beautiful room."

"And to place the auk here at the entrance. As if to speak for every other creature in the hall. *J'accuse.*"

Should she show him the bustard? Maybe not.

"Why do you love it so much?"

He shrugged.

"Because it's such an old man. And like a child. Because it never had a chance."

After that, they walked back to the hotel, a rather long walk via the Cluny Museum, where the unicorns lifted his spirits right up. "There's our Emily," he said. That was in August of 2000, a wonderful wonderful trip. It was on that trip that Margret thought she might be pregnant; they'd stopped using the diaphragm the previous winter. That night, walking home after dinner at a very old brasserie, its mirrors so old, the silver so peeled, they were like black pools, she'd told Charles her period was late. Only a few days, but . . . She remembered it so well because he'd said, Maybe there's a little auk in there. On the plane ride home, the blood and the cramps had come, stronger than usual, ten days late.

The book was on her lap, the glossy jacket smooth under her hand. She opened to the middle, leafing through the section that had pictures and descriptions of every auk on display in the world's museums. She hadn't looked at the book since the Christmas day she'd given it to Charles. She turned the pages slowly. Audubon's auk. The Prince of Denmark's auk. The Prague immature. The Amiens auk. The Lille auk. And here, the Paris auk. It was bird no. 31. She turned the page to see the photograph, and there it stood, just as she remembered it, high-headed, a little king. And there was his handwriting, in black ink, tiny underneath.

8-26-00 *w/ Mar*

She had the letter by her side, the registered letter, just received. It was from the Labrador Aviation Authority, apologizing for the lengthy delay, but explaining that after extensive analysis of records, et cetera, the readings showed that Cessna serial number X359748, piloted by Dr. George Fenner, with passenger Charles Ashur, had passed its landing destination of Saint John's and flown due north, turning south at fifty degrees latitude where it circled Funk Island, circled twice, and met with heavy fog blanketing the island and surrounding seas. The plane went down southeast of Funk Island.

She slipped the letter into the book and closed it.

She didn't need this report to know. She had always known. For years he'd wanted to fly over Funk Island, a barren plateau in treacherous waters, its silt knee-deep in auk bones. He said if he were younger he'd have gone there on a dig. But not now, he said, just to fly over would be enough. Just to fly over and look down. Like a little boy.

Twenty-eight

"I'M COMING WITH YOU," Emily said. "I need a break, an escape, a minivacation. So you're taking me to the Point this weekend whether you want to or not."

Margret didn't want to. She had some work in the little upstairs, a loft-like attic with four dormers. There was an extra cot up there, and a long table bought locally at a school sale. Charles had used the table when he had piles of books and needed to spread out. Now, Margret was keeping her birds up there, for storage, feeling like Tippi Hedren in Hitchcock's movie, only these birds behaved. She didn't want Emily to see them, because she didn't want to explain them, but unfortunately the lock on the upstairs door had never worked. At the same time she really couldn't say no to Emily, who asked so little of her and was in a professional funk. Her latest show, Clay, got a surprisingly nasty review in the *Times* and was not selling well. The stonecutter coming in next was a repeat, which didn't exactly thrill Emily. And the show scheduled for mid-April, Arachnid, bit the dust when the artist, a weaver who created strange imagery within weblike structures by pulling and twisting threads, had called to say she couldn't deliver the number of pieces they'd agreed on. She had carpal tunnel syndrome and had finished only three.

"But she had ten when I signed her up!" Emily exclaimed, as they zoomed down the Garden State Parkway. "I said, 'What happened to the ten you showed me in Vermont?' And she said, 'They weren't good enough so I unraveled them.' Can you believe it? I say they're superb and she unravels them. I said, 'Your show is printed into the schedule.' Well, that made no impression on her at all. None whatsoever. These people know nothing about New York. And I really needed those webs. They were knockout."

Emily rolled down the window to let a whoosh of winter into the car. It was late January and they'd left the city at two in the afternoon, just ahead of the rush hour, and were now going sixty past the Tom's River exit.

"I could kill that stupid woman," Emily said. "This on top of my lousy review."

"No one gets one hundred percent good reviews."

"I know. It was only a matter of time."

"Like four years. You've had amazing press."

"Yes, I've been lucky. But don't you think there was a personal agenda in that review?"

"Which line?"

"Emily Edwards, who thinks she can reinvent the potter's wheel."

"More snarky than personal."

"I knew I shouldn't have done pottery. I hate pottery. But it was such exquisite pottery. And yet I really do hate the idea of all that sloppy wet clay and people getting all oozy and sexual with their thumbs forming curves. Like that scene in *Ghost*, and the million and one seductions one imagines taking place in pottery classes all over America."

Emily was on a roll.

"Emily Edwards—from Chalice to Clay. From silver to pots. Or to pot, I should say."

"You're blowing this out of proportion. Can't you pull your June artist up into April? Who *is* your June artist?"

"This guy who does chandeliers, iron and mercury glass, some in a celestial motif with orbs and stars and others with deep-sea figures, spirals and puffer fish. Very Jules Verne."

"They sound fascinating."

"They are. But it's too much like the World show. You know? Just too soon. I mean, I will if I have to, but it doesn't feel right. God, I wish I smoked. Now is just the time to light up a cigarette so I could blow the smoke out vehemently. Do people blow smoke out of their noses anymore? You don't see it much. I wonder if you can get cancer of the nose from blowing smoke out of your nose?"

"My grandfather Snow? He once held out this little tin to me and opened the lid. I was about five. And inside was this moist-looking brown stuff I thought was chocolate. He put his finger in and lifted it to my mouth, and when I tasted it, expecting something delicious, I got this spasm of . . . I can't even describe it. So bitter, it was like a bite. I spat it out and he laughed. He wasn't being mean. Just playful, I think."

"And your point is?"

"Chewing tobacco is both dangerous and gross."

This cracked them up.

"He worked in the steel mills, right?"

"Yeah."

They got to the Cape May Acme around six and bought groceries; then they stopped at Collier's and bought two bottles of red, two of white, and then at the last minute some Grey Goose, vermouth, and olives, Emily suddenly in the mood for martinis. Even though it was cold they rolled both windows down to enjoy the drive along Sunset Boulevard, so pitch black and spooky. In January no frogs would be hopping across, but one did have to watch for low-flying owls and the sudden, sulfurous eyes of raccoons. The lighthouse high beam was already circling, searching the corners.

"How long before the house heats up?"

"Pretty fast. I put the red rug down in November."

Margret was always amazed at a what a tight little house it was, despite its creaky floors and sticky windows. So many houses at the Point weren't winterized. She turned the wheel and heard the crunch of the gravel driveway, always more eloquent in the dark. They each took a shopping bag, and Margret unlocked the front door, turned on the front light and the living-room lights, and went straight to the thermostat. When Emily went out to the car for her overnight bag, Margret dashed up the back stairs to the attic, pulled the door shut, and set a box of books on the step in front of it.

"Martini time!" Emily called, coming in the front door. "But first let me flop on my couch."

The living room had two couches arranged in an L shape and

covered in white duck, and one upholstered chair, a chintz with big red roses. Emily, when she visited, always slept on the couch under the side window. Margret and Charles had kept the walls bare, except for the one that didn't have a couch or windows. There they'd hung a collection of paintings and watercolors, all of them containing stark horizon lines. Sky and sea, sky and field, sky and snow. There were three low Chinese tables scattered about, rosewood squares, one ornately carved, for books and drinks. Charles hated coffee tables, hated feeling trapped behind heavy objects. Margret brought a throw from the bedroom, just in case Emily was chilly. But already the house was warming. She mixed the martinis and brought them out.

"Yummy," Emily said, eating an olive with a little white onion inside. "That shot of brine is divine."

"Are three olives enough?"

"For now."

Emily had flipped off her shoes and stretched out on the couch.

"Oh, did I need this," she said. "I know I'm always making fun of the Point, but once you're here, it's as if New York City doesn't exist. You forget what quiet really is. It's almost frightening, the silence."

"It's like a drug."

"By the way, I'm not wildly hungry. Should we just have a little pasta with pesto?"

"Fine with me. I'll start the water boiling."

"Don't yet. Let's chat over our marts. Tell me more about Jack."

"But I told you everything already."

"We didn't discuss it in depth, because we've hardly seen each other since you left Saks. Was he as handsome as ever? How has he changed? Why doesn't he have a girlfriend?"

"He wanted to know why *you* don't have a boyfriend."

"We really were meant for each other, Jack and me—in another life, I guess. So go on."

"When he came into Ouest, you should have seen the heads turn. And not just women. You don't see men like that in Manhattan. Not that there aren't gorgeous guys in New York, but there's something about Jack."

"That lean green eastern aura," Emily said.

"He's almost old-fashioned now. His starched white shirt and his beard, and smiling so much. And his sport coat rolled up in his backpack."

Emily motioned for a refill. "But do you think he'll ever marry?"

"It's hard to imagine. I'm not even sure he's only straight. It's not that I've seen anything happen, or he's said anything. But he has a kind of autonomy, an unholdable quality that makes you feel boundaries don't matter."

It suddenly hit her what it was. Something akin to the homeless men in the north end, with that quick warmth and narrow path and the backward glance that says don't follow.

"He's like an English explorer," Emily was saying between sips, "going off to make his fortune in the wilds."

"Well, not quite. I mean, he works for Genentech."

Margret brought out the pasta, and they slid to the living-room floor and ate there, each with her own Chinese table.

"Wait," Emily said. "The wine's in the freezer."

She went into the kitchen.

"It's cold enough," she called to Margret, "and we really should have wine with the pasta."

She brought out a bottle and two glasses.

• • •

The plates were in the sink and they'd opened a second bottle of wine. It wasn't what they usually did, but Emily insisted. After all, it was Friday night, they didn't have to be anywhere tomorrow, why not blow off some steam? And it was such lovely chardonnay, Chalk Hill, Emily's treat, one hundred dollars for two bottles.

"It's downright cozy now," Emily said, back up on the couch. "Now how do you like Lord and Taylor? You know, I've never forgotten bringing home my dress for the high-school prom in a box from Lord and Taylor. Remember when stores used to pack dresses in boxes? And now they just stuff them in a bag. It's one of so many things that's gone."

"Like telephone dialers."

"For that matter, rotary phones."

"And baked alaska."

"Oh, no, they have it at the new Le Cirque. But hats, they're mostly gone."

"Except for Philip Treacy."

"Cocktail hats," Emily said. "And going out dancing. I recently watched that old movie *The Best Years of Our Lives*, and it showed people in dinner clubs, looking so glamorous and dancing. We should call Azam and get him to bring another Martha Graham guy. What did he say to you? So, you see, I'm not just a Graham man? . . . We should go out dancing. It would be different, don't ya think?"

"You mean like a double date?"

"Nooo. Just friends having fun."

Margret didn't say anything.

"You know," Emily said, pouring herself more wine, "I didn't tell you this, but he called to ask why you weren't returning his calls. He said he thought you might like to go to a movie or something."

Margret's face was getting warm.

"He's such a sweetie. I don't see why—"

"You know very well why."

"It's not about him; it's about being out in the world. And I saw you two dancing at the gala and you were having fun."

"Because I was drunk on those damn manhattans you ordered. I got really sick that night."

Emily looked confused.

"You're angry about manhattans?"

"I'm not dating," Margret said.

"Right."

There was half a bottle left. Margret got up and took it into the kitchen, corked it, and put it in the fridge. Then she came back into the living room.

"Well, that was obnoxious," Emily said. "But when Margret has decided to end a conversation"—she said it singsongy—"it's over." She cocked her head and smiled. "Margret is done, so we can all go home."

Emily lifted her chin. She was studying Margret as if she'd never seen her before. Margret regretted having put the wine away like that, but didn't know what to do now, so she sat down on the other couch, staring back.

Emily angled her body toward Margret and leaned forward.

"Do you ever put anyone else first anymore?"

The question floated there.

"Do you ever think of me?" Emily asked. "And even now, saying this to you, I have to be careful with you, because of Charles. But have you ever thought about *my* life? How all those years you had that wonderful man"—her face seemed to lose structure, as if something had slipped under the skin—"and I had no one? I've never had anything like what you've had. But it's me who has to whisper around you. And walk on eggs. And watch every word. How long"—her voice broke on the word "long,"—"before someone is careful with me?"

There were tears in her eyes.

Margret moved quickly to the other couch, sat beside Emily, and put her arm around her shoulders, while Emily, who really wasn't a crier, wiped away each tear with her finger. From eye to eye, each tear caught before it fell.

"I'm sorry," Margret whispered, hugging her. "I'm sorry."

"I must be more tired than I thought," Emily said. "And I drank too much. Let's get my couch made up."

Margret woke in the blue-green bedroom. She remembered that Emily was out on the couch and that this uneasy feeling was because of their fight. Not a fight exactly, more Emily telling her what a bad friend she'd been. And even as she'd wanted to plead, *You can't understand*, she knew Emily was right, that Emily had been giving more, way more, to the friendship. I could tell her about Joe, she thought, tell her what happened in the Boiler Room and how he'd said something similar. But then Em might take it wrong, see it as criticism, being lumped with Joe. Margret hadn't told Emily so many things, and she'd played down leaving Saks, said nothing about the snow, only that she was ready for a change and she could always go back.

It was eight fifteen in the morning and the house was still. Emily was either asleep or maybe already out doing a run. Margret got up, her head a little throbby, and on the way to the bathroom looked into the living room. No Emily. Once in the kitchen she wondered if she should make coffee or go to Wawa for some, and then she heard a sound, a floorboard creaking upstairs. She ran to the stairs and looked up. The door was open.

"Emily?"

"You get up here right now."

That damn door. She ran up the stairs and saw Emily standing at the long table in her pj's, looking at one of the boxes. Then Emily looked at Margret.

"What are these?"

"Just something I'm playing around with."

Emily looked odd. Margret couldn't tell if she was peeved or puzzled?

"So this is what you're doing when you don't pick up the phone? Why didn't you tell me about these?"

"Because there's nothing to tell."

Emily lifted one up and held it at arm's length.

"That you're spending your time arranging stuffed birds in shadow boxes is nothing? At the very least it's an extremely strange hobby."

She studied the box she was holding.

"They're like your windows for Flow, only smaller. Did you order these birds from somewhere?"

"I found them."

Emily raised her eyebrows.

"I found them near buildings where they crash during migration. It's a collection."

"Taxidermy is a kind of folk art," Emily said, picking up another box, a vertical, the one with the hermit thrush. The inside rims and back were painted a deep lavender, which Margret had waxed and then overlaid with black, then silver, for a stippled, twilight effect. The box contained a tall forest of bare branches, and on the ground, dried sprigs of white lilac, a pale understory. Here the thrush was positioned with its bill raised, about to sing. Oh, that bright eye turned out well. And then something Margret had found in a Cape May junk shop, an old enamel watch face without hands. She'd hung it on a branch—a pale moon.

"Tell me about this," Emily said.

"It's a hermit thrush. They only sing in the forests where they nest. Some say they have the most beautiful song of all birds. It figures in the poem by Whitman—that's why I used the white lilacs."

Emily moved to the box with the brilliant Blackburnian.

"And this?"

Margret had been through so many sketches with this one, trying to get simpler, closer. Finally, she lined the entire box with sand gathered at the Point and mixed with glue. Before it dried she combed it into fine, tight waves, like the waters depicted on the walls in Sennacherib's palace, with those little curls for tides and crests. It was a painstaking process. Into this void she placed the warbler in its dive.

"He's the sun," she said. "I posed him so you could see the stripy head and blazing breast."

"Mar. The birds are beautiful, but it's the world in the boxes that's compelling. There are eight here. Do you have more?"

It was clear where Emily was going.

"It's illegal," Margret said. "You're not allowed to take these birds even dead from the ground. You're not allowed to stuff them. I did it anyway, but if they were displayed, I could be arrested."

"Oh, please. No one made a peep about that sparrow in my window, which I now assume was yours. Do you have more?"

"Four, soon five, in New York . . . but this isn't a joke. The guys from Fish and Wildlife just swoop in. I talked to an antiques dealer whose tortoise sewing scissors were taken at customs."

"Don't tell Fanchon about that; she'll be crushed."

"There are dealers who specialize in hundred-year-old mounts, which are theoretically legal because they predate the law, and still they can't display the stuff. It all goes out of the back room, like a speakeasy."

"Enough. It's my risk to take. I knew you had an amazing eye, but this is something else."

"Obviously they're influenced by Cornell."

"All shadow boxes are. There's no getting away from it. Gloria Vanderbilt had a show of Lucite boxes about a year ago, down at K S Art, and it wasn't an issue at all. She used nineteenth-century iconography and girlish things, dolls, crosses, glitter; it was memory and desire, sort of Frida Kahlo in an ice cube. You know, hot and cold. But these are coming out of a whole other tradition. Naturalist collectors and museum dioramas. I mean, didn't Audubon stuff and wire birds as models?"

Margret nodded. It was constantly surprising how much Emily knew. She was now looking at the black-and-white warbler, so zebra-like in his jungle of pressed ferns.

"But dioramas feel dead and these have a breathing feeling, like secret rooms somewhere."

"That's what I was trying for. Air."

"They're dark, but not a human darkness."

"I tried not to use man-made objects, except when I had to."

"Uh-huh. It's as if the birds themselves found these places."

Margret knew she'd created something. And now someone else knew too. Emily was beaming.

"We'll go to the Ebbitt Room tonight to celebrate. We can plan it out. I wonder what the title of the show should be? I know. How obvious. Windows!"

SPRING MIGRATION

Twenty-nine

MARGRET THOUGHT SHE WAS GOING to burst with pride. The invitation said five to seven, and here it was five thirty and the gallery was full. There were people she didn't know, art-world people, she guessed, maybe birding people too. And there were people she knew well: her parents over at the hermit thrush talking with Jay Marti and his beautiful wife, Cara; her aunts Bett and Bethany by the palm warblers; and two Connecticut cousins just ahead of them, looking at the ovenbird. Tom and Tina and Stephen had arrived as a group and then fanned out. And ohhh, Sasha was just coming in the door. Sasha! He'd actually left Eleventh Street to come to Twenty-fourth.

"Daaaling," he said, exhaling the last puff he'd taken at the door, looking like a vestige of Saint Petersburg in his black twill redingote and skintight jeans, his platinum hair brilliantined like Count Vronsky and expensive scent coming off him, something, she thought, by JAR. "Let me look at you."

She took a step back so he could see her in her new dress, a sleeveless sheath of pearl gray mousseline de laine, courtesy of Tina, who'd called Margret when the invitation came and said, "I've got your dress. It's Lanvin with a Balenciaga hang and genius seaming over the bust, simple and perfect for you. We'll use my discount. So get over here." Even with the discount it was expensive, but her parents told her they'd pay, and she had on her pearls and her hair was down and she'd bought a new pair of oystery slingback pumps. It all felt like a dream, like she was floating, but it wasn't a dream; she knew how much work went into her birds.

"Already you're drifting away," Sasha said. Then he gave her three kisses—left cheek, right cheek, left cheek, because Russians did three not two—and then went to look at the show.

Emily was working the room. Margret had seen her work countless rooms at countless parties, but it was strange to think, She's working the room for me. Emily was now standing next to a tall man and nodding. They were looking at the thrush.

"Margret."

It was Nan Schifman. She gave Margret a quick hug.

"We had no idea you were an artist," she said, plucking a glass of champagne from a passing tray. "The invitation took us totally by surprise. I mean, we've loved your windows, but *this* . . ." She made a small arc with her glass of champagne.

"I'm glad you're here."

"You know, with work, and now with redoing the London apartment, though it really isn't the smartest timing because the dollar's dropping, well, I've been so tied to the phone that it's just a treat to get out."

Margret just kept smiling and nodding.

"Lee's still looking at the boxes. I told him to pay special attention to the blue warblers."

The black-throated blues. The box was filled with a bower of branches painted bone, ivory, and cream, while the back of the box and the inside rims had steep color, a midnight blue she'd leafed with tiny silver stars. The two birds flitted within. Tamino and Pamina.

"Do you like that one?"

"It feels like morning and night at the same time."

Tom had come up behind Nan and was hovering impatiently enough that Nan glanced over her shoulder. She turned back to Margret and said, "I'll find Lee. He'll want to say hello." Then she trickled into the crowd.

"So, doll," Tom said, looking absolutely the same as the last time she'd seen him and sounding as if there hadn't been a five-month silence. "I have to go. But I feel like now I know where you've been. Shall we say, *snowed* into these boxes?"

They both laughed, and with a whispered "brava," he left just as Emily brought up a young couple for introduction. Margret worked hard to concentrate on names, but it was hopeless. There seemed always to be another person waiting to say who they were, and what they liked, and congratulations, and by the time they moved on, the name was gone. It was only six, with another hour to go, but the ebb and flow of the party around her, as if she were the only fixed object in the room, it made her feel like that auk on the rock, alone in the froth. Off to the side she saw her mother, who waved at her with a champagne smile and then burst out laughing at something Bett must have said. When her mom first saw the boxes, she'd been speechless. Well, not speechless, but there wasn't a single canted remark. She simply said,

"They're beautiful." And her dad looked at Margret as if refocusing, and said, "They really are just yours."

"Mar. This is Matthew Dunning from the Museum of Natural History. He's a curator there."

"Ornithology," he said, shaking her hand. "Nice to meet you."

"And you."

He was somewhere in his thirties, in jeans and tweed with unruly brown hair, a real nature-guy smile in his dark blue eyes, which were level with hers. She knew his type. He was a grown-up version of the bird boys they saw at the Point, the ones who manned the hawkwatch platform and the dyke at Higbee's, calling specks going over based on wingbeats, a *zeet*, a frisson of color in the coverts. It was bird-watching raised to the state of feathered calculus, a level of perception she'd seen Charles silently admire, seen him silently feeling it was a place he'd never reach. You had to start so young, or you had to bird all day every day, and he was already so brilliant but not at this. And yet he wanted this too, even as he knew there wasn't time. It was too late; he was already near fifty.

"I'm in charge of the collection," Matthew Dunning was saying. "I collect old taxidermy, though now it's pretty much out of my price range."

"I saw a lot of stuffed birds growing up. My grandfather was a birder and also an entomologist. He had a magnificent black-crowned night heron. Lord Heron, we called it."

"Did he bird with a shotgun?"

"You mean the days when you didn't look, you took?"

"Yeah. Those ravishing euphemisms."

"No shotgun, because he wasn't that old. Though he did tell me about Franklin Roosevelt turning green from the arsenic."

"So the heron wasn't his work?"

"It was a mount from the 1880s, I think. In a huge glass dome. Whoever did it put a piece of mercury glass among the reeds, to be the marsh. I used to look it at and think I could dive in there and get to another world."

"Beyond the looking glass?"

"More like *The Little Mermaid*, the real story, by Hans Christian Andersen."

"I've never read the original, just seen those pink Disney dolls all over the place."

"Well, it's pretty punitive, sort of Protestant gothic. But I always remembered the underwater palace that had walls of coral and windows of amber. And I guess I've always thought birding was like that too, like you're going through a curtain and leaving human time behind."

"Time," he said. "I'm not going to ask the sixty-four-thousand-dollar question, because why ruin the fun. But we both know these birds aren't old."

Margret didn't know how much he was going to make of this. She wasn't going to lie, but she didn't have to answer either.

"I would never kill a bird," she said.

He tipped his head back as if thinking about it. "Let's just say I'd kill for these mounts. The museum's short on passerines."

She wanted to ask him which he liked best, but that would presume he liked them, and he might really disapprove of what she'd done. And yet of everyone here, his opinion mattered the most in a way, so she said, "Is one better than the others?"

He looked down, so she looked down too, at his scuffed loafers. Then he looked up and said, "The Blackburnian's dive is perfect, the position of the wings. But the hermit thrush . . . I can hear it. Anyway, I wanted to meet the maker, and now I have. Maybe we'll cross paths birding sometime."

"I'm mostly in Riverside Park."

"Alas, I'm in Central."

He put out his hand and they shook a second time. As Matthew turned for the door, Margret noticed two of Charles's Columbia colleagues moving into the gallery. What would they think?

"Bethany and I are going back to the hotel"—it was Aunt Bett whispering in her ear—"and we'll meet you for dinner at eight." They were all going to Gramercy Tavern after the party. Her parents, aunts, Emily, and herself.

And then Azam was standing in front of her, looking much as he had the night they met, sculpted in heaven and dropped to earth.

"The girl who never returned my calls," he cried softly, his green eyes light on hers, but steady.

She hadn't returned his calls, because she couldn't. She hated what she'd done, the weakness of it, but the memory of the pleasure of it wouldn't rinse away. She didn't know what to say.

"It's fantastic," he said, gesturing toward the boxes. "Like little theaters in the sky. And the forest too."

"Azam," Emily exclaimed, zooming in for a kiss. Then she whispered to Margret, "The *Times* is here," then zoomed off, leaving Margret and Azam staring at each other.

"How have you been?" she asked, knowing she should be saying, I'm sorry.

"Dancing, rehearsing, touring. And also making my own dance. I'm trying to."

"That's wonderful."

"Maybe. It's not so easy. But Margret . . ." He smiled crushingly and then took her up into one of his hugs, that faint scent of lemon in his hair. When he let her go, Sasha was standing there, looking from Azam to Margret.

"Who is this Raphael standing over you?" he said, eyes narrowed. He was always suspicious of too much male beauty.

"Sasha," she said, "this is Azam, a dancer with the Martha Graham Company. Azam, Sasha is an artist and illustrator."

"A dancer," Sasha said dubiously, holding out a bloodless hand.

"Isn't she great?" Azam gushed.

"Yes," he said slowly, this time narrowing his eyes on her, "she *is* great." And then he was bumped from the side by a hip twenty-something to whose sleek back he gave a lashing look. "Voilà. Too many people. I'll call you tomorrow to analyze your elegies." And with a quick bow and twirl, he was gone.

"It's our end of the table," Azam said, as Lee Grovenor walked up in Russia's wake. Yes, it was Margret, Azam, and Lee.

Azam took Margret's hand in his. "I have to go too. The theater."

"I'm glad you came," she said. And she realized it was true, because even with that long cool hand holding her smaller one, those beautiful fingers curling, she felt herself on the other side of something, as if that night between them was in a box, behind glass, breathing darkness and sadness but no longer tormenting.

He turned his smile from Margret to Lee, shook his hand, and left.

"Congratulations," Lee said.

"Thank you. And thank you for being here."

"You're welcome."

Since the dinner party Margret had thought of Lee as a friend, but she'd forgotten how hard it was to get him talking.

"It's been just about a year since your dinner party."

"It has, hasn't it? We haven't done as much entertaining lately. I've been traveling for work, and Nan's trying to redecorate the London flat from New York."

"That can't be easy."

"No," he said, looking at her expectantly.

He really was an owl. Happy in silence.

"Nan said she liked the black-throated blues," Margret said.

"It's her favorite."

"I think of them as Tamino and Pamina."

"Man and wife," he said, "wife and man, attain the level of divinity."

Margret knew the line. It was from *The Magic Flute*. Pamina sang it with Papageno, the bird catcher.

"That *is* what the box is about," he continued, "isn't it?"

Margret loved Lee. Not a wanting-him kind of love; she just loved what he was.

"But you like another one better?"

"The sparrow," he said.

It was the last box she'd done. She'd filled it with dead leaves, stacked sideways one atop another, overlapping like strata in stone, so that the eye faced hundreds of edges and ledges of shadow. The bird, a humble little song sparrow, was laid in low, a wing faintly unfolded like Marat's fallen arm, its half open, sunken eye made with a mix of Elmer's glue and black paint. The sparrow was hard to see from more than three feet away, blending with the potato beiges of the leaves, the russet browns, compressed color in a forest floor.

"It's something like Veruschka's *Transfigurations*," he said, "but sadder."

"It was strange that I made it dead. I didn't decide it. I just knew it should be."

"Why is the show called Windows?" he asked.

"It was Emily's idea, because I do windows. But it made another kind of sense, because the birds were killed crashing into windows. Do you think . . . ?"

Lee seemed not to be listening. His head was turned toward the entrance of Flow, where a murmur, a blur, *something* was coming through the crowd, a change in the atmosphere and heads turning. In her inky satin Emily shot past, swift, and Lee looked questioningly at Margret, then back to the growing commotion. Margret pushed through to get a view. Maybe an actor had come in. An entourage. She saw four big men in suits. One of them stood in front of Emily, holding a gold badge to her face. Mom came up and gripped Margret's arm.

"What's going on?" she asked.

Margret wanted to say, "I don't know," but she did know.

The men swept through the crowd, people shaking their heads amid the rising level of sound, and began taking the boxes off the walls. They were walking out with them, one in each hand. Emily was practically nose to nose with the head guy.

"This art is private property," she said, "and many pieces are sold."

"They are officially unsold," he said, thrusting a document into her hand. "You are in violation of a U.S. statute, the Migratory Bird Treaty Act, and this art," he said, "is being seized under Section 706, which restricts any wildlife that is taken, possessed, transported, or sold illegally."

"*Be careful!*" Emily cried as one of the men went by with three boxes, the third slipping from under his arm. She reached to take it from him and the chief extended his arm, barring her from the box.

"Tell them to be careful," she implored. "These boxes are fragile."

"You're lucky we're not arresting you."

Emily rounded on him. "You have nothing better to do? This country's at war, and you're confiscating *shadow boxes*?"

He chose to ignore her, took a last look at the empty walls, and strode out like Elliot Ness, guests hissing as he passed. Margret's mother was looking fraught and offended, a unique combination, while her father was making his way over from across the room. People were looking at each other, stunned but already recovering, and Emily, who had seemed so small next to that man, now looked rather dashing up on a chair, clapping for attention.

"Obviously, the show's over for tonight. But the party isn't over til seven. So have another drink, leave your address in the ledger at the front desk, and I'll send you an update on the show once we've spoken to our lawyers."

Margret still hadn't moved. Rooted in a party that had imploded, she just stared at the empty walls, all her work gone. Emily hadn't yet said a word to her. She was busy talking to a woman with a notepad.

"What happened?" her father asked. Her mother looked like she'd been hit with a brick.

"Using these birds was illegal," Margret explained, "even though they were dead. And stuffing them too. It's really two violations."

"But I see stuffed ducks all the time."

"They're game birds, Dad. These aren't."

"Did you know that when you did all this?"

It was not something she could explain. It was never something she could explain.

"Yes."

People began to drift out, and Emily finally came over, her expression consoling, her eyes bright.

"I'm sorry, Margret. We got caught. I'll call my dad, and we'll see what our options are."

"Do you think it was Matthew Dunning? From the museum?"

"I don't know. Was there time for it to be him?"

Margret shrugged and shook her head. She didn't know either.

"Are you okay?" Emily asked.

"I'm too stunned even to be embarrassed. I mean, at least we weren't arrested."

"Violations result in fines," Emily said, "rarely arrests. By law this can't cost more than two thousand dollars. Why don't you and your parents go ahead to the restaurant and I'll—"

"You still want to go out?"

Emily grabbed Margret's shoulders.

"It was a big success. Eight of the boxes were sold. Do you know who took the hermit thrush?"

Margret shook her head no.

"*Einstein on the Beach*. Robert Wilson!"

"The tall guy you were talking to?"

"Yes. With that kind of recognition, you're made."

"But it's all gone."

"The boxes are gone. You're not."

Thirty

New York, N.Y., April 16—One is used to strange sights at Flow, Chelsea's unpredictable, high-profile purveyor of the guild arts. And one is used to stuffed birds at Teddy Roosevelt's pile on the park, the American Museum of Natural History. What happens when you put the two together? The Feds. Just as Flow's cocktail party for its new show, Windows, was in full swing last Saturday, officers from the U.S. Fish and Wildlife Service arrived with an order to confiscate all artwork, which they did in less than ten minutes. Flow owner Emily Edwards and artist Margret Snow were not arrested, but will likely be fined.

It has been almost four years since the city's last legal skirmish in an art gallery, when Mary Boone displayed a bowl of live bullets in her gallery on Fifth Avenue. She was arrested and jailed for one night. This time, the art in question was an exhibition of surreal shadow boxes, each containing one or more stuffed birds, species like the hermit thrush, blue-headed vireo, song sparrow, and warblers.

All of these species, according to Chris Nutall, a spokesman for Fish and Wildlife, "are protected by the Migratory Bird Treaty Act. We are very serious about enforcing these laws. When birds migrate through our lands, we are their caretakers."

Edwards maintains that the birds died during migration, crashing into the plate-glass windows of office buildings and skyscrapers. "It's not like the artist was out there with a gun," Edwards said. "If the true concern is the death of birds, then there's a bigger issue that Fish and Wildlife should be addressing, and that's how developers use glass in urban landscapes."

Nutall concedes the point. "Birds do die on migration once they land in cities." But he defends the ban on taxidermy, no matter how the bird was obtained. "Stuffed birds are beguiling. People see them in dioramas, in bell jars, and then they want one too. It becomes fashionable and then proliferates. There's been a lot of taxidermy flooding the New York market lately. Usually it's through private sales that are hard to track. But this was brazen."

Says one downtown dealer who spoke on the condition of anonymity, "I buy in the Midwest and from universities that are deaccessioning their collections. There's a huge appetite for really good taxidermy, especially birds. I have three different designers, famous ones, who get calls the minute something comes in. But it's all down low, even though the old stuff is technically legal. The government doesn't want to hear that. They confiscate for the fun of it."

In the hour or so that the Flow show was up, the point was

proved. Eight of the thirteen boxes, priced from two thousand dollars, were already sold.

"Shadow boxes are hard to do," said Theresa Shilts, a curator at the Museum of Modern Art, "without seeming like Joseph Cornell knockoffs. These were strong in their own way."

Nancy Raglan, who says she came to the opening because she's a bird-watcher, enthused, "You can tell Ms. Snow knows birds. They don't seem trapped in these strange settings; they seem at home."

Said Matthew Dunning, a curator in ornithology at the American Museum of Natural History, who was also at the opening, "I'm a nut about taxidermy, a great, lost art. And this work was very fine. Warblers are difficult, because they're so small, so it doesn't surprise me that a woman did this." When asked if it bothered him that the work was illegal, Dunning said, "There is nothing like seeing these creatures up close, to study feather patterns and body structure. I see the need for the ban, but I also see the loss."

Preparing for her next show, Verne, a collection of mercury glass chandeliers and sconces, Flow owner Emily Edwards was philosophical. "Art often flies above the law. Look at *Lady Chatterley's Lover*. James Joyce's *Ulysses*. In our own era, the photographs of Sally Mann raised legal concerns about the consent of children. Margret Snow's boxes were like rooms in a world that nature hides from view. I'm saddened that more people won't be able to see this show." The artist, Margret Snow, who has designed windows for Saks Fifth Avenue, Lord & Taylor, and Flow, had no comment.

The article appeared on the first page of the *New York Times* Arts section, below the fold, with a color photo of Emily seated at her black lacquer desk at Flow and a smaller picture of one of the boxes, the Blackburnian. Emily would be thrilled. The photos were money in the bank. But Margret turned back to section B of the paper, which she read again with disbelief: "Experts' Pleas to Pentagon Didn't Save Museum."

The National Museum of Iraq, fondly called "Baghdad" by Charles and his cronies, all of whom had done research there at one time or another, had been sacked by Iraqi looters while American soldiers stood by and watched. She'd read the first coverage of the story on Sunday, the day after her show opened and closed, and could even then hear cries of outrage from scholars around the world. She had met some of them at a conference in London she attended with Charles, serious men who married late, supremely cultured yet with firelight in their eyes. They were the spiritual sons of Austen Henry Layard, the man who uncovered Nineveh in the mid-1800s, proving that Assyria truly existed and wasn't some biblical fantasia. And they were the scholarly offspring of James Henry Breasted, the University of Chicago Egyptologist who shifted the study of Western civ's origins from ancient Greece and Rome to the lands of Iraq and Iran. "I really should change my middle name to Henry," Charles once said.

Just such men had come to the memorial service at St. Paul's Chapel. They had come for Charles. He was, he used to joke, the second Assyrian Assyriologist in history; the first being H. Rassam, who discovered Nineveh's dying lions. One of the men who came, Charles's mentor at Chicago's Oriental Institute, could hardly bring himself to speak. He sat like stone in his chair on the aisle. When he came through the receiving line, moving slowly, his old eyes watery and red, he took Margret's hands in his two hands, mottled, veined. He said, "I loved that boy."

The article just got worse. The Pentagon was defending its inaction, claiming the military "had never promised that the buildings would be safeguarded." It was simply beyond belief. Charles would have been stunned and heartbroken. She could just hear him, in wonderment that the warmongers knew so little about military history, had no idea that the museum's artifacts and reliefs were right up their alley, all about preemptive right and the power required to keep peace. "The Assyrians were like the Borg," Charles sometimes said, "assimilating everything in their path." And what a path. An imperial swath cut north, south, east, and west. Then chiseled into marble, basalt, rock. He would have been insulted too, in his soul. This sort of war would not have been waged on a white country. It made her ill.

"American forces followed the military's plan to secure oil wells, dams and other critical sites . . . ," she read. "But they did not try to guard the National Museum. . . ."

The phone rang.

"Can you believe the publicity?" Emily trilled from downtown. "Front page of the Arts section. But Mar, that's not the best of it. I had a meeting late yesterday with Matt Dunning at the Museum of Natural History. It was Matt, me, and the museum's lawyer, Alexander Kolb. He's a former United States attorney who's now with Cadwalader. And get this: he took my dad's class at Michigan Law. He said, 'I know Dick Edwards. The go-to guy for the truly screwed.' Anyway, if a man could be a martini, he's it."

Margret didn't know Emily wanted a man who could be a martini. That aside, she hadn't heard Emily sound like this since, well, since Jeremy.

"Olive eyes and a face like flint." Emily was soaring. "Like Pasha in *Dr. Zhivago.* You know, working his jaw."

They'd both loved Pasha. He was hard where Zhivago was soft.

"We spoke Russian. Just a little, but I'm amazed at how much I remember."

Margret really wasn't in the mood for this.

"Em, I'm running late. Can we talk later?"

"Let me just say this fast. Matt Dunning doesn't want your birds rotting in a warehouse. He wants them for the museum, and he wants Alex to get them from Fish and Wildlife. So that's what the meeting was about."

"Do you think it can happen?"

"Alex thinks it can. The downside is the boxes will have to be dismantled."

Margret was silent.

"But Matt did say he would welcome your input on how to display the birds. He really respects what you've done."

"And you don't think he cued the Feds so he could get the birds?"

"I don't. He could have just hired you to stuff some birds."

"I guess so. I'd like to believe he's a nice guy."

"Oh, everything's turning out so well," Emily sang.

"How can you say that? Your gallery's empty and my boxes are destroyed."

"I *am* angry that more people didn't get to see your work. I've been getting a lot of calls about it."

"Really? What are people saying?"

"They want to know if there's any way to see the boxes. And if you're making them under the table."

"It's not like anyone can stop me, unless they follow me around. I still can't believe the government found out."

"Well, maybe someone saw one of the invites."

"Yeah, but how? It's not like you advertised in the *Times*. Does

Fish and Wildlife read arts listings? I doubt it. And I don't think you ever used the word 'taxidermy' anywhere."

"I didn't."

"When I told people about the show, I just said shadow boxes; I didn't even mention the birds. Maybe Joe did it. Maybe he saw Tom or Tina's invitation. And yet, I don't think he would."

No, she thought, he wouldn't.

"Mar."

"What?"

"It doesn't matter who. They were going to find out anyway. Sooner was better than later."

"No. Later would have been better."

There was silence on the other end, a silence strangely aloof, not really sympathetic. It was Emily on that chair in the gallery, so swift, so in control.

"How did you know what the amount of the fine would be?" Margret asked. "And that it would be a fine and not jail time?"

"Because I did research, as any responsible entrepreneur would do. I was following up on what you told me."

Margret knew Emily too well. She knew this tone. She knew this lightness was defensive. She knew.

"*You* told," Margret said. "It was you."

"Now just listen before you judge. Just because they knew about the show didn't mean they'd come. I put it out there and left it to fate, yes. Why not? You were never going to be able to make a career with those birds because it's against the law. I made a decision. To put you on the map and me in the spotlight."

Margret's mouth was hanging open.

"As for the sales, there was never going to be a profit, because again there was a finite amount of time before we got caught. You now have collectors who want to buy your work. Reviews may still come. We took pictures of everything. You can build on that."

"What work?"

"Your eye. Your imagination. You don't need birds."

"You sold me out."

"You're not being reasonable."

Margret couldn't cry, speak, move, or think. Couldn't see beyond her knees, her feet, the floor. She could hardly breathe.

"*Please* don't be mad at me," Emily begged.

"I don't know what I am," Margret said. And hung up.

Thirty-one

THERE WERE A LOT of notes and calls after the *Times* article appeared. Distant relatives, Columbia acquaintances, long-lost friends from Vanderbilt, even her best friend from grade school, whom Margret hadn't heard from in twenty years. She'd gotten a call from the visuals manager at Tiffany. It didn't get any better than Tiffany. He wanted to take her to lunch, and that was exciting. Matt Dunning called to give her an update on the birds, which were indeed going to the museum. He envisioned a warbler diorama with one tree, a New York City tree, and different species feeding in different sectors, just as they did in life. "I once had eleven species in a Central Park pin oak," he said. "I see it like that." She had to remind him that all told she'd stuffed only ten species of warbler—"Ten'll do"—and that the ovenbird would be happier on the ground. "Of course," he said. It comforted her to know the birds would have a home together.

That morning, the vice president of the Linnaean Society had called to see if she might give a lecture on her recent experience. "They won't throw vegetables at me?" Margret asked. "They'll be fascinated," he assured her. She told him she'd get back to him.

And now this. She was sitting on the couch with the mail on her lap, staring at a typewritten note on letterhead stationery. It said Jonathan Brookoff Dance Company, in sans serif type. Clipped to the letter was a xerox of a short story, "The Nightingale and the Rose" by Oscar Wilde. She went back to the letter, which read:

> *Dear Margret Snow,*
> *My name is Jonathan Brookoff, and I am the head of my own small dance company. I am planning a new work for my next engagement at Dance Theatre Workshop, based on the Oscar Wilde short story, "The Nightingale and the Rose" (see attached). The premiere is next October. This piece is of a bigger scope than usual for my company, and it will require our first set, more of a mise-en-scène really.*
>
> *I am writing to you because I went to your opening at Flow and was struck by your beautiful boxes. It occurred to me you might bring a unique perspective to the stage. Do you have any interest in designing for the theater? Could we meet and discuss the possibility? I can't pay much, but I've got a following and I get reviewed (see clips).*
>
> *My number is below, so I hope you'll call. Oh, please note the highlighted line in the story. I don't know why, but it made me think of your boxes.*

Margret flipped to the story, turned the page, and saw lines marked with yellow: "Yet Love is better than Life, and what is the heart of a bird compared to the heart of a man?"

Margret read the story from beginning to end. It was about a nightingale who trades her life for a rose, a bloom forced from her own blood on a thorn in the night. She does this for the young student she loves, who has foolishly promised a red rose, out of season, to a vain young woman he admires. When he brings her the rose, she spurns it, preferring to wear a jewel, the more costly gift of another suitor. The rose is thrown into the street.

So all the themes were there. Art and life. Ecstatic sacrifice versus banal desire. The loss inherent in love. All so effortlessly pressed into the writing. Wilde loves beauty, Margret thought, but he isn't afraid of emptiness. She could see that the stage should reflect that.

A hanging window frame.

A perching bough.

A latticed archway climbing with ivy.

And somehow, the barren rosebush.

She wondered if it was appropriate to suggest that the final rose not be a prop, but a dancer. Don't get ahead of yourself, she thought. It's only a meeting. Don't go in with preconceived ideas. See how he thinks. Still, she could see the night of the transformation, the moon laying a silver path across the floor of the stage, and the path withdrawn at the approach of golden dawn.

Margret walked to the east window. The sun was high and south of Saint John the Divine, where it always was around noon.

You know what you need to do now?

It was in this room he'd said it.

Store windows are stages.

That Friday night, before they'd ever kissed, even then he could see what she might do. And he'll never know I got there, she thought, that he planted the seed and it grew. She leaned her head against the jamb and closed her eyes.

Don't you dare think of leaving.

I don't want to leave.

Thirty-two

CHARLOTTE WAS ASKING TO SEE MARGRET. "Your grandmother has a question she says only you can answer," Margret's mother said on the phone. "And only in person. So please take the train up, and sooner rather than later, because none of us are getting any younger."

The Beecham house was one of those coveted old colonials, yellow with white trim, angled into the expensive wedge of land between Brattle Street and the Charles River. You could walk to the house from the Harvard T station, about half a mile, which is why Margret always used a backpack when she came up to Cambridge. It had once itself been a backpack of a town, but boy, the Square had changed. It was shiny now, full of franchises you'd find anywhere. Starbucks, Origins, Abercrombie & Fitch. It wasn't scruffy anymore, no longer a place of wire rims and dirty jeans, dusty bookstores and student dives.

Margret knew Cambridge mostly from her August visits, and like all university towns, it was somewhat forlorn in August and seemed to be saying, go, go to Gloucester.

By the time she was sixteen, Margret could appreciate the scruffy intellectual aura, the almost migratory sensation of the place, summer students about to leave, undergrads about to arrive, and always the inevitable hangers-on, scholars uncertain, unfinished, unable to leave the nest. She wasn't in such a hurry then to get to the shore, wasn't as keen to swim, bird, or help Milton with his insects. The day or two before they left, she longed to go sit with a frappé at Café Algiers, or to leaf through volumes of poetry at the Grolier bookshop, or to hang out in the Square at twilight. She would think of reasons to run out, chores that needed to be done. It must have been so transparent. We need more milk; I'll go. She'd watch the summer-school kids pass by, living it up, and the grad students who'd stayed on for the summer, so romantic in their narrow striving, their pallor of the stacks. She'd walk very slowly back to the house, to the ticking clock and the panes of glass. It was like a Vermeer in there, circles, squares, and the lengthening light, except for Molly's leaping welcome from low haunches, her clickity nails on the parquet floor, the most memorable of Beecham dogs, an incredibly sweet German shepherd.

Margret rang the bell and waited. Charlotte used to be quick to the door, but now she took some time, the bustle gone. Her beauty, however, remained. Charlotte opened the door and held out her arms for the deft hug and back pat she always gave. Her face, framed by white hair cut to the chin and tucked behind her ears, was etched with fine wrinkles that were whiskery, adding to her look of a pampered pussycat. She really should be perched on a pillow, Margret thought.

"Come in, dear. How was the trip? Are you hungry? I can heat up some coffee and make you a sandwich."

Charlotte, in ivory slacks and turquoise linen, was already heading to the kitchen.

"I ate on the train," Margret said, following. "But I'd love some coffee. And I brought milk"—she pulled a carton from a brown paper bag—"just in case."

Charlotte was notorious for having only skim milk in the fridge.

"Do you mind if I make a quick call for messages?"

"Of course not. But while you're at it, why don't you take your backpack right up to your room?"

Nothing much changed in the house. Even the smells were the same. The green Rigaud candle in the hall. The lavender in the bathrooms. The powdery scent in the bedroom Margret always used, the little blue room that had once been her mother's. In Milton's study, uninhabited now for fifteen years, an antiseptic smell, not unpleasant, still clung; though where it clung was anyone's guess. Margret sat down at his old oak desk.

She'd left Emily a message that morning, from Penn Station. They hadn't spoken since the phone call, and in that time Margret had wrestled over the whole fiasco—not just Emily's scheming but all the good things that had come of it. Would these things have come with only a show? Or did the raid make the difference? And who, finally, was more wrong? Emily for using the boxes? Or Margret, for using the birds in the first place? It wasn't as if Margret hadn't been complicit to some extent. One could argue that she should be thanking Emily, not hanging up on her. Just before boarding the train, Margret called Emily's apartment, knowing she'd get the answering service. She said she was sorry for hanging up, that she loved Emily and missed her, and that some nice things had happened. She said she was on her way to Boston and would be back on Sunday night.

Margret didn't carry a cell, so if Emily returned the call it would be to 113th Street. Margret was nervous. What if Emily didn't want to make up? What if she was done with the friendship, fed up? Margret picked up the phone and dialed. There were two messages. The first was Jay Marti, reminding her of a meeting on Tuesday. The second was Emily.

"Thank *god* you called. I've been bursting to talk to you, 'cause when I can't tell you things it's almost like they haven't happened. And this is too great to leave on a message, but it's about him. We had dinner last Sunday and I'm seeing him tomorrow night, and he's so smart and articulate, but totally grounded, and we just never stop talking and . . . well, I guess now I've told you. But there's so much more to tell, so call me. And *yesss*, I love you too. So call."

It was infectious, Emily's happiness. It was surprising, too, how well it fit her. Hearing this happiness made Margret sad for the years Emily had gone without real attention, real empathy, from her. But then Emily had told her this much last January. How strange it all was. Emily wouldn't have met Alexander Kolb if she hadn't sabotaged the show. And there would have been no show to sabotage if Margret hadn't made the boxes. And there would have been no boxes if it hadn't been for the birds. So in a way, it was a gift from them. Well, it would be a fun phone call, and she'd sneak it in tonight, once Charlotte was in bed.

She looked around the room. Lord Heron was where he always was, on the cabinet, striding through the sedge with radar red eyes and those strong green legs. He really was majestic, his tall, blown bell jar fitted to an oval platform of warping wood, and his long black bill like a broadsword. She went over to the cabinet and studied the floor of the mount, the marsh of mercury glass, a silver pool surrounded by moss more than a hundred years old and reflecting the white belly feathers of the bird. A tiny eternity it was. A fen, she thought, so exquisitely, poignantly scaled.

There on the bookshelf was the little box that had once fascinated the cousins. It contained five wheel bugs in profile, *Arilus cristatus* in graduating sizes from one-week nymph to fifty-day adult. Unique among assassins, this species had an armored prothorax, a spiked hump that resembled the cogged wheel in a watch; hence, its name. Stegosaurus bug is what the boys had called it. But it really was so Captain Nemo, that outlandish cock's-comb a bit like the *Nautilus*. Milton could never hypothesize a purpose for that hump. A baroque embellishment, he called it. Anyway, the frightening thing about *Arilus cristatus* was the beak. Viewed from above, the insect was nothing to be afraid of. But viewed from the side, you saw a long dagger slung beneath head and neck, where there was a groove for it to sheathe in. It could deliver a vicious bite that caused searing pain. And yet, wheel bugs were rarely seen. Most people lived their lives not knowing they existed.

That was Milton. He loved secretive creatures. Rails, herons, Family Reduviidae. When he died, a cerebral hemorrhage that caught him in the cool darkness before anyone was up, it didn't seem such a terrible way to go, down in the kitchen, preparing his thermos for a dawn doing what he loved. Scanning, stalking, listening alone.

"Coffee's ready."

Margret came down the stairs and through the dining room. Charlotte had set the kitchen table with cups and saucers, two plates with scones, and was pouring milk into the Old Paris creamer.

"Mom said you had something you wanted to ask me."

"It's about my memory, which isn't what it used to be. I can remember minutia from my childhood, but not last week's weather. Do you want some butter for your scone?"

"No, thanks."

"I can't remember where the place is," Charlotte said. "Milton mentioned it now and then."

"What place?"

"He told me where he wanted to be scattered, but now I can't remember. I thought I'd written it down—the way to the glen—but I've searched all the drawers where I put things so I won't forget them. And nothing. Anyway, I need to know so when the time comes we can be scattered together."

The glen? She must mean the glade.

"But I thought you'd scattered his ashes," Margret said.

"Why would you think that?"

"I don't know. I just assumed it was something one does soon after. So are his ashes here?"

"Of course. And that I haven't forgotten. They're in the cabinet in his study. I put them in the big brown biscuit tin."

Margret was dumbfounded.

"Couldn't you have found something better than a biscuit tin? And a brown one at that?"

"Why? He loved those biscuits. Do you want another scone?"

Margret shook her head no. Theater of the absurd, she was going to tell Mom.

"Back to my question. Do you know where the place is?"

"If you mean the *glade*, yes."

"That's it. The glade. I was thinking glen. Can we go tomorrow to see it?"

"It's a jaunt; it's in the nature reserve near Cape Ann."

"Good. We can swing by the shore house and see if the caretaker has mulched the beds. Meanwhile, we're having dinner at Bett's tonight. So in about an hour, I'd say, we should be ready to go."

"But that means we're leaving at four thirty."

"Just in time for cocktails."

"And the drive home!" Margret regaled over the phone, down in the kitchen once Charlotte was asleep. "I had one hand on the dashboard and the other on the door. She was oblivious. Though at least she goes slow. But enough on that . . . tell me about Alexander. You've gone out once already."

"Sunday," Emily said, "and a second date tomorrow night. I don't even know how to begin. I mean, we speak the same language. Like we're picking up where we left off in another life. And he's so handsome, though I suppose some people might think he's too pale and severe. You can see him listening. But he's sharp when he talks, right to the quick of things."

"I hear a difference just in the way *you* talk about him."

Not blithe, Margret thought, but carefully, on that tightrope of wanting him to be the one and fearing he's the one, because then what if you lose him?

"He's leaving Cadwalader. He says he's tired of corporate work and misses prosecution. So he's going back into government. I love that."

"So he's sharp like your dad, but he's going after the bad guys."

"Yeah."

"And what was the first date like?"

"It was really simple. We met midway at Balthazar, because both of us were coming from work, and we just stayed and stayed. When we left, it was really late and deserted. We started walking to Prince Street, and then he just stopped and kissed me. One of those in-between kisses that are so romantic."

"Like in old movies."

"Yeah. And then he walked me all the way home. Thank god I had on those lowish Pradas. And then goodnight kisses at the door. I'd forgotten how wonderful kissing is. You know, it's been a long time."

"I know."

"But I'm not going to rush this."

"There's no reason to."

"I just can't wait to see him again."

The next morning Margret volunteered to drive because she couldn't stand Charlotte's rolling stops. Charlotte shouldn't be driving at all, she thought; her eyesight wasn't great and her night vision was awful. Margret settled behind the wheel of the car. The old blue coupe was long gone, though still mourned by Mom, who thought it symbolic of something, though just what she never quite said. Charlotte's latest car was a white Volvo, yet another one that looked good with her hair. Margret turned the key, noting the sturdy purr, and took Charlotte's directions to I-95, where her own memory kicked in, the northward drive as familiar as a face.

"So, Charlotte, I had dinner with Jack a few months ago."

"How is he?"

"He's fantastic. Great job, good perks, handsome as ever."

"You know, Margret, I've been wondering something."

"Uh-huh?"

"Do you think Jack could be gay?"

"Wow! I didn't think you knew what gay was."

"Oh, please. Just because I don't discuss these things doesn't mean I don't know about them."

"Okay, but why do you ask?"

"It's just a feeling I have. He's not married yet, for one thing; he's so noncommittal. But there's also that air of availability he has."

"Here's the difference. I always saw him as being unavailable. Or rather, uncatchable. But maybe they're the same thing. Because I've wondered about him too. Have you ever asked Aunt Bett?"

"Heavens, no. My three daughters can have infinite success in the world, but one little comment from me, it's criticism. I really can't say anything. I've become positively meek."

Charlotte would never be meek.

"Anyway," Margret said, and here she slowed down, "when I saw Jack, he told me something I'd never known. That you were married to Milton's older brother Ned. How could I have reached thirty-two without knowing that?"

"Because it was put to bed long ago."

"But I'm interested to know about it."

"I'm not sure it's your business to know about it, or Jack's, for that matter."

"But here you were just wondering about Jack. And it is family history."

Charlotte sighed.

"When I was ten, my family moved to the same block as the Beechams. I loved Ned from the first minute I saw him, at a church luncheon. I had on a pink dress I hated. He was the tallest of the boys, and his hair was slicked down. He was three years older than me; Milton was one year older, and weird, always off to the side, in the ends of the day, dawn and dusk with his bugs and birds. But Ned, he was a dream, with deep dimples and his warm laugh, the kind of laugh that includes everyone in the room. Being older, he paid no special attention to me. Not until I was at Boston Conservatory and he was at business school. We crossed paths at a concert and then he did pay attention. And then came the war. We married before he and Milton went overseas, a quick marriage, as people did in those days. A year and a half later the plane crashed in the English Channel."

It was a series of snapshots really. The pink dress, the slicked hair, the concert, the marriage, the crash. In water, like Charles, but in war. Margret let the car fill with quiet.

"It was . . . well, I don't have to tell you. The sun goes out. And there's no word for that."

Charlotte was looking straight ahead, as if seeing what she was going to say.

"That's what a premature death always does. The sun goes out. Obviously it wasn't unexpected. There were countless deaths. But bad things didn't happen to Beechams. Then this did. And I hadn't gotten pregnant, so there was nothing left of Ned."

"And then?"

"It wasn't my finest hour. They sent me to a place . . . for a rest. I wasn't there long, a few weeks. It has a dreamlike feeling to me now, not a good dream, but not a bad one either, just fragments. Milton was back. He came to see me every other day. He said, Leave here. Go back to the conservatory. Finish your degree; Ned would want that. So Milton was taking care of me. And maybe himself through me. I was comforted by the ways he was like Ned. The eyes, the hands, that they were still in the world. But eventually I loved him for something else, something I needed, how tough he was. It was a strange way to form a marriage, but there you are. He gave up science and took Ned's place in the bank. I don't think he minded; he never said he did. You're like Milton. You're tough."

Margret didn't know what to say.

"By the way, dear, I'm sorry about your show . . . the birds and all."

"It's okay. It's not like I was raised to be a taxidermist."

"I should say not."

Margret saw the turnoff, pulled in, and parked the car.

"Okay, Charlotte, this is the reserve. I'm going to write this down, starting with 'Park in the visitors area.' "

Taking the notepad with her, Margret went around to the passenger side so Charlotte could lean on her if she needed to. Charlotte waved her away. They walked slowly across the gravel, and Margret wondered if Charlotte could manage this.

"Now, things might be changed from the days when Milton and I used to come here."

He had died in the autumn of 1988, when Margret was seventeen. That was her last August in Gloucester, so it was fifteen years ago. They had always entered on the left side, and though there was fancy new signage, and now a color-coded map of paths—the .5-mile, the 1-mile, the 1.5-mile—the left entrance was still there. If Margret remembered correctly, the glade was reached at that baby-toe squiggle on the one-mile path. You left the path at that point, wove through a stand of cedars, and it was just beyond—a secret place.

"So it's about one mile total," Margret warned.

"Why do you think I wore my walking shoes?"—a spike of irritation—"Let's go."

Margret was surprised that so many landmarks had lasted. The huge gray rock, vaguely the shape of a ram's head, still flanked the footbridge, which was now aluminum. The five weeping willows along the creek, much bigger now, their boughs brushing the bank, were the same waterfall of green. The second wooden footbridge, also aluminum, led to the long straight path through a meadow.

The sun was high but it was a cool day, the first Saturday in May.

There were warblers above, stitching the air with song, the first flush of spring migrants, but Margret ignored them, concentrating on the path.

Charlotte walked steadily and silently as Margret announced the landmarks, then jotted them down in the pad. And then the path looped and there were the cedars. Margret motioned for Charlotte to follow her off the path, and just as always, beyond the cedars, a peculiar clearing opened under oaks and locusts. It was the glade, just coming in green, but so much the same. The grass wasn't wavy, because it wasn't long enough yet, and the log was gone, no doubt moldered away. But the greens were tender, and the sun was visibly working, burning off the dew.

"This is it," Margret said. "The glade."

Charlotte walked into the center of the clearing and looked around.

"I used to lie in this grass," Margret explained, "because by August it's so long, it's like a fairy tale."

"And what did he say here? Exactly."

"He said maybe in Downing Meadow so he could be with the wheel bugs. Or the bayside marsh, with the bitterns in the spring. Or here, with the wood thrush. And then he said again, maybe here."

Margret went to where the log had been.

"This is where the log we ate on was, but we could probably sit on that one."

She pointed to a more recent fallen tree, then walked over to it and sat down.

"Do you want to sit?"

Charlotte came slowly over and lowered herself to the trunk.

"So this is where you two had your chats?"

"We ended up here, ate lunch, and then headed back."

"And not too many people came here?"

"No one ever did. You can see this grass hasn't been walked on. You're not supposed to come off the path, and most people don't."

"Milton probably felt he owned the place. He donated a lot of money to conservancies."

"I don't know how or when he found this spot, but I always thought it was magical."

"It is. I'd be happier here than in a buggy old marsh."

They both started laughing.

"Let's skip the house," Charlotte said. "We'll go home, have a rest, and then go to the Ritz for dinner, just us."

"Why not?" Margret said, and they laughed some more.

Margret let Charlotte lead the way back, watching her walk, noting the trace of jauntiness still there, and every now and then the hand lifted to brush back her hair, a gesture touched with glamour, the curving pianist's fingers, the delicate turn of her wrist, a woman raised to be watched, and to perform. They emerged from the reserve, and as they walked back to the car across the gravel the shadow of a butterfly fluttered on the ground before them. It was still early for butterflies, and Margret looked up for it, up and around, but saw nothing. Once, when she was walking north with Charles along the Hudson, on the Cherry Walk, the shadow of a butterfly danced across the path in front of them. They'd looked up and around to see what species it was, but already it was gone, southward they assumed. Margret said to Charles how life was like that, how something behind you, and so small—a movement, a tone, a word—can throw a shadow in front of you. And he'd said, Wouldn't it be terrible if it couldn't? What would the world be then?

Thirty-three

IT WAS SPRING SONG in the trees. It was parulas and black-throated blues, slurry scales in the boughs. She heard the two-note lisp of a blue-winged warbler, like Daffy Duck sputtering, and the yip of a redstart and the chestnut-sided's *pleased-pleased-pleased-to-meet'cha.* It was elating, all the noisy flitting and zipping above one's head, the sun brushing the tops of trees in a waking radiance of life. Milk-glass larva feeding on seeds, last fall's galls and beetles out from under bark, all these emerging insects were a feast to sing about, to feed on before the next flight north.

It was eight A.M. and Margret had the morning to herself. She stood at the top of the stairs at 115th and leaned against the retaining wall, scanning the branches above. It was a fallout. There'd been a clear sky and south winds the night before, and hungry birds were working the sweetgums, oaks, and locusts, fresh with shoots. She focused her binoculars on a flash of orange high in a crown—a dazzling Baltimore oriole.

Margret came down the steps and decided to go through the Women's Grove. Usually she went straight to the north end, but there was so much song in these trees, too much to ignore. She cut down across the sloping lawn to get to the Sanctuary entrance, then took the cedar path in, very slowly, listening intently. There were sopranos and soubrettes, mezzos and tenors, and from time to time the unreasonably loud call of the ovenbird, like a nickel in a bucket.

The grove was empty except for Margret and the Sanctuary's caretaker, an older man she'd seen from a distance for years. Charles used to talk to him sometimes, said he was a retired history professor and a superb birder, but Margret kept her distance. She knew he'd seen her pocketing feathers, and once a catbird's nest, and she was always afraid he might say something about it. He was up ahead, maybe twenty yards, but he seemed to be waving her over. There wasn't any reason not to go over. So she walked a little faster. When she got to him he smiled, so she smiled back.

"How're you doing?" he asked.

"Pretty good. Six species of warbler."

"I had a prairie in the north end, just at the entrance."

"A male?"

"A beaut. I'd show you where but I have to get these pines planted, fifty of 'em."

He motioned toward a white plastic bag on the ground, a bunch of pathetic-looking twigs on top of it. They had only a few needles and almost hairless roots.

"I was supposed to have some kids from AmeriCorps, but they were hijacked to Ninety-sixth Street."

Margret was still looking at the twigs.

"That's fifty?"

"They're small."

She picked one up and held it to her nose. The wisp smelled deeply of pine.

"I could help you," she said.

"Well, if you would dig the holes, I could tote the water. We'd be done in an hour."

"Okay. Where do you want to plant them?"

"Over by the fence."

He counted out ten pines and handed them to her. Then he showed her where to start digging, not too deep, just enough so the roots hung straight. "Dig the holes at least four feet apart," he said, "in spots where sunlight will get to them all summer, which is hard to tell now when the trees aren't in full leaf, but try to guess." Then he left to get the water, and Margret began to dig. The spade cut easily into the soil, still wet from the previous day's rain.

It was pleasurable, spading into the earth, chip notes in the treetops and sun shooting through the boughs. It was satisfying, her foot on the shovel and the earth coming open in dense wedges, not neat wells but dark fissures receiving the sun, the odd worm snapping and twirling. She finished digging the holes, then leaned on the shovel for a breather. She was remembering the summer her cousins dug a foxhole in the empty lot in Gloucester, how exciting it was, and how they wouldn't let her dig because she was too small, and a girl. Margret walked the shovel back to the first hole, where she'd left the ten small pines. She heard a note, faint and far away. She waited, suspended. Then it came. A green song from the ground, from the north, a cathedral of green—the wood thrush. Its fluty woodwind, those liquid trills, rang through the grove and flooded Margret's heart, a vaulting beauty momentarily hers. She breathed deeply, as if to hold the beauty longer in her breast.

Who'll sing a psalm?

Margret knelt to the ground. With her left hand she positioned a pine over a hole and with her right hand brushed in the dirt, kneading the clumps so they would fall loose around the roots, the smell of the soil so close and cool and clean.

I, said the thrush, as she sat in a bush, I'll sing a psalm.

A little more dirt, she thought, a little more. And then the tiny pine was standing on its own. She gave it a long look, saw that it was straight, and with both palms flat, closed the earth around it.

ACKNOWLEDGMENTS

I want to thank Tim Wisgerhof, the former window director at Saks Fifth Avenue, and stylist Stacey Goldfedder for so patiently illuminating their craft. I am grateful to Rebekah Creshkoff, the founder of Project Safe Flight, for explaining the history of her organization to me, and to Doug Taylor, for sharing his knowledge of antique taxidermy and its position in the marketplace. Bruce Schwendeman, of the venerable Schwendeman's Taxidermy Studio in New Jersey, generously vetted my chapter on the skinning of birds.

With admiration, I acknowledge the following sources: Julian Reade's *Assyrian Sculpture*; Jeremy Gaskell's *Who Killed the Great Auk?*; and Errol Fuller's *The Great Auk*. The *New York Times* article of April 16, 2003, from which I have quoted, was written by Douglas Jehl and Elizabeth Becker.

ACKNOWLEDGMENTS

My thanks to first readers Jackie Dector and Ruth Peltason, to smart and sunny Vicki Lame, and to my discerning copy editor, Patricia Phelan. With deepest gratitude I acknowledge my editor at St. Martin's Press, Michael Flamini, so cultured, witty, and intuitive; and my agent, Alice Martell, a force of nature.

Finally, for her unfailing advice and support, I thank my sister Caryn Jacobs.